THE WITCH'S SON

Haifa Mlouka

ISBN: 978-9909-01-158-4

For my fourteen year-old self who started writing on a whim and never looked back

"Wholeness is not achieved by cutting off a portion of one's being, but by integration of the contraries."

—Carl Jung

1
EREBUS

The hospital corridor stretched in an endless spiral ahead of him. Through the darkness, the striking glow of yellow eyes followed his every move. They swayed with the prowl of a predator. Tracking. Hunting.

Theo froze, disoriented in the aftermath of the usual blackout. Three months of avoiding magic, three months of struggling to coexist with himself. His fingers instinctively curled.

The eyes surged forward. Something slammed into his chest, driving him backward, the weight of it like a sack of stones dropped from height, knocking the breath out of him. He gasped, soundless, and then a ragged inhale tore its way back in.

The lights above flickered, making the hallway twirl in waves of dizzying flashes.

Theo tried to stand, but his legs buckled. His magic's familiar tingling sensation crept up his arms, but he crushed it down. Not again. Never again.

Vision darkening at the edges, he scanned the empty path before him for the door to his girlfriend Mina's room. She would never believe he got lost. Mina was waiting for him, alone in that cold, dark place where she had been trapped for months. Nothing else mattered now.

As he tried to focus on the door, Theo's vision blurred into a haze of white lights and dark corners.

Low, inhuman growls drowned out even the hum of the building's ventilation. He fumbled for his phone. His thumb found the flashlight button, and the light pierced the darkness of the empty hallway.

Theo slammed into a wall as the lights finally ceased flickering. He pressed his back against the harsh concrete, counting his breaths. He tried to move, but his jacket snagged on something sharp and yanked him back. He wrenched free.

The growls grew louder. A silhouette stood motionless across from him. Under the buzzing fluorescent lights, the figure stretched too long, angled the wrong way.

Theo yanked himself free and crawled forward, his palms pressing into the slick floor.

The figure still didn't move. The faint vibrations of an unnatural human groan thrummed through the building, making Theo's bones bristle.

Theo kept inching forward. He bumped into a stretcher flat against the wall. He grabbed the edges and shoved it forward. The dark figure was simply gone, like the air itself had swallowed it. A chill ran down Theo's spine.

His body reacted without thought. The shadows at the edges of the corridor twisted and bent toward him, a living thing he hadn't summoned. The darkness obeyed, wrapping around his wrists like hungry vines. Familiar. Cold. Alive…

The shadows responded as they had during that night three months ago. He had no semblance of control over them; they fed on his emotions, growing stronger with his fear and desperate, useless rejection.

Theo stopped short. A noise behind him. He turned. It was right there. It recoiled as the shadows swarmed around it, encasing it in a writhing mass. Panic flooded him, but it was too late to stop them—they had already taken control.

The shadows lashed out, striking with a force he hadn't intended. The figure staggered, driven back a few feet, before it steadied itself and kept coming.

He backed into the icy wall behind him, heart thudding against his ribs. And there was the figure, close now; a man in a torn server's apron and hat, towering over him. His eyes were nothing but yellowish holes that almost glistened in the dark. His head tilted permanently upward, toothless mouth hanging open. His nails extended like talons, filthy and encrusted, clicking against each other like a metronome, the sound growing louder with each passing breath.

The air vibrated with a thousand whispers, voices from every direction. In the chaos of noise, one name stood out—"Casimir."

The name was vaguely familiar, yet it made no sense. He couldn't place it.

The man slammed into him. Hot, fetid breath washed over Theo's face as his head collided with the wall, the impact cracking through his skull, and he dropped to the floor, his shoulder taking the brunt. His arm went numb.

He got to one knee. His vision swam. The taste of the man's breath lingered, sickly and vile.

Theo rose, standing on weak legs. He lifted himself enough to stumble. The second blow took him across the back of the head. He went down hard, flat on his back, eyes too heavy to keep open as the ceiling lurched above him.

A whooshing sound hummed with the echo of the hallway, cloth against the dark, or wings. Both of which didn't belong there. Theo pushed out a slow breath, ready to give into oblivion, when his gaze locked on an owl flying toward him from the end of the corridor. Its eyes gleamed with intelligence, almost human.

An owl inside a hospital…

The thought followed him under.

2
FAMILIAR

Consciousness returned in fragments. Goosebumps stung his skin. An aching soreness in his neck and back greeted him as he struggled to move. Colors and shapes sharpened into focus, the absence of the hospital's bland smell, his sheets, his bed, his apartment.

Theo's eyes burned as reality assembled itself around him.

Sketches of the strange faces from his dreams covered the walls, but someone else stood by the window. Her red hair gleamed like a flame, cascading in gentle curls to her mid-back. When she turned to face him, imperfectly placed freckles dotted her nose and cheeks, complementing her caramel-colored eyes.

"Welcome back." The lingering shadows recoiled as a smile brightened her face. Her hand on his shoulder was too warm, like it had been there longer than he realized.

Theo blinked, a slight tingle spreading through his spine at the contact.

"You passed out." The girl leaned against the wall, arms crossed, like it was the most normal thing in the world.

"Who are you?" Theo rubbed his eyes. The memories of the man's eerie presence flashed through his mind. "What are you doing in my house?"

He shot up, his heart racing. The room was charged with an energy he could not place. The few wards he placed should have prevented anyone from entering. Unless…

He scanned the room, his suspicion growing.

"Calm down." The girl waved him off with a dismissive laugh. "I didn't break in, if that's what you're panicking about. My name's Scarlett. I know this is too sudden and unexpected, but I'm your familiar. You can trust me." She shrugged. "I was drawn to your power. I felt a connection. It's hard to explain."

Theo shook his head. That wasn't possible.

"I don't know what that means." He struggled to his feet, his movements clumsy from the lingering effects of the attack.

"A familiar is a magical partner," she shifted her weight on her other leg. "When you're in trouble, I feel it." She tapped her temple, a cunning smile on her face. "Oh, and we can do telepathy. Cool, right?"

"You've got the wrong guy."

"Right, then explain the shadow show at the hospital." Scarlett's smirk cut through his denial like a blade. His lips twitched.

The owl…its intelligent eyes…It had no business being in a hospital corridor. He'd filed it away as another piece of the night he couldn't explain. Until now. She was the hospital owl.

Now that she had mentioned the magic, there was no point in pretending anymore. Three months of hiding, and it took one night to blow it all away.

He studied her face, weighing his options.

"If I tell you anything…you can't tell anyone. Ever," Theo said, his voice low, meeting her gaze. It was too calm. His secret was already slipping out, and the burden of it made his head throb.

The last time he had used magic he had lost control and put his girlfriend in a coma. The memory, vivid and unrelenting, still haunted him.

"I said you can trust me." She nodded, crossing her hands defensively.

"I don't need you—I don't know you," he huffed, waving her off as he walked to the fridge. "There's the door or the window. Whatever suits you."

"Interesting." She waited.

"I don't need a lecture, alright?"

"Look, I hate that I have to be the one to tell you this, but…" Scarlett sighed and raised her hand to her creasing forehead, her brows knit together. She sat on the bed and rubbed her thighs with her palms. "You need to sit down. Something happened at the hospital."

He turned to her. Her eyes held anger wearing grief's face. He sat beside her.

"Everyone escaped when the Yak attacked, but Mina…I went to her room and found blood and the flowers you gave her scattered on the floor. She's gone."

The words hung in the air. The world tilted, sound fading to a distant hum. He had known, somewhere deep down, but hearing it made it real.

"No." The word escaped before he could stop it. "No, she was just…she was in a coma. Why would that thing—"

His hands trembled the same way they had after what happened that night, whenever he thought about magic, about losing control, about Mina.

"I need to be alone," he said, voice cracking. It took him a few beats to grasp the doorknob. The weight of it all crushed his chest, giving way to something inexplicable.

***

The door opened with a creak as Theo stepped out, a chilly breeze hitting his face. He wished it was strong enough to numb the stirring in his guts.

The street outside was nearly empty, only the distant thump of club music and the sickly glow of streetlights broke the silence. Theo walked with his hood up, hands shoved deep in his pockets, staying in the shadows between the light pools.

You know what you have to do.

He stopped, legs buckling, the whispers slithering through his mind. The pavement bit into his knees as he clutched his head.

"Leave me alone!" A scream tore from his throat as his fists struck the ground. The earth beneath him cracked. The dust, a choking reminder of what he'd lost.

"Theo." Footsteps pounded behind him. "Are you okay?"

Nor. Six months of living together, and the guy still disappeared at night, whispering behind closed doors. He always seemed to know more than he let on. He was also the only person who'd left food in the fridge without saying anything about it.

Theo tried to force a clueless smile, but his back muscles popped, making him wince instead.

"Hey." Theo let Nor pull him up, feeling the weight of his own body like a stranger's.

"What are you doing here?" The words came out flat, mechanical.

"I was…clubbing," Nor chuckled, a trickle of sweat glistening against his temple. "What happened to you?" His eyes narrowed.

"It's nothing. Just…one of those panic attacks." Theo forced a laugh that sounded brittle. "Happens. Don't worry about it."

"Alright." Nor's face went slack, his hand dropping from Theo's arm. "You can talk to me, you know?" The words barely carried.

When Nor stepped closer, Theo backed away.

Seeing Nor's confusion at his repulsion, Theo closed his eyes, searching for words in the darkness.

"Thanks. I appreciate it." His voice caught, the lie tasting like ash.

Nor moved closer, extending a hesitant hand, then pulling it away almost immediately.

Theo averted his gaze as warm tears spilled down his cheeks. He lifted his hand to his face, wiping at them in aggressive strokes.

"I'm heading to the shop," he said, already turning. "My brother's coming by."

He walked away before Nor could respond, before Nor could offer sympathy he didn't deserve. Nor wouldn't understand, anyway. He was just his roommate.

How could anyone understand? Theo himself couldn't separate his grief from the darkness growing inside him.

***

Theo ducked through the small wooden entrance of his plant shop. A now nauseating blend of floral and herbal scents hung in the air. The smell had changed since Mina's coma. Before, he'd kept everything alive and well-stocked into their respective bottles. Now, the rosemary lay on the top shelf, their edges yellowed out. The sage and the mint hung dry at the entrance, turning dark green. He lowered his hood as he approached the shelves beside the basement stairs. Even the chamomile flowers—Mina's favorite—sat on their own specialized shelf, wilted and sad, their vibrant white petals turning black at the edge.

His fingers brushed a dusty leather surface, and for a moment, time stopped. Mina's journal. The one she never let him near. It smelled like old leather and some type of floral incense. He should not touch it. Not after everything. Before her coma, the journal had been Mina's constant companion, always clutched close, her eyes never leaving it. The last time he'd seen her with it; her trembling hand had been holding the pen, hovering over the page. Her head tilted down. He had asked once what she was writing. She'd smiled and changed the subject, and he'd let her. That was Mina. She'd deflect with a smile that made you feel your question was the problem. Once she'd read him a line aloud from the middle of a page, something philosophical about sunrises and sunsets and the space between. She'd closed the journal immediately after, like she'd shared one piece too many of her mind. He'd thought about that line for months, until…

Now the journal was heavy in his hands, he couldn't bring himself to open it. He clenched his fingers tighter around its weathered edges. What if this was not something he should know? But a part of him could not let go, as though the writing inside was pulling him in.

He plopped down on the dust-layered top basement step and flipped open the cover. The familiar scrawl of Mina's handwriting struck him with a jolt of melancholy. It was comforting in a way—so familiar—like a reminder of everything they had been through. Every moment of their precious time together, observations about him, details he'd never known she noticed.

But as he read deeper, her words grew heavier. *"I can't move on. I'll become what I must to fix this."*

That one phrase pierced through him like a burning needle. She had been just as lost as him, always desperate to fix the things he could not change.

He turned the pages, his fingers numb. She had filled all the blank spaces. Pieces of her she had never shared. Her fears and her insecurities. And now, reading it, its grasp tightened around him, the emptiness pulsing like a phantom ache, in the depths of his being.

He had to do something. Bring her back. The desperation would not disappear.

The journal slipped from his hand, falling with a thud like a dead weight, its pages fluttering as if Mina's life was passing before his eyes. But her last words lingered, unshakable, pulling at him.

The words 'Fix it' clung to his head like a restless echo in an empty room, but instead of fading, they grew louder with every second. He couldn't possibly live with that knot, that guilt pushing in. Letting go was not an option. Not like this.

The shadows stretched and winded around him like a comforting, hungry embrace. It didn't feel like magic. It was a predator. One that recognized him. One that had been waiting for the right moment to strike.

You could use them. You could end all this pain. A distorted version of his voice whispered in his ear. Just a little more…control.

The magic, the rituals, they were all within his reach. If he just extended his hand, he could fix it. Theo squeezed his eyes shut, hoping to repel them, but their reach was never far enough.

A dark pull exploded in his chest, threatening to consume him. His grief transformed, reshaping itself into something darker, an impulse that demanded control. Grief and the need to fix blurred together, but none of that mattered. The shadows, the magic—they were within reach.

"Theo?" Scarlett's voice sliced through the heavy, oppressive silence of the room. He blinked, suddenly aware of the shadows at his feet, his hands still clutching the journal, almost ripping it. He hadn't even realized how tight his grip was.

Scarlett stood in the doorway in front of him. Her eyes narrowed to slits as she took in the scene. Theo looked up at her, dropping the journal at his feet. The tails of the shadows receded to the dark corners.

Scarlett stepped closer, her arms hung stiffly at her sides as she approached him.

"What're you up to?" Her voice was steady but filled with concern. Theo's heart thumping as the fog in his mind cleared. He could not explain what he was feeling. He couldn't tell her what he was about to do. Because it wasn't just grief.

"I thought I told you to get lost." The words slipped out before he could stop them, his voice thick with a strange feeling. "Are you deaf?"

Scarlett didn't back away. She stepped closer, her gaze softening as she picked up the journal.

"I know what you were thinking," she said.

Theo snatched the journal from her hand more roughly than he intended and held it tighter than before. The urge to take control was stronger than his willingness to let go. The thought of losing her was unbearable.

"I'm not that stupid," he whispered, almost to himself. "I was just in my head." It was not a complete lie.

"I understand," Scarlett's voice reached a softness he would've never thought her capable of. "But it wouldn't have worked, you know? It wouldn't bring her back the way you think."

Theo looked down at the journal, his grip loosening. The shadows had faded, but the grief lingered. Scarlett's hand on his shoulder was a grounding comfort. Her presence allowed him something he could not give himself alone—the chance to sit with his grief.

He nodded and let out the breath he had been holding, along with the tension in his body as his muscles loosened. He was not alone. And that, in itself, made the darkness feel just a little less suffocating.

The silence stretched between them, heavy with unspoken questions. Scarlett observed him, her expression shifting from concern to something more serious.

"I lost someone dear to me too." She moved closer, her steps light and quiet. "I got obsessed at one point." She shook her head as her eyes drifted to the far wall. "I was ready to do anything to see him. Even necromancy." She pulled a sharp breath through her nose and closed her eyes as if banishing some memory away. Theo squeezed his eyes shut, not wanting to imagine what she must have gone through.

"What I'm saying is." She reached a hesitant hand to his shoulder. It was so warm, it almost burned. "Don't make the same mistakes I did and learn to let it go."

"But I need to know what happened, at least." Theo looked up at her, tears burning at the corners of his eyes.

"Of course," she breathed, as if worried about startling him. "We need to talk about that thing at the hospital, then."

"You actually know what it is?" The word came out sharper than he intended as Theo lurched forward on the step, catching himself. "It looked disturbingly human."

"It's far from human." She shook her head and leaned against his workbench, her casual posture at odds with the gravity in her voice.

"What is it?"

"It's called a Yak," she said it like that should end the conversation.

"And?"

Her jaw tightened. "Puppets. Always controlled by a master." She looked away. "Takes a special kind of sick bastard. And it means the attack wasn't random."

Someone had ordered Mina's death. The thought made bile rise in his throat. His grief was twisting into something darker.

"If you were their target, they can come back anytime," Scarlett said, resting her head against her fist. She shifted in the chair as she turned her gaze to the window, where a bird flew by in a flash.

"Who would—" Theo broke off as the shop's bell chimed, cutting through his questions. Footsteps approached.

"It's my brother," Theo muttered. "You need to—" But Scarlett was already shifting. Her form blurred and shrunk until an owl perched where she had stood. The transformation was so smooth it could have been a trick of his tired mind.

"Were you talking to yourself?" Kai's laugh filled the room as he entered. "Don't tell me all this time alone in the shop has finally gotten to you."

"Just…thinking out loud." Theo forced what he hoped was a genuine smile, but something about Kai's sudden appearance was off. He hadn't told Theo he was coming until yesterday.

Kai paused, his eyes wide as they landed on Scarlett. But, just as fast, he continued walking, a forced laugh leaving his lips.

"Where did it come from?" Kai settled into a chair, his gaze flickering around the room. His movements were too careful, like he was watching for something. Theo kept his expression neutral.

"Yeah, she won't leave me alone." Theo stifled a scoff as he caught Scarlett's un-owl-like eye roll.

"So, how've you been?" Kai's voice softened and his expression grew more serious.

"You know, keeping busy." Theo tried to steady his breathing when shadows moved in the corners. He backed into a table, blocking the shifting shadows from Kai's vision. The movement was too clumsy.

Theo darted his eyes to Kai, making sure he didn't notice. He was busy studying the ceiling with that same scrutinizing gaze. His fingers tapped lightly against the surface of the table.

"Right," Kai said absently, like he was not interested in knowing the answer to his own question.

Theo pushed a sharp breath, too aware of the moving shadows hidden behind him.

"Hey," Kai began, voice shifting slightly, "something's been on my mind lately." His gaze drifted into the distance. His eyes pulled down, and he looked like he had not slept in days.

Theo's stomach dropped. "Tell me." He aimed for lightness but missed. Kai's tone was too casual compared to his creased expression.

"I wanted to ask if—" Kai looked anywhere else but at him as if forced to speak. "Wanna go to our parents' house with me? You haven't been back there in years, have you…?" He trailed off, an awkward chuckle escaping his lips.

Theo's mind raced, but the lie slipped out without thought. "I go there all the time."

"So, what do you say?" Kai's fingers drummed against the table, an anxious rhythm. "We'll go through some stuff for old times' sake."

Theo blinked, the suggestion unexpected.

"Now?" The word was out before he could stop it, a knot of suspicion tightening in his gut. Kai had shown up unannounced, and now this. It didn't sit right.

Kai's gaze shifted for a moment before he answered, almost too quickly. "Actually, work's calling me back earlier than expected." His tone was strained, a little too rehearsed. "Is Friday okay?"

Why the brief visit, followed by an excuse to leave so soon?

Theo stared at his brother for a beat.

"Sure. Friday works."

"Okay, we'll meet then," Kai's voice softened and his shoulders relaxed, his expression was still guarded. "About Mina…" he said. "I'm sorry."

Kai left and Theo stood there, mind churning. Kai always came and went like this—unannounced, brief, guarded, like he was hiding something. After the door clicked shut, the silence turned heavy, as if his brother's absence had physical weight. Yet Kai's apology barely broke through his numbness.

The familiar grief came crashing back like a tumult. Mina's face flashed in his mind—her laughter, the warmth of her hand in his. All gone. His breath grew shallow as the silence pressed in on him further, doubling the emptiness in his heart.

He was alone with questions that had no real answers. Kai was hiding something and someone had tried to kill Mina.

The darkness in his mind whispered that it had solutions for all of this. Simple, permanent solutions. Scarlett hooted softly from the ceiling, as if reading his thoughts.

3
MAGE

Theo's fingers drummed against the nightstand as he sat on the bed. His eyes burned as he stared at his phone. He typed another message to Kai.

"*I want to talk.*"

The empty message thread mocked him. Always the same shit with Kai. He never answered when Theo needed him. Not after their father's death. Not now after Mina.

Mina.

Her absence still gnawed at him. Her smile, her laughter. And Kai? Gone too. Off on his mysterious "work trips" when Theo needed someone to talk to, someone to share the weight of it all.

Theo's jaw tightened, his thumb hovering over the screen again. What was the point of even sending the message? He'd sent fifty-four messages since Mina went into the coma. He knew because he'd counted. That was what he did now. Count. Unanswered messages, days since the last time he took care of the shop, nights since he'd slept. The numbers had started to get of hand.

Frustration clawing at him, Theo threw the phone on the bed. It bounced once and clattered to the floor.

He jolted upward, breath snagging in his throat. A bullet? A gunshot? His heart slammed against his ribs as he stared at the phone.

What just happened?

Theo stayed pressed against the foot of the bed until his breathing steadied and the panic subsided. Shadows shifted at the edge of his vision. When he looked, they vanished. He blinked hard. The phone lay still in the middle of room. Nothing moved.

He craned his head to the ceiling. The day was still going downhill. He spared one last glance at the phone on the floor, left it there, and ambled out the door.

On his way to the balcony for some fresh night air that might clear the clog in his lungs, Theo spotted the kitchen lights open. He detoured toward it and the first thing he saw was a dusty cookbook flung open in the middle of the table. Nor stood at the far right, in front of the open fridge, wearing a blank stare.

"You two fight?" Theo held back a laugh as Nor flinched, his feet floating off the ground for a second. He jerked his head in Theo's direction, his cheeks flushing with a hint of embarrassment.

It was rare they cross paths at night. It felt orchestrated. There was no escaping the situation.

"Oh…hi." Nor slammed the fridge door, almost sending the whole thing through the wall. "I didn't see you come in."

"Well." Theo dragged his feet and threw himself against a chair, gripping the book and reading some strange egg recipes. "You *were* in the middle of an intense glaring match with the poor fridge." He couldn't help himself. It was right there.

"I was asking it for ingredients it didn't have." Nor scratched the nape of his neck and joined Theo at the table. He sat down and released a loud sigh, his smile fading. "I cook when I'm…" he paused as if measuring his words. "Going through stuff."

Theo said nothing. His heart clenched. Every conversation Nor had tried to start, every one he'd shut down.

"I'm sorry if I come on too strong sometimes." As if reading his mind…

Theo shook his head, trying and failing to dismiss it as nothing. His fingers crushed the cookbook's spine, cracking the binding.

"Sorry," he muttered, setting the book down with exaggerated care.

"No worries." Nor sent him a soft smile that crushed his soul.

"Speaking of you finding me crawling in the middle of the street," Theo fixated on a rogue piece of wood at the edge of the table, plucking at it with his fingers. His heart thumped louder than the growl of the fridge's engine in the stillness, under Nor's expectant gaze.

"I just lost someone." His voice came out wobbly, strangled. "My girlfriend, Mina. She—" The words stopped.

How much should he tell him? He could not possibly say things about magic, sentient shadows, and a flesh and blood puppet.

"She was in a coma, and now she's gone." He settled. The sentence was a string of mumbles and shallow breaths.

"That's horrible," Nor said, his tone steady. "No one should have to go through that." There was no surprise in his voice, no shock in his face as Theo studied his unblinking eyes.

His reaction was measured, almost prepared.

Theo narrowed his eyes for a moment, then shook his head and sighed.

"Well, it's part of life," Theo said.

A beat of silence.

"You should get some sleep." Nor stared at him. "You look like you haven't in days."

"Yeah," Theo heard himself say as he pushed off the chair and somehow found himself already out of the kitchen, Nor following closely behind heading to his room.

As he was about to turn the knob of his door, Nor's voice drifting in, muffled behind the barrier of the door, drowning out most of his words.

"Yes, I found it…" The coldness in Nor's tone sent a chill down his spine. "…he's back. I'm guessing for his brother."

Theo stepped closer to the locked door, straining to hear more.

"Yes, sir. I've been following him. I believe he's headed to the farmhouse…yes with his brother." Nor's voice faltered at the last word and Theo's shoulder slammed too loud against the door frame.

Fuck. He froze, waiting for Nor's voice to stop short, for footsteps, for discovery.

Nor's voice emerged again, firm and serious like he had never heard it before. The words drifted in and out of earshot.

"…yes his girlfriend…I was late…yes, sir."

Theo pressed his ear back against the thin wood of the door.

His girlfriend. Nor had said it like he already knew her name. Like he already knew.

After a stretch of silence, he stepped back as the call ended, the weight of suspicion settling heavily on his chest. Was Nor watching him?

***

Theo stared out the window as the landscape blurred by, the road to the family house stretching in a sea of green.

Theo's stomach clenched, but not from hunger. Nor's voice kept looping: *Headed to the farmhouse.*

Did he pose as his roommate to get some information? What did he want with Theo?

"So, where were you all these months?" He turned to Kai, breaking the silence.

Kai shot him a look in the rearview mirror. "I was working. You already know that."

"I know," Theo sighed, darting his eyes back to the window. "You just never tell me what you do besides 'work for the government.' Are you some kind of secret spy?"

"We're not talking about this again," Kai snapped, his grip tightening on the steering wheel. "I'm not supposed to tell you anything. I thought you understood that."

"Whatever," he muttered, trying to ease the tension, though his mind was elsewhere.

His eyes flicked to the road ahead, but his thoughts kept wandering back to the phone call. Was Nor playing him? Was this some sort of game? How much did he know? Who was he really?

As they pulled up to the house, the sight of the worn farmhouse came into view, but it was different this time—distant, unfamiliar, as if he had never been there before. It was like stepping back into someone else's memory. A memory he did not recognize.

Pushing the car door open, Theo stepped out, the gravel crunching beneath his shoes.

"You've been here before, right?" Kai asked, looking up at the house with a mix of melancholy and something like disdain.

"Couple of times," Theo lied, voice flat as he tried to keep the detachment out of his tone.

The porch steps felt wrong under his feet, his senses numb to the unfamiliar creaks of the old wood beneath them. Too unfamiliar for a place he had supposedly grown up in. The weight of the house, of its history, pressed down on him, yet it still felt like a stranger.

Kai stormed ahead, flinging the door open with a loud groan of protest from the hinges. "Come on," he called over his shoulder, his tone cutting through Theo's thoughts.

Theo followed, trying to shake the unsettling feeling. Dust and mothballs hit him like a slap. He knew he had been here. But there were no memories, no echoes of laughter, just blank space, like walking through the abandoned life of a stranger.

The living room was withered, with its brown plaid sofa and pictures on the wall. He stopped at a framed photo of a family he didn't recognize. A younger version of Kai, a woman with eyes he almost knew, and a guy with Theo's face standing slightly apart from the others as if they weren't in the same room.

It was all so…far away.

Theo went straight to one room, throwing his duffel bag onto the bed with a tired sigh. He opened it, pulling out his you-never-know knife and tucking it into the drawer under the desk, quickly hiding it away. The door creaked open, and he froze, closing the drawer a little too forcefully.

Kai barged in without knocking, eyes gleaming with impatience. "Hey, Teddy, do you want to go through the boxes in the basement now?"

"Later," Theo said, pushing past him to flop onto the bed. He let his head sink into the pillow, trying to lose himself in the softness, the quiet. "I'm kinda beat."

Kai didn't argue, instead throwing a glance at the window. "Okay, tell me if you need anything."

"I will. Thanks," Theo said, his thoughts still swirling. But before he could settle, a soft flutter of wings behind him.

Scarlett, in her owl form, landed lightly on the edge of the bed.

"He doesn't know you're a witch, does he?" she asked, her voice soft and probing.

"I already told you, nobody knows." Theo sat up, not meeting her eyes. "And I want to keep it that way." He reached for the knife again, but the weight of the conversation hung in the air.

"Why's that?" Scarlett's eyes gleamed with curiosity. She plucked at the fraying edges of the pillow beside her. "It's not a big deal. I'm sure he'll understand. Being your brother 'n all."

Theo paused, the tip of his finger tracing the sharp edge of the knife. He didn't know why it was so important to keep it a secret. The fear of rejection, of being seen as different. The fear that his own family—his brother—would turn on him.

"I doubt it," he breathed. "*I* don't even understand my magic, and…I don't want him thinking I'm a freak."

"But…you already are." Scarlett let out a soft snort. "College dropout, unknown parents, creepy plant shop. Should I continue?"

"Fine," Theo groaned, burying his face in the pillow. "You made your point."

The worst part was that the plant shop was the only thing he'd ever been good at, and lately he couldn't even keep a cactus alive.

She laughed, the sound light, but there was something sharp beneath it. Something that poked at his senses.

"Which brings me to your friend Nor." Scarlett's voice turned cold as she changed the subject. Theo snapped his head up too fast, doubling his vision.

"He's a little suspicious." She narrowed her gaze, crossing her arms against her chest.

"Why? What's suspicious about him?" Theo frowned, sitting up again. "Also, not really my friend."

"I don't know. I have a hunch." She shrugged as if that was a real thing to go by. "Maybe he followed us here," she said, her voice low and conspiratorial.

"Why would he do that?" Theo chuckled, trying to dismiss the thought that crept up on him before Scarlett even said anything. "He doesn't even know anything. I think."

"Oh," Scarlett said. "You're not sure about him either." it wasn't a question.

Theo hesitated, the knot in his stomach tightening. Maybe she was right. He and Nor were never close, after all, and there was too much evidence of his suspicious behavior to ignore.

"Fine, yes." Nor's phone call flashed in his mind. "Go keep watch and leave me alone." he pointed at a tree branch that faced the open window.

"Smart," Scarlett nodded, winking, before she darted out the window.

She flew off and his mind was still reeling. There was something wrong, something in the air. He couldn't place it, but it was a feeling he couldn't ignore.

Suddenly—the familiar presence, the pulse of magic, something powerful swirling around him.

"Don't you feel that?" he asked, his voice strained.

Scarlett flew back inside, her eyes wide. "What? Don't tell me you changed your mind."

Theo raised his head, scanning the room. "It's the same thing I felt at the hospital," he whispered, barely hearing his own words.

A growl sliced through the quiet, deep and guttural, vibrating in his chest, rattling his teeth.

Theo jumped to his feet and headed for the door.

It exploded inward, splinters of wood covering the ground. Theo's world slanted to its side. Dust, the taste of blood where he had bitten his tongue, something massive and stinking filled his vision, crushing him against the wall behind him. Scarlett pulled him to her by the wrist and he stumbled to his knees.

"Run!" Her voice was a high, piercing sound. She released him and flew straight at the creature with inconceivable speed.

"No," Theo said, more to himself than to Scarlett, and grabbed his knife from the ground.

There was a sound like a bat hitting wet concrete. Then Scarlett was on the floor, coughing up blood, and the Yak was staring at him.

The knife handle slicked with his sweat. His hands would not stop shaking. The blade wobbled uselessly as the thing's yellow eyes locked onto his.

Casimir. The name cut through his panic like a shard of glass. Not his thought. Never his thought. *Casimir, Casimir,* louder now, until he wanted to claw at his skull to make it stop.

The monster crushed the knife, shattering it under its filthy claws. Theo backed away, fear rising in his chest, his gaze locked on the creature's twisted face.

Scarlett flew past him, the wind rushing around them. She slammed into the Yak, pushing Theo to the ground as she flapped her enormous wings. She dug her foot into its chest and ripped out its heart. It let out a low hiss as its skin blackened, the stench of decay filling the air.

A short beat after the corpse thudded to the ground and before Theo could process anything, Kai walked in.

Great timing.

"What is happening?" His voice was unexpectedly level.

Theo froze, staring at his brother. Scarlett, having shifted back into her form, flew out to the tree after she muttered an "oops, you're on your own."

There was no way Kai would buy any story he came up with.

Theo turned back to face him and tried to keep a convincing steadiness to his voice.

"You—how did you—" He shook his head, his mind too scrambled to form a coherent sentence.

Kai's face went slack, his face tracking the destroyed wall and the creature's remains. An impossible scene. Cold settled in Theo's gut. Kai faltered for a moment, his confusion giving way to…disappointment?

"Theo, what the hell happened?" His jaw worked as he visibly contemplated moving forward or backing away.

"I don't know how to explain this," Theo's voice came out sharper than he would have liked. He looked at the door, wishing Kai would leave so he could figure out what to say.

Kai's scoff came out wrong— too calm, too knowing.

"Don't bother. I get it."

Get what? How could he get this?

"No—what?" Theo said, looking past Kai at the remnants of the battle, the echoes of the monster's growls still lingering. "Just let me—"

Kai's eyes narrowed, suspicion flickering across his face. "I need some air."

"I don't want to drag you into this, Kai…" Theo's voice faltered at his brother's name.

There was a long silence, one of those that Theo knew all too well and hated with all his heart.

With a heavy sigh, Kai turned toward the door. "I will be back." His eyes flared with something Theo could not read.

With one last glance over his shoulder, Kai left, slamming the door behind him. The sound of his retreating footsteps was a relief.

As the door clicked shut, Theo didn't have time to breathe before Nor burst through the door. His expression was frantic, eyes scanning the room as though expecting something to jump out at him.

"Hey, are you okay?" he said, his breath heavy. His eyes moved over the room—Theo, Scarlett, the Yak's remains—and back to Theo.

"Told you he followed us," Scarlett mumbled.

Theo stared at Nor, ignoring her comment. "Did you do this?"

Nor looked like he'd been slapped. "What? no, of course not. I heard noise and came running when I saw the thing."

"Oh, that's good." Theo blinked, relief surging through him. "It was a—"

"We'll talk about that later," Nor interrupted, stepping further inside. "There's something you should know about me," he locked eyes with Theo. "I shouldn't have kept it from you."

Theo rubbed his temples, frustration building. "What are you talking about, Nor? What thing?"

Nor didn't answer immediately. He stepped closer, his expression dead serious as his eyes darted to the window. "Where's your brother?"

Theo blinked, confusion clouding his mind. "What are you—he's gone out." His voice was low and strained. "He—"

"I'm gonna tell you about why I'm really here." Nor's expression darkened. "About your brother. Everything."

Before Theo could react, the walls breathed in around him. Shadows crept at the edges of his vision.

He wanted to deny it, to reject whatever "truth" was coming his way.

"You need to come with me first," Nor said, his voice brokering no argument. "Before they find you."

Before who found him?

Theo swallowed, trying to shake off the sudden, suffocating heaviness.

"Wait...no," he muttered again, though it was more out of disbelief than conviction.

Nor and Scarlett stared at him, waiting. Their faces blurred together.

Who could he trust? Who was lying? His brother, his roommate, this familiar he barely knew?

"Give him a minute." As he was about to ask where they were going, or curse at Nor—there was no way for him to know—Scarlett jumped in, her arm dramatically stretched in front of him like a shield. "We're not leaving here until you spill everything."

Nor clicking his teeth, jerked his head toward the rotting corpse still laying in the living room. "Fine. Let's sit."

Theo realized he was nodding.

4
HAVEN

"Kai is a witch hunter known as The Crow." Nor's posture stiffened, his gaze narrowing.

Theo looked at the table. There were scratches in the wood. He stared and counted them, trying and failing to shake off the thought.

"A what?" His voice came out more wobbly than he wanted. "How do you know that?"

"I work in a place called Praetor Magum," Nor sighed, his voice darkening. "I've been following this sudden emergence of these Yak things." he gestured vaguely with his hand. "Then I discovered your brother. I've been following him for a few months."

The words wouldn't land. Witch hunter. Months of following. Everything at once. He couldn't separate one betrayal from another.

"So, you knew about the hospital attack, about—Mina?" The word came out like a wound reopening.

Nor said nothing for a moment.

"I did." His expression softened slightly, but his tone remained even. "I was late…I'm sorry." He looked at the floor.

Theo stood up and sat back down. There was nothing to do with that information except hold it.

"But the thing with your brother is more important right now. It's not just Kai."

Theo swallowed bile. "The whole organization."

Nor didn't answer. Which was answer enough.

"Why?" The word scraped his throat raw. His voice was steadier than he felt. "Why me?"

Nor paused and spoke in a voice that carried a weight far beyond his years. "Your magic, it's—" He glanced at the ceiling where the chandelier swung, dancing with the wind. "A few months back, a surge doesn't go unnoticed. It was like a flare. They track events like that." He met Theo's eyes. "And so do we."

"But I haven't used magic in three—" Theo gulped involuntarily as the memory static flashed in his mind. The whispers. The shadows. The magic. Mina on the floor.

He stumbled back a step, gripping the edge of the table for support. When did he stand?

"This is not happening," he mumbled, almost pleading.

Nor stepped forward, his eyes unblinking. "After the hospital, I've been tracking the Crow's movements. He's been back longer than you know." He shook his head. "I don't know what they do with the witches they detain. And I don't want to find out."

Silence stretched. The shadows hovered at the corner of his vision, waiting for a slip.

Kai, a witch hunter. Theo's own brother hunting witches—hunting him.

And Nor—

A sharp tug twisted at his insides, an echo of that same unsettling feeling, like ink in water. The tension between him and Nor stretched. A dark thread ready to snap.

"And you? Did your bosses tell you to follow me too?" The words slipped out before he could stop them.

"Not really. Back then, we didn't know you were the source of the surge." Nor didn't flinch. "It wasn't about you specifically. You were…unforeseen."

"So you pretended to be my friend?" Theo's voice was quieter now, colder. The black hole in his chest growing by the second, feeding off his pain.

"At first." Nor's expression faltered slightly, but he quickly masked it. "But I want us to be friends. You're the one who keeps rejecting my friendship." He met Theo's gaze for a moment. "Look, I was sent to investigate the Yak presence. For some reason, it was most concentrated in your area. I wasn't even there for Kai, let alone for you."

Theo didn't respond, but his mind churned. Whispers of self-doubt flooded in, wreathing like fog around his thoughts.

Was that supposed to make him feel better?

It only pulled him deeper into the crushing weight of inevitability, of a life spinning out of his control.

Scarlett stiffened beside him, exhaling a loud breath, but said nothing.

"Another thing about Kai," Nor said, his tone suddenly calm. "Every time I followed him, I always lose him at the bridge. I don't know where he disappears to after that."

"So?" The word came out strangled, as he tried to hold himself together. Theo counted how long it'd take him to get to the door.

"If you don't believe me, come with me tonight. You'll see for yourself." Nor shrugged. "Maybe I'll have better luck with you guys."

Theo recoiled, his fists clenching so hard his nails bit into his palms.

Was it really Kai?

The nagging question remained, gnawing at him.

"Fine, but you could be wrong." His voice cracked, but he pressed on, ignoring the way his vision darkened at the edges. "This *Crow* could be anyone."

"Great, let's go." Scarlett's high pitched cheerful voice cut through the silence, though the hesitation and slight twitch of her lips were not fooling anyone. She jumped to her feet, startling Theo.

Nor gave her a small nod, and they moved toward the door. But Theo lingered, his thoughts racing.

They left the building, the crisp air hitting Theo's face as they hopped into Nor's truck, which was parked behind a tree. The drive was suffocated with silence; the only sound the tense intakes of breath.

As they arrived near the bridge, Theo slowed his pace, pulling Scarlett back a few steps. "Hey." His voice was rough like he hadn't spoken in hours. He held the question in his mouth a second longer, dreading the answer. "You think he's right?"

Scarlett pursed her lips and nodded.

"I thought you were on my side." Theo shook his head, not ready to accept it.

"I am. But I'm also sure about this." She gazed at him. "I've got a feeling."

"A hunch, right?" He laughed, the sound thin.

The certainty in her eyes was worse than doubt. He wasn't sure if that comforted him or scared him more.

"Yes, but not just that," Scarlett said, her voice as steady as her expression. "You mentioned your brother travels a lot, acts weird sometimes—all that evidence stacked against him." She clicked her tongue, kicking a small pebble in her path. "Smells fishy to me."

She was right. The timing, the secrecy, the way Kai always disappeared…Theo opened his mouth to respond, but—

"We're here." Nor's voice cut through his thoughts. "The Brooklyn Bridge is where I lose him."

Theo's mind was racing. It was too fast, too convenient. He had to prove them wrong. It could not be Kai.

"Doesn't make sense." Scarlett narrowed her eyes. "Why would he come here? The place is always stacked." Theo barely heard her, his heart pounding as he pushed ahead.

The tension gnawed at him as they raced toward the bridge. But there was no sign of any Crow or any Kai.

Theo tugged at his hair, frustration building with every passing second.

"See?" Nor's voice cracked as he looked around. "Where could he go from here?"

"Wait, I just remembered something," Scarlett said, raising a hand as if struck by a thought. "I heard…maybe seventy years ago, about a hidden bunker inside the bridge—a Cold War-era bomb shelter."

Seventy Years?

"That sounds like a stretch," Theo muttered, keeping the questions about her age to himself, as an uncomfortable uncertainty twisted in his gut.

"But worth checking out." Nor shrugged, not looking convinced by his own words. "It's our only lead."

They split up, scanning the area for any entrance. Scarlett shifted into an owl and flew off, the sound of her wings cutting through the tension.

Theo froze in the middle of the bridge, his eyes darting between the shadows, mocking him.

"Guys, I think I found it." Scarlett's voice rang out from a distance, restoring feeling in his legs.

Theo turned to Nor, his breath catching.

"You sure?" He called back as they ran to Scarlett, who was standing in front of a small, hidden door, the air thick with the weight of whatever they were about to uncover.

"Good job," Theo said, offering a brief nod as he clapped her on the shoulder. He barely registered his own movement.

"Let's see," Nor mumbled as he crouched in front of the door, examining it.

Multiple deadbolts pressed against it like belts. They were clean and almost glossy, contrasting with the rustic age of the door.

"Can you break it?" Her hands at her sides, Scarlett's chest heaved.

"I'm sure I can." Nor stood upright, his face unreadable.

Theo blinked.

"Well? You need a countdown?"

Nor's expression hardened, cutting through a moment of hesitation. His muscles tensed as he clenched his fists, veins popping like tubes beneath his skin. His nails stretched forward like predator claws, hardened and thick.

Nor swung his hand like a lion at its prey, the noise against the rust of the door was deafening, clanging in Theo's ears forcing his eyes to squeeze shut.

A moment later, the once pristine locks, now hung dangling like useless wires against the door.

"There," Nor rasped, swaying on his feet and sweat dripping from his face.

"You okay?" Theo stepped closer, steadying Nor with a hand on his shoulder. Nor nodded as he turned to him. His eyes reflected his appreciation for the question.

"Didn't know you could do that," Theo nodded.

"Yeah, well…" Nor looked down, still catching his breath, and shrugged. A mix of exhaustion and something like vulnerability in his eyes.

The corner of Theo's mouth moved. It was closest thing to a smile he'd managed all night.

"Alright, let's head down, then." Nor gestured to Scarlett—who was poorly concealing a smile—to push the door open.

"Right," Theo hesitated for a moment, his mind spinning from the chaos. All of it pressing down on him like a vise.

But there was no time for thinking. Not when everything was changing before his eyes.

5
HUNTER

It was well after dark when they entered the bunker. At the top of the stairs, the wet walls shimmered under the moonlight, casting pale shadows. But the deeper they went, the light faded. The stairs creaked beneath Theo's feet, each step an echo of his growing unease. He stared down at the cracked wooden steps awaiting him. The shadows twisted at the edges of his vision, just out of reach.

"Hey Theo, can you turn on your flashlight?" Nor stuffed his phone in his pocket. "I'm out of battery."

"Sure." Theo stiffened at Nor's request. For a split second, he thought he had told him to use magic. Every time he tried to use it, something inside him stirred awake.

His phone slipped in his sweaty hand.

He tightened his grip, trying to still the chaotic thrumming beneath his skin. He pressed the torch button, leaving behind a dirty thumbprint.

A flicker of blue light sparked, briefly distorting his vision. The shadows recoiled, swirling like smoke as the light expanded, illuminating their surroundings.

A sharp, acrid scent of smoke filled the air, but it wasn't enough to mask the damp odor emanating from below.

Theo's fingers twitched against the cold stone walls he used as guiding crutches.

Do it. You know you want to.

The whisper vibrated in his ears and he almost lost balance and slid down to the bottom of the stairs.

Each time he reached for his magic, memories of that night with Mina flashed through his mind. No control. Hurting her. The whispering voice promised strength, answers.

Theo pressed his nails into his palm until they left half-moons in his skin.

"Come on," Scarlett urged, walking ahead. "Let's see what's down there."

At the bottom of the stairs, The ceiling was lower on one side, shored up with a wooden beam Nor had to duck under. The smell of damp stone and old wood clogged Theo's nose.

A sudden bang echoed in the distance. Theo froze, the shadows growing thicker around him. He inhaled, trying to shake off the dark tendrils creeping inside his chest.

"What the hell was that?" Theo heard himself whisper, his voice hoarse.

The light flickered out and darkness swallowed them whole as they crept forward. Theo's breath came in quick gasps.

"It's dead." He waved his useless phone in the air and buried it in his pocket.

"Perfect timing," Scarlett sighed, exasperated.

Just a little more. The voice was louder now, pushing against his mind.

I could fix this. Just let me take control.

Theo clenched his fists, pushing the thoughts away, but the shadows crawled at the corners, restless and unsatisfied.

"How are we supposed to find him if we can't see?" Scarlett broke through his haze, her voice distant, as if the darkness was swallowing her too.

"You're an owl," Nor said, trying to mask his annoyance. "You can see in the dark, right?"

"Right. But that's just me. What about you two?"

Theo's throat was dry. "We'll find a light switch."

"Scarlett, you go find it and turn it on. We'll wait here."

"That's a great idea," a muffled voice came from behind them. Theo whipped around, his heart leaping into his throat.

The figure in the shadows was indistinct, but the weight of his presence, as if the darkness itself had shape and form and the shadows were alive, breathing, waiting for the confrontation to escalate.

"Who's there?" Theo's voice was sharp with the panic he couldn't quite suppress.

The lights flickered on, revealing a man standing at the foot of the stairs. Theo held his breath. He knew that face, even shadowed under the hood.

"The Crow." The name leaked from him in a whisper.

The man took a hesitant step forward, his gaze locking on Theo.

"Teddy?" That voice…

Theo's heart slammed in his chest. He couldn't breathe. No, his mind screamed. No, it couldn't have been him. Kai was his brother.

Theo took a step back, a cold sweat breaking out across his skin. "No. You can't be—"

"I can explain." Kai gulped, the sound so loud, it bounced against the vastness of the bunker. "Please stay calm."

But Theo didn't hear him. His mind was racing. The brother who had stayed by his side, and now—now this?

"You're The Crow. I knew it." Nor's voice broke through the haze of confusion.

The man—Kai—shifted, his face momentarily unreadable. "I don't know what you're talking about."

Theo's stomach churned. Was it really him? His mind couldn't make sense of it. The shadows clawed at him, growing restless. He needed answers. Needed something solid to hold on to, something to ground him, but everything was slipping away.

"Enough!" His voice cracked, unrecognizable. "What the hell is going on here?"

Before he could react, Kai was moving, his speed unnatural. He lashed out, slamming a punch into Nor's jaw, sending him sprawling to the ground. The shadows surged, swirling around Theo's body like a cloak. The darkness tugged at him, urging him to fight with everything he had. But at what cost?

"Nor!" Scarlett said, rushing to his side, but Theo's focus was solely on the man in front of him—his brother.

Theo turned, fists clenched, a strange emptiness settling in his chest. "I'll take care of this."

The darkness pulsed in rhythm with his heart. The magic, a raw, hungry force, clawed at his mind. The more he fought it, the deeper it pulled. For a second, he squeezed his eyes shut and opened them to find the shadows darker and deeper. He was losing himself in the pull of them.

"Teddy," Kai pleaded. His glistening eyes and creased brow made Theo's jaw lock. "You don't have to do this. Let's talk."

"You can drop the act." Theo took a slow breath, his eyes narrowing. "You're not fooling anyone."

"Act?" Kai flinched. His voice was a whisper, almost too soft to hear. "Tell me, brother, what do you think you know?"

Theo clenched his fists tighter. His body was shaking, his breath uneven. He raised his hand, and one of the shadow tendrils caught Kai's dagger from his grasp. With one quick motion, it lunged the sharp edge into his brother's shoulder. Kai crumpled to his knees, a scream tearing through the silence.

The darkness had grown stronger, feeding off his anger, his fear—then gone.

Theo's head was blank as he blinked at his hands. Kai was at the far end of the room, on the floor.

"Shit." Theo stumbled to the unconscious body and lifted Kai off the ground, heaving him over his shoulder.

"We need a doctor." He glanced at Scarlett, who was still holding a groaning Nor in her arms. "For both."

"I'm fine." Nor nursed his jaw. His feet tangled together, and he almost tripped.

Scarlett nodded and helped Nor up the steps.

Above ground, the street was dark and quiet, save for the scuttling rats and the occasional cat slinking through the bushes. The street lamps flickered sporadically, casting long, jittery shadows that made Theo's pulse quicken. His steps grew larger as the paranoia crept in. They were always watching him.

"We need someone good who won't ask questions," Theo muttered, the familiar weight of the shadows gnawing at his insides, the dark power stirring within him like a living thing, waiting to escape.

"Don't worry." Scarlett's voice broke through his thoughts. "I know someone."

"If you're thinking about giving them to some witch doctor, forget it. He won't want to treat a hunter," Theo replied, trying to focus on the practical rather than the creeping anxiety settling at the back of his skull.

"You're right. But you'll see. We won't have any problems." Scarlett's tone was steady, sure of herself in a way that made Theo feel both reassured and uncertain at the same time.

"If you say so," Theo grunted, changing their course. "Wait…Where are we headed?"

"Just shut up and trust me, okay? You'll see when we get there." Scarlett rolled her eyes.

"Fine." A heavy sigh escaped him.

6
DEADWEIGHT

"A club?" Theo shifted Kai's dead weight on his shoulder, sweat trickling down his neck. "Pretty sure they need stitches, not a DJ."

"Your medical expertise coming from where exactly?" Scarlett's lips quirked, but her eyes stayed sharp, scanning the street. "The plant shop first aid kit?"

A bass sound from the Pythonissam Club hit them before the neon did. The steady pulse made Theo's teeth ache. He nearly dropped Kai when recognition clicked.

"Jeez," he muttered, watching moths batter themselves against the purple sign. "Of all the places…"

"Having flashbacks about a certain green hair incident?" Scarlett's teasing carried an edge now. "Because we don't have time for another color-changing catastrophe."

"Hey!" Theo's pulse tightened as fragments of the past returned. "How long have you been watching me?"

"A while," Scarlett said, with a glint of amusement in her eyes. "It was fun."

Last time he had stumbled through those doors, he had been drunk enough to pull a prank on Mina when she was mad at him to cheer her up.

The attempt backfired, and he turned his own hair green instead of hers. He had woken up face-down in a booth, surrounded by empty shot glasses and wilted roses.

He had never drunk since.

Theo didn't laugh. He squeezed his eyes shut, trying to stay focused and ignore the creeping sensation he was always being watched, always being drawn toward something darker.

Inside the club, the air was thick with sweat and perfume, bodies writhing to the pulsing beat of the music. Eyes bore at the back of Theo's skull as he passed through. The weight of their gazes was like stiff fingers tracing his skin.

"Why are they staring at us?" he asked, unable to shake the unease clinging to him.

"I don't know," Scarlett's voice was tight. "Maybe because you're hauling an unconscious guy and I'm stumbling with a half-conscious one?"

"Hey," Nor opened one eye, his words coming out muffled against his teeth. "I'm a bit dazed." he shoved Scarlett to move on his own but stumbled and fell back against her shoulder.

"Ow!" she protested. "Don't do that again." Her hand was petting her upper arm.

Nor's reply was a stifled groan.

They were acting like they had known each other for years. Theo wished he could have that kind of connection. He *had.* It was gone.

In a corner of the club, they stopped in front of a black door, the oppressive heat and noise from the dance floor suddenly muffled.

The atmosphere shifted as Scarlett let go of Nor, who stood upright, caressing his jaw, and turned the doorknob. It opened, revealing a long staircase, descending into the depths of the building.

"More stairs?" Theo groaned, rubbing the back of his neck.

He flinched and almost stumbled down as Nor emerged behind him.

"Will you just stop complaining already?" Scarlett rolled her eyes and gestured for them to follow her down.

With a sigh, Theo shuffled forward, his steps reluctant. He was too aware of the shifting tension in the air—the anticipation of something that wasn't quite right. The magic inside him rippled, hungry for release, but he forced it down like he had done so many times, only this time it was harder.

The staircase was silent, the hum of the club's music nowhere to be heard, replaced by the muffled sounds of voices—low, guttural murmurs.

As Theo stepped into the room, the noise stopped. The laughter died. Every pair of eyes turned toward him, and for a moment, the weight of their gazes was like a thousand hands pressing on his chest. He stood still, trying to appear unaffected. Focus. Control. Just get through this.

"Would this have to do with the people hunting me?" Theo muttered under his breath, his voice carrying more bitterness than he intended.

Nor stiffened at his side at the remark. Theo's stomach boiled with frustration. What else was he hiding?

Scarlett moved quickly, her pace picking up as she guided him forward. "Keep your head down."

Theo followed her, his mind racing. The voice was quieter now, but still whispering in the back of his mind. It was always there, waiting for his weakest moment to strike.

They stopped in front of a white door with a sign reading "Doctor" in black letters. The room was sterile, harshly lit by flickering artificial lights. The smell of antiseptic filled the air, and the sound of a clock ticking on the wall was disturbingly loud in the silence.

As they entered, Theo's gaze swept over the gleaming stainless-steel instruments, the vials of liquid arranged like the tools of some unsettling ritual. Everything about the room was clinical and cold. The stark white bed in the center mocked him, its clean sheet unsettlingly pristine.

"Scarlett." a voice called from behind. Theo turned. A slender man emerged from the crowd, his presence almost ethereal against the harsh backdrop of the room. His dirty blonde hair was messy, and he wore oversized combat boots. As he drew closer, the exhaustion etched into his features spoke of sleepless nights. The bags under his eyes were a dead giveaway that he wasn't just a man who treated the injured, but one who lived in the shadows, a doctor who didn't ask questions.

"I wasn't planning on coming," Scarlett said, "but we have two injured guys. I need you to treat them."

Theo extended a hand cautiously. "You're the doctor?"

The man smiled faintly. "Hello, Theo. I'm Peter Darce." He turned to the still form of Kai. "What do we have here?"

"My—A witch hunter." Theo nodded grimly. "The Crow."

"Oh." Peter's eyes widened with recognition.

"You know him?" Scarlett scoffed.

"Yeah, I worked at Praetor Magum for a while." Peter's gaze flicked to Nor for less than a second. "They talked about him…a lot."

As Peter set to work, Scarlett and Theo sat in the waiting room, a heavy silence hanging between them. The voice was still there, clinging to the edges of his thoughts, but he pushed it down. Now was not the time. But the ache in his chest—the coldness of the power that never fully released him—was never far.

"Hey," Theo spoke up, breaking the quiet. "Do you remember the conversation we had after I got attacked at the hospital?"

Scarlett didn't look at him, but she tensed, the weight of the question hanging between them.

"Yeah," she whispered. "That Yak. I tried to find out who was behind it."

"So?" Theo leaned forward, eager for answers, but Scarlett didn't respond. The door to the office opened just then, and Peter emerged, looking grim.

"Their injuries aren't that bad, but they'll need to stay the night."

"Then we'll all stay here until tomorrow," Theo nodded, relieved but still on edge. "If that's not a problem."

"No problem at all," Peter replied with a tired nod as he turned to Scarlett. "You can stay as long as you like."

Before Theo could respond, a crash echoed through the room, followed by a low, guttural growl. The Yak. It was back.

Scarlett didn't hesitate. As the Yak surged into the room with inhuman speed, its yellow eyes locked onto Theo, she leaped in front of him, using her body as a shield. The Yak's claws flashed in the dim light, but before they could strike,

Theo pushed Scarlett aside, fury bubbling inside him. He would not let it take her down again.

The Yak's talons locked around Theo's throat, lifting him off the ground, and his vision swam with the pressure.

Mind screaming for control, the shadows howled, urging him to stop holding back.

As the world closed in on him, Theo's fingers twitched. A knife came flying out of nowhere, slicing the Yak's face and freeing him from its grasp.

"You're not that scary," Theo muttered.

The Yak flickered like bad television static, its form dissolving into the club's shadows. Theo tasted blood, his teeth chattering from leftover adrenaline. Then fire bloomed between his shoulder blades—the creature's parting gift.

He stumbled, catching himself against the bar's sticky surface. Through watering eyes, Scarlett transformed. Not the graceful shift he had seen before, but something brutal. Her wings carved through the air with precision, talons catching the neon lights as she struck. The sound was worse than the sight—wet rope snapping, followed by the dull thud of the Yak's head hitting the floor. It stopped near his boots, mouth seeping, jaw still working, and eyes rolling until they fixed on Theo with an ugly expression.

He stilled for a moment.

His mind seethed, an insatiable void pressing against the corners of his mind. A steady, low vibration of energy that yearned to be released.

Scarlett shifted back to her human form, her features softening as she looked at him. She pulled him by the wrist with more force than grace, her grip steady despite the unfolding chaos.

"You okay?" she asked, chuckling. "Don't die on me *now*, would you?"

A choked laugh escaped him and he opened his mouth to respond, but found his body betraying him. The pain from the Yak's claws was still sharp, a searing reminder of how close he had come to death. He tried to lift his arms, but they were leaden.

"I can't move my arms," he rasped, the weakness in his voice a stark contrast to the power that usually flowed so easily through him.

"Get a hold of yourself." Scarlett's voice was firm, but there was a softness to it too, as if she were trying to help him stay grounded in an increasingly unstable world. "We need to get out of here now."

"Yeah, thanks," Theo chuckled bitterly, trying to muster some semblance of strength. "I feel so much better."

A sound came from behind the cabinet. Theo's muscles tensed, expecting another Yak, another attack. Scarlett froze, her hands suspended on his shoulders as she was trying to lift him up.

Peter crawled from behind the cabinet, coughing and covered in dust.

"You okay, guys?" His eyes were slits as he wiped his dirt-smeared face.

Theo sighed as relief washed over him, and Scarlett released a breath at the same time.

"What about Nor and Kai?" Theo's voice was weak, but his mind was still sharp. He pushed against the fog of exhaustion and pain, his thoughts shifting. "Where are they?"

"While you were fighting that thing," Peter moved on to dust his pants and white coat, now turned light brown. "A group of hunters took Norman. I recognized their uniforms," he paused, chest rising and falling like he'd been running. "And before you ask, no, your brother wasn't with them. He took off alone."

Theo's mind whirled. Kai was a hunter. Why would he not go with his hunter friends?

"Why would they take Nor?" Theo frowned, his mind struggling to catch up. "Do you know where they would have taken him?"

Anxiety surged in his chest, and the shadows knew it.

Peter hesitated, his gaze flicking to Scarlett in less than a second. "Probably Infernales. It's their high-security prison for…witches and such."

"Ah, shit." Scarlett ran a hand through her hair as he turned to her. "We're not going there."

"Why not? We're just gonna be like those 'oh well, good luck out there' people?" Theo's arm restriction gnawed at his nerves as he shifted to a more comfortable position. "He's a friend."

"Theo…" She trailed off and shook her head as if the words she was about to let slip were not for his ears. He clenched a sore fist and bit the inside of his cheek.

"Okay. We'll get him back…" The tone of her voice was reluctant yet decisive, like she had gone through a whole debate in her head and the opposite side had won.

"Really?" Theo jerked his head up to look at her. There was a scowl etched on her features, but Theo kept quiet, not wanting to stir up anything he was not supposed to.

Whatever went through her head, everyone had the right to keep some pieces protected in a vault.

"And your brother too…" She sighed, but there was a smile in her voice, "if you want that, of course."

Theo nodded, absent.

Kai. There he went again, disappearing, running away.

What a coward.

The shadows stirred at the edges of his thoughts. More present, more violent. The need to give in to that darkness, to let it swallow him whole, was constant, and yet, looking at Scarlett reminded him of the fragile humanity he still clung to.

Theo said nothing as she helped him to his feet again.

With a grunt and a surprising ease, she lifted him onto her shoulder and walked out of the club. The weight of his body slumped against hers, and despite the overwhelming pain, a flicker of relief sparked within him at her presence.

7
ECHOES

Theo lay on the bed, eyes closed, replaying the fight in his mind. He'd lost, and Scarlett had saved him. Again. Frustration simmered in his chest. He sat up, careful to avoid pulling at the half-healed cuts on his back and reached for Mina's journal on his nightstand. The slightest friction against the raw wounds sent sharp, burning pain radiating through his body.

A knock at the door pulled him from his thoughts.

"Hey, it's me," Scarlett called before stepping inside. "How are your wounds?"

"Still burn." Theo ran a hand through his hair, irritation creeping into his tone. "Damn it, I can't do anything."

"For God's sake, stop being a baby. They'll heal eventually."

"Eventually?" He dropped onto the bed, book in hand. "We don't know what they're doing to him there." He shook his head and jerked it toward Scarlett. "Nor, I mean."

She leaned against the doorway, arms crossed to her chest, tense and rigid.

"We have to move fast." He threw the book to the side, and it landed perfectly in the center of the pillow. "Today."

"Are you kidding me?" The sharp shift in her tone caught Theo off guard. "We can't just barge in there." She stood upright, her arms back at her side.

Theo leapt to his feet. He did not know she had a state of being other than calm and collected with a side of sarcasm.

"Then we make a plan." He walked toward her, his boots squeaking on the floorboard.

"I don't—" Scarlett opened her mouth to speak but interrupted herself when Peter came up behind her.

"What are we doing?" He shoved his hands inside his dirty coat pockets. Why he was still wearing it was beyond Theo.

"Yes, Peter can come with us." Theo didn't know the reason behind Scarlett's reluctance. Maybe she didn't care that much about Nor, or maybe she didn't think it was worth the risk.

"Backup, right?" Theo nodded, hoping that would be enough to convince her. Rescue missions needed at least three people.

"Right." Scarlett massaged her temple and walked away, leaving Theo stammering for what to say to turn her around. "I'm gonna get some air," she yelled when she was out of sight.

Peter shrugged and followed behind.

As the door clicked shut, Theo exhaled heavily, pacing the room. He paused, shoving the thought away. They should go get Nor.

Before he could dwell further, Scarlett barged back in, her face flushed and her eyes piercing.

The air must have been refreshing.

"Fine, we'll do it." The words tumbled out in a rush.

"Let's go." Theo grabbed his coat. Whatever changed her mind, Theo was in its debt.

"Wait..." Scarlett stopped him. "We should go somewhere first. For weapons and stuff."

"I don't know. You're the one with the hunches."

Scarlett sighed, rolling her eyes. "How about the bunker? We could find stuff there, right? And maybe—just maybe—make a plan."

"Ha. How didn't I think of that?"

"Shut up." She bumped her shoulder against his arm as they left.

***

The bunker was quiet when they arrived, sunlight slanting in through cracks in the walls. Theo had expected chaos and filth, but the space was pristine. A large table dominated the central room, illuminated by a map of the world. An empty, unwashed coffee cup pinned the African continent and the chair was slanted in a weird angle.

Had Kai come back here? Theo kept the thought to himself.

The next room held rows of computers and communication devices, their screens dormant.

As they ventured deeper, they found shelves lined with books and files, an arsenal of weapons displayed on the walls.

"Yep. This is our secret base now," Theo said, a smile pulling at his lips.

"I'm grabbing weapons," Scarlett announced, already heading to the shelves.

"Find me a good knife," Theo called after her, heading back upstairs.

Reaching the surface, he stepped outside, letting the fading sunlight wash over him. The horizon was a bright kaleidoscope—orange, red, and purple, blending seamlessly as the sun dipped lower. Shadows stretched long and sharp around him, their edges wavering like they were alive. Scarlett joined him, her presence quiet but grounding.

"One thing I remember about my mother." Theo stared at the horizon, searching his hazy memories. "She used to drag me to watch the sunset every day. We'd sit on top of a mountain, just watching in silence."

"That's nice," Scarlett said.

"Yeah." Theo lowered his gaze to the pebble-filled ground. "Funny how something so small can mean so much."

"She sounds like a wonderful mother." Scarlett looked at him with warmth.

"I don't know." Theo sighed, the shadows retreating. "That's literally all I remember."

Scarlett said nothing as she placed a hand on his shoulder.

Theo nodded, some of the tension easing out of him. "Let's get Nor back."

***

Theo crouched low beside Scarlett and Peter, his eyes locked on the building ahead. The shadows stretched long across the ground, the night air climbing up Theo's back in a tense shiver.

"See that building?" Scarlett's voice broke the silence. "That's our target."

Theo took a moment to reply, his eyes darting across the building.

"We have to be careful," Scarlett went on, her tone strained, as if lost in thought. She cast a brief look at him as swiftly as she turned away, a flicker of something—fear?—flashing in her eyes.

Theo kept his voice low. "You don't have to say it. I'm not stupid."

Scarlett shot him another glance, the tension in her jaw tightening, but she said nothing. Her gaze flickered toward Peter for a moment, then back to the building. Her fingers drumming her knee nervously.

"How're we getting in?" Peter murmured, breaking the silence. He grimaced, but his usual nervousness was apparent in his tone. "Knock on the door and tell them the secret code?"

Scarlett shot him a sharp look, her eyes flashing with irritation. "No," she blurted, but refrained in a flash. "I mean, I'm not sure."

As much as she tried to hide it, her voice was sharper than usual. The subtle tension in the set of her shoulders, the way her hands clenched at her sides, as if she were holding herself back, gave her away. He held his tongue—he knew better. Though she tried to cover it up, she'd been on edge since they heard the name of the prison. Her discomfort seeped through him as if he were the one afraid.

"Hey listen," Peter whispered to Theo as if noticing the shift. "I've never seen Scarlett like this before."

Theo glanced at him, intrigued. "What do you mean?"

Peter hesitated before responding. "It's just…She's never been this obviously on edge."

Theo turned to look at Scarlett, who had stiffened at the conversation. Was he reading too much into it?

"Guys," Scarlett waved her hand, cutting them off. "You know I can hear you, right?"

"Oh, sorry," Theo muttered. But the question lingered in his mind—what did he really know about Scarlett?

"It's fine," she said with a slight shrug. "He's right. I *am* a little scared, as much as I hate to admit it. Let's just say I have memories of this place that I'd rather bury for good."

That gave Theo pause, his heart dropping for a brief second. He opened his mouth to speak, then closed it instantly as Scarlett put up a stopping hand.

"I don't want to talk about it." The vulnerability in her voice was raw, unexpected. He studied her closely, his mind working through the implications of her words.

"Well, if you don't wanna do this—"

"I have to do this," she interrupted sharply, her voice steely. "I'm your familiar," she said, almost as if she was trying to convince herself. "Besides, not going in there was the reason for the bad memories. I was weak."

The lie, the hesitation in her words. Theo had learned to read people, but Scarlett was harder to decipher.

"If you wanna stay behind, I would totally understand—"

"Oh, shut up." She slapped the back of his head, but her tone was warm, almost playful. "You're lucky I'm here."

Theo rolled his eyes. "Yeah, because where would I be without your endless wisdom?"

"Dead in a ditch," she shot back with a grin. Then her expression softened. "Seriously, though. You can't do this alone."

He hesitated, her tone catching him off guard. The way her words felt more real, more genuine, hit him harder than he expected. "Thanks for the pep talk."

The unmistakable sound of footsteps snapped Theo's attention back to the present. It was too close. His grip on the knife at his belt slipped with cold sweat.

"Guards," he said, "two of them. They're coming this way."

Scarlett didn't flinch, but her body tensed.

Without sparing him a glance, she nodded. "Let me handle it."

Scarlett was already there, and it was over in a flash. One guard crumpled from a strike to the head, the other subdued before he had time to make a sound. Her movements were too fluid and quick for Theo to keep track of them all. But not enough for him to miss the slight tremor in her hand as she finished. It was quick, almost imperceptible, but it didn't escape him.

Scarlett stripped the black and white camouflage military-looking uniforms from the unconscious guards on the ground fast. Theo looked away.

"Hey, what about me?" Peter interrupted his thoughts, pulling him back to reality. "There's only two if you hadn't noticed."

"This one is for you." tossed the second uniform at him. "I'll be extra stealthy." She shrugged, trying to mask the strain in her voice.

8
INFERNALES

Theo and Peter quickly pulled the guard uniforms on, adjusting the ill-fitting clothes as best as they could. They couldn't afford to stand out.

"Wouldn't they recognize you?" Peter asked, his voice low, but there was a nervous edge to it. "I mean…they would, right?"

Theo nodded. "Yeah, we thought of that. But we'll just have to take the risk."

The coarse fabric of the uniforms scratched against his skin, a constant reminder of the foreign roles they were trying to play. Scarlett was already looking ahead, her sharp eyes scanning the entrance, calm and composed, her movements precise as ever.

She glanced back at them, her lips pressing together in a brief, almost imperceptible smile. "Ready?"

Peter let out a small laugh, but it felt forced. "Of course!" He squealed.

Theo turned to him, managing a tight smile. "Just stick close and follow my lead."

Theo pulled his cap down to hide his face. The sound of their footsteps echoed in the empty hallway as they entered. A rhythmic reminder of how close they were to the danger inside.

As they moved forward, a familiar unease tugged at Theo. The air was stagnant and cold, thick with the remnants of all the souls imprisoned here. His head throbbed, a sharp pressure building, as if it might burst.

The prisoners who must have walked these halls. He snapped himself out of the thought.

Focus.

They entered the mess hall, the clatter of distant voices filling the space. Armed guards stood watch over rows of cells, their expressions blank, but their eyes sharp.

The noise was distant, like an echo in Theo's head, as his mind focused too much on the grim faces of the prisoners. The smell of unwashed bodies and the cold, damp air hung in the room, gnawing at his senses.

Scarlett was a few steps ahead, sticking to the shadows. Her posture was relaxed, though her senses were alert, scanning the room. Theo and Peter moved through the space as if they belonged. His gaze flickered over the prisoners—some hollow-eyed, others too gaunt to be real.

"You think Nor's here?" Peter whispered, glancing around.

"Let's keep moving," Theo said, trying to keep the tremble out of his voice.

They passed row after row, moving slower now, scanning the cells for any sign of Nor. But as they walked, Theo's focus fractured, his mind pulled in too many directions.

He froze, an invisible hand clasping over his mouth. His ribs heaved against a tightening pressure as if they were bound by ropes, straining to inflate his lungs. He wanted to run; he needed to get out.

Instead, he wobbled, the edges of his sight fading as he steadied himself, though the feeling lingered. His head throbbed, his skin painfully taut. For a moment, his chest was constricted, the air too thick to draw in.

Scarlett, a few steps ahead, didn't seem affected. She glanced back at him, but her movements didn't falter.

Theo clenched his jaw, forcing himself to keep moving. The pain didn't matter. He would not stop. Taking a deep breath, he pushed through the suffocating pressure, but each step was heavier, like walking through mud, and the walls were closing in by the second.

"Theo?" Peter's voice was distant, worried. "What's happening?"

"We need to move," he said, his voice tight, giving nothing away.

***

Theo approached the back door and gripped the handle. The cold metal bit into his palm as he twisted it open, and winced at the quiet creak. Behind him, Peter was close on his heels, his footsteps clumsy, but quick. Scarlett barely made a sound as she moved silently in their dark corner.

Theo motioned for them to follow him, his gaze flicking over his shoulder. There was no time for mistakes. They couldn't afford to stand out.

They moved down the dark passage. Theo's mind was sluggish, but he pushed through it. The weight of Peter's nervous energy behind him, and Scarlett's strange, quiet and constant presence in the background, were not helping.

Focus. Nor was waiting.

They reached a door, and Theo paused, pressing his ear to it. Two voices. He could hardly make out the words, but the tone of the conversation raked at his nerves and the feeling of unease that had been gnawing at him all this time tightened in his chest.

He moved to open the door, but before he could, Scarlett stepped forward, faster than Theo expected, unlocking the door with a swift and silent motion.

The room inside was empty. Theo stepped in, scanning the surroundings, but Scarlett didn't wait for him to give the all-clear. She was already moving toward the next hall, her steps deliberate. Theo followed after making sure Peter was close behind.

As they moved down the hallway, Theo's thoughts kept drifting.

They came to the foot of the stairs and a man with a thick British accent, low and deep, rattled the silence.

"I assume you had a talk with the new prisoner…I know he's your son. But you must not forget," the man said, "he's Casimir's friend."

Casimir.

Before he could react, heavy footsteps rang out, growing louder. He needed to hide, but there was nowhere to go. Behind him, Scarlett had already shifted into her owl form, her wings barely a whisper as she darted into the shadows.

Peter didn't have the same instincts, but he followed silently as Theo blended into the corner. He barely breathed, the sound of footsteps growing nearer. The man's voice faded in and out of hearing, and Theo's fingers dug into the wall. He couldn't see them, but he could hear the heavy steps of the guards as they passed.

Theo shifted in place, just enough to look and catch a clear sight of the guards. His eyes widened as they dragged something—no, someone—toward them. A prisoner. His heart stopped when he recognized the bloodied face. It was Nor.

The guards forced Nor to slump against one of them, his arms wrenched behind his back, wrists bound tightly with fraying ropes. Blood streaked down his temple, and his body hung limp as they hauled him forward. The muscles in his shoulders looked strained from the awkward angle, and Theo could see faint marks where the ropes had bitten into his skin.

Theo's body stiffened, paralyzed by the sight of Nor being dragged like a rag-doll, bruised and half-conscious. Before panic could fully overtake him, a sharp, sudden noise—footsteps echoing down the hall—ripped Theo back to the present. He pressed himself further into the shadows, praying the guards wouldn't notice him.

The guards heaved him down the corridor, Nor stumbling as his legs buckled under him.

How had he let this happen?

Peter shifted beside him, a barely audible breath escaping his lips, but Theo couldn't tear his eyes away from Nor. His mind raced. They had to help him, but the guards weren't far. The plan had been to find Nor, but not like this.

Scarlett was gone now, out of sight, but the weight of her presence remained still. She seemed like a person who had always handled things on her own, but the sudden appearance of Nor—the sight of him hurt—drove something deeper in Theo. They weren't leaving without him. No matter the cost.

"Keep moving!" The guards continued past, oblivious to the quiet corner they had hidden in, dragging Nor further down the hall.

They dumped him into a chair in the center of the room, and the rough motion wrenched a groan from Nor's lips. They quickly tied his arms down to the armrests, trussing him. His wrists, already raw and bloodied, strained against the ropes as he tried to shift, but the bindings were unyielding.

Theo's breathing quickened. He turned to Peter. "Let's go get him. We can't waste any time."

Before he could move, the room grew colder as a tall figure walked in—a man in a dark coat and top hat, his presence suffocating. The guards straightened at his arrival, stepping back as he walked to a corner almost out of Theo's vision. The darkness shadowed a portion of his face.

Theo pressed himself tighter against the wall, barely daring to breathe. From his vantage point, Nor sat bound in the middle of the room.

When the man stepped closer, Nor's head snapped up, the faint glow of his blue mage eyes sharpening as recognition dawned.

"No," Nor whispered, his voice trembling. "This can't be happening."

The man stopped in front of Nor at arm's length, his expression unreadable. Then he smiled, slow and unnerving. "Hello, Norman."

Nor's voice cracked as he muttered to himself, "This can't be real."

"I assure you, I'm very real," the man said, his tone as smooth as ice.

Nor quickly hardened his expression. "What the hell is going on here?" he said, anger lacing his voice.

The man clasped his hands behind his back, his calm demeanor only heightening the tension. "We did not get a chance to talk after—" he trailed off, his expression faltering for a second and then back. "I owe you answers."

Nor looked like he recognized the man, but who was he? Why did Nor seem so shaken? Theo strained to hear every word of the exchange.

"Answers? How long've you been working with the hunters, John?" Nor jerked forward. The chair scraped against the floor with a sharp screech.

The man stood firm, a distant look in his eyes. "Believe it or not, I'm here to help you."

Nor shook his head. "Help? You want to *help* me? After all these years?"

"I know this is hard," John said, his calm demeanor unwavering. "I'm not like them, Norman."

Nor darted his eyes away as the man stared at him with something Theo did not recognize.

"There's something you need to understand," he finally said, "about the witch."

"I don't know any witch." Nor lied, but the hesitation in his voice betrayed him.

"Theodore," the man said, his voice deliberate. "The witch's son. Or as some call him…Casimir."

Theo forced himself to stay still. *Casimir?*

Nor's face paled. "Prince of Darkness, Casimir?" he whispered. "What does he have to do with Theo?"

John leaned forward, his hands settling on Nor's shoulders, his voice low and grave, but laced with unexpected warmth. "Your friend is in great danger."

"Spare me the warnings and cut these damn ropes," Nor growled.

The man's entire face turned into a glare, his tone darkening. "There's something you need to understand about your friend, Theodore. He's in more danger than you realize."

Nor shook his head. "You're not talking about the Yak that's been following us, are you?" he said, his voice strained.

"That's the least of your worries," the man said firmly. "When Theodore arrives—"

"Dad…" Nor's loud defeated sigh and voice broke him off. "What are you doing?" He shook his head as he slumped back, his chest heaving. The rope still held, but his body sagged in defeat. Only the sharpness in his eyes marking his refusal to surrender.

Theo's chest dropped. He couldn't tear his eyes away from the man's face as it softened at the word.

Nor stared at his father, his face a mix of confusion and anger. "Why did you never look for me?" his voice rose with bitterness, and Theo could feel the hurt radiating from him. "How could you just—"

Theo thought he heard it first—soft, uneven footsteps echoing from somewhere just out of sight. He ducked lower and glanced at the darkened hallway, catching the faint glint of movement.

9
TRUTH

The room grew colder, the tension thickening. A figure emerged from the shadows. A tall woman, dressed in black, her stark black hair falling in waves that seemed to blend into her leather jacket in the dim light. Her feline green eyes gleamed with a predatory sharpness, scanning the room as she surveyed Nor with a smirk.

"Morgana." John stepped aside, his voice barely a whisper as he acknowledged her with a slight tilt of his head before retreating into the shadows. The guards straightened as she strode past them.

"What do you want?" Nor's voice cut through the air, defiant and sharp. Even in his beaten state, he wouldn't give them the satisfaction of fear.

The woman crouched in front of him, tilting his head up with almost playful aggression. "Ooh, straight to the point," she said, her voice thick with amusement. "I like that."

Nor spat blood onto the floor, glaring at her through swollen eyes. "Just get on with it if you're going to torture me."

She laughed, a cold, jarring sound. "Torture? Oh, not yet." She leaned in closer, her smile disappearing into something harder. "First, you're going to tell me everything you know about your Theodore." Her voice dropped to a whisper.

Peter shifted beside him; the panic radiating off him in waves.

Theo's eyes searched the room for any sign of Scarlett. She was gone. His mind raced. They couldn't leave Nor behind. But how could they get to him without alerting every guard in the prison?

"And your little friend behind the wall," the woman's gaze drifted past Nor as if she knew Scarlett's exact position.

Relief fluttered through Theo as the faint whoosh of Scarlett's wings echoed, growing distant. Nor's shoulders relaxed at the sound.

Nor slumped back in the chair, letting out a heavy sigh, his eyes still locked on Morgana, daring her to make the next move.

After an endless stretch of quiet, Morgana let out a exaggerated sigh.

"Ugh, you're no fun." She flung her hands up, swinging the dagger carelessly.

Nor held his ground, eyes narrowing as he studied her.

"What?" she asked, voice dropping to something colder, arms crossed in challenge.

"Who are you?" Nor asked, his voice laced with suspicion.

"Oh?" Morgana chuckled, the sound bouncing off the walls. "I guess John didn't tell you."

"What are you talking about?" Nor's confusion deepened.

"You'll find out soon enough," she smiled. "Now tell me everything I need to know."

"You can go to hell," Nor scoffed. "I'm not afraid of you."

"Been there, done that." A brief wistful look crossed her face before it disappeared behind the aggressiveness she came in with. "You have such beautiful eyes." She moved closer to him and tipped his chin up as the dagger traced under his socket. "Shame about that."

Theo's fists clenched tighter. He couldn't watch anymore. His mind raced, calculating the next move as Morgana's hand moved closer to Nor's eyes.

"Ready?" Theo turned to Peter, his voice a low whisper.

"Huh?" Peter's wide eyes searched Theo's face.

There was no room for hesitation.

With one sharp motion, Theo gestured for Peter to go to the other side while he darted forward toward Morgana, who was still looking down at Nor, oblivious to their movement. Theo picked up the pace, and with the momentum of a jump, he threw himself in Morgana's direction, closing the gap between them. Peter followed, his body hitting the ground with an echoing thud as he knocked Morgana off balance.

She staggered, her dagger falling from her hand just as Theo wrenched her away from Nor.

For a moment, her calm cracked—wide eyes, parted lips—but it was gone in a blink. A slow grin curled on her face as she sized him up.

"You must be Theodore," she said, twisting out of Theo's grip with unnerving ease.

As she was about to strike back, a loud screech echoed through the room. He didn't need to see her to know who it was.

Scarlett—her majestic owl form descended from above, wings slicing through the air like sharp blades. She slammed into two of the guards that were running through the door, her talons tearing into their chests and faces with unnatural precision.

Hope flared in Theo's chest. He grabbed Morgana again, slamming her against the wall. Her grunt of pain barely registered as Theo caught sight of Nor, struggling against the ropes, wrists raw and bleeding. His stomach churned at the sight.

Morgana shifted, moving like liquid, her free hand flashing to her waist. A dagger appeared as if conjured from nowhere, the blade gleaming.

Pain pulsed through his arm as she slashed it. He staggered back, clutching the wound. Morgana juggled the weapon in her hand like a toy before Scarlett struck her, her talons grazing Morgana's shoulder and breaking her rhythm. The dagger slipped from her grip, clattering to the floor. For the first time, Theo saw her falter.

With a desperate surge of strength, Theo pinned Morgana's wrist to the wall, his hand pressing against her throat as he fought to keep her down. She clawed at him; her nails scraping his skin, but Theo held firm. Peter rushed to his side, helping to hold her down.

Morgana's smug smile never faded. "You think you won?" she rasped, but the mockery in her voice stayed firm. "Don't kid yourself."

Theo ignored her, though the smugness almost got to him as her hand twitched of its own will. He breathed the frustration away and augmented the pressure on her wrist.

Peter stumbled his way to Nor, helping him out of the ropes. They had the upper hand.

Scarlett was still fending off the guards when one of them found her blind spot and shoved her to the wall with sheer force. She crashed against the hard stone, her wings ruffling at her sides as her eyes fluttered open and shut, and she stumbled her way to the vent, her wings drooping like heavy anchors.

Theo's breathing came fast and shallow. He looked up, distracted, just as Morgana shifted beneath him. Her boot stomped down on his foot. Pain shot through him as he stumbled back, the world spinning.

Guards poured into the room, their sheer numbers suffocating. Theo barely had time to register the oncoming tide before Morgana's elbow drove into his ribs, sending him sprawling. His vision blurred as he crashed into the stone floor.

He tried to get up, but pain exploded in his skull, his eyes rattling in their sockets. His legs buckled under him and his cheek fell against the cold ground as the world disappeared.

***

Theo's head throbbed, each pulse of pain sharp as glass shards slicing through his temples. The acrid smell of damp stone filled his nose, mixing with the metallic tang of blood. Hot rope bit into his wrists, raw skin chafing against the fabric with each movement.

"Where…am I?" Blinking against the light filtering through the barred window, his voice cracked, swallowed by the oppressive silence. Did anyone even hear him?

"No clue, dude," Peter's voice, familiar but distant. "I tried everything."

Theo shifted, discomfort prickling his skin. "What happened?"

Bitter humor laced Peter's voice. "That lady knocked us out. Then the guards started kicking you for no reason."

"What?" Theo frowned, the confusion thickening in his chest, suddenly aware of the soreness all over his body. "Why?"

"You're a target, man. Everyone hates you here."

Theo swallowed, his limbs feeling leaden. "I can't feel my body."

Peter's voice softened, a mix of worry and indifference. "Are you okay? You got knocked out pretty hard."

"Yeah." Theo's words were far away. "The voice in my head is still there," he muttered, regretting immediately.

"A voice?" Peter's disbelief was sharp.

Theo's throat tightened as he nodded. Might as well admit it. "It never stopped."

Peter was quiet for a moment, looking at his feet as if he were contemplating his life choices.

"Maybe I know someone who can help," he said, still looking down.

For one lucid second Theo imagined what it would feel like to stop fighting it. Not a loss of control. But his choice. The path was there. How easy it would be to slip into it. Instead, he pulled his knees to his chest and stared at the wall.

"Her name is Iliana. I'll tell you about her when we get out of here," Peter said, voice low, like it was a secret. "But you should be—"

"Hello, prisoners." Before he could finish, Morgana's voice sliced through the air like a knife.

"What's up?" Theo blinked, irritation crawling up his spine. She was here. Of course. He looked at Peter, who gave a low, urgent whisper.

"Don't answer, you idiot."

"Theodore." Morgana's voice was too sweet, too sure of itself. "It's good to meet you at last." She stared into his eyes, and there was something cold in her gaze that made Theo want to flinch. "Your reputation precedes you."

Unease settled deeper. "What reputation?"

She kneeled before him, her presence overwhelming. Her fingers brushed against his cheek, and he had to resist the urge to jerk away. "Oh, you know nothing about yourself." She pursed her lips. "Shame."

"Who the hell are you to tell me about myself?"

"Calm down," she laughed, soft and mocking. "I'm not telling you anything."

Theo's stare never wavered. The words were sharp on his tongue, but he swallowed them, unwilling to give her any satisfaction.

"You know," she said, "we only captured your beloved Norman because we knew you'd come to the rescue. He means nothing to me." She leaned closer, her breath too warm on his skin. "Don't make friends. They're only weaknesses."

Anger flared in Theo's chest, a deep, furious rush of it that almost made him lash out. But he controlled it, keeping his eyes on her with an intensity that might have burned her alive if he could've made it real. Instead, he turned his face away from her touch.

Morgana laughed, a cold, triumphant sound. She moved away, her heels clicking sharply against the stone floor.

"Aren't you adorable?" she said, ruffling his hair as though he were a child. "I'll be back. Gotta decide what to do with you."

The moment she was gone, Theo exhaled sharply, the tension draining from his shoulders. "What a bitch."

Peter's laugh was dry. "You don't say."

Theo shifted again, the ropes digging deeper into his skin, the cold creeping through his clothes. He strained to listen, trying to catch the faintest sound above. His ears picked up the muffled voices of Morgana and John, the words sharp and filled with something like hatred.

"We talked about this..." Morgana's voice carried, rising with anger. "...what side we're on!"

Theo leaned forward slightly, trying to catch more. John's voice was harder to hear, but he made out a few words: "...what you are to me...he would hate me and think I abandoned him..."

Theo's jaw clenched. He wasn't sure who they were talking about.

The floorboards creaked above, the voices rising in tension.

"Selfish old bastard, you only think of yourself...he already hates you. Did you ever think about how I would feel?"

A bitter knot formed in Theo's gut. They were talking about Nor. He wasn't sure who John was to Morgana, but there was a heaviness to their words, connected to the chaos surrounding him. Whatever John was hiding, it tied them all together. He needed to know. He would make them talk once he was free.

"It's been hours," Theo muttered, exhaustion settling into his bones. "I don't think she's coming back."

"Yeah, me neither," Peter was yawning, his voice thick, like he was already half asleep.

"Dude, were you asleep?"

"I guess I was."

Theo shook his head in disbelief, his stomach sinking. "Let's get out of here."

Peter blinked at him. "Wait. What if it's a trap? What if they're waiting for us to make a move?"

"Then let them wait." Theo nudged at the rope holding his hands captive. "We're not staying here another minute."

His thoughts were already in motion, considering the door, the layout of the prison. The space between them and freedom. He used his tied-up hand to reach for the knife hidden in his boot. His movements were slow and careful, fingers slipping over the hilt, the weight of the blade in his palm grounding him for a moment. With a sharp, focused motion, he sawed at the ropes, his wrist stiff, the knife sliding through the fibers with frustrating slowness. It took time; the ropes resisting him, but finally, they gave way. Then he hastened to cut Peter free; the blade slicing through the fabric with more difficulty than Theo hoped, but the eventually came undone.

As he tucked the knife back to his belt, a sound echoed down the hall—quick footsteps, heavy with purpose. Theo froze, eyes darting toward the door.

"Someone's coming," he whispered, barely able to breathe as his pulse spiked. But it was too late. The door creaked open, the figure silhouetted against the dim light from the hallway.

"Scarlett?" Theo breathed out, his shoulders relaxing.

"Finally, I've been looking for you everywhere," she gasped. "What happened?"

"It's all his fault." Peter pointed at Theo.

"I'll tell you later," Theo said, already moving toward the door. "Come on, let's find Nor and get out of here."

"Wait." Scarlett's hand closed around his arm, pulling him to a halt. "I know where he is."

Theo chuckled, relief flooding his chest. "Even better. Let's go."

The mess hall crawled with guards. Theo moved with purpose, following Scarlett and staying close to the shadows. The guards focused on their duties, their chatter drowning out any awareness of their surroundings. They slid between the columns, ducked behind crates, and shifted across the floor with practiced ease. Every step had to be measured, every movement precise.

"Okay," Scarlett whispered as they approached a corner. "Anyone could be in there, so we've got to be—"

Theo didn't wait. With a swift kick, he sent the door crashing open. It slammed against the wall with a violent bang.

"Or we could do that," Scarlett remarked dryly.

Inside, a figure slumped in a chair, head hanging low.

"Nor."

Nor's head jerked up, eyes widening as he saw Theo.

"Theo, thank God." His shoulders relaxed.

Theo rushed forward, his fingers trembling as he worked to untie the ropes around Nor's wrists. Why did everything feel so wrong right now?

"You okay, buddy? You look like hell."

Nor gave a weak laugh. His voice strained. "Better than you."

The words cut through the tension like a slight relief. Still breathing. Still alive. Theo exhaled, still not fully believing they were here, in this moment.

Scarlett moved in beside them, clinging to Nor as he stood. The sight of them together, so fragile and yet…real. Theo's stomach twisted. What did he miss?

Nor froze, clearly startled by the contact, and then hesitated before wrapping his arms around her. It was slow, careful, like something unsure, but the tension in his muscles was palpable.

"Sorry," Scarlett muttered, her voice quiet and distant as she quickly pulled away, her words too soft in the heavy air. "You okay?"

Nor blinked, still processing, before a faint smile tugged at his lips. "I am now."

What the hell was happening? The weight of it—the confusion, the unresolved tension—pressed into his chest.

But before he could make sense of it, Scarlett chuckled under her breath, shaking her head as if to clear the moment. She turned away, walking back to Peter's side, and Theo stared after her, holding back a laugh.

His own chuckle escaped before he could stop it, though it was dry, barely more than a strained exhale. "That was unexpected and…awkward."

Nor's fist connected with his arm. The punch wasn't hard, but it was enough to snap him back to the present. "Shut up."

Theo grinned despite himself. Yeah. What a mess.

"Guys." Peter's voice sliced through the moment. He waved his hands impatiently. "Let me remind you we're still in prison. Not exactly the place to have a moment."

Theo's stomach dropped, the reminder like a cold splash of water. Right. Focus.

"I agree." Morgana's voice cut through the air, sharp and unforgiving.

Theo's body stiffened at the sound of it, his muscles locking as if primed for a fight. Not again.

"You."

"Me." Morgana's smile bloomed, wicked and knowing, like a snake baring its fangs.

A low growl of frustration rose in Theo's chest, but he bit it back, unwilling to give her the satisfaction. Instead, his eyes shot to the shadows where John emerged, his figure tall and looming.

"Enough of this nonsense," John said, his voice gravelly, yet with an edge of calm, "we're not your enemies."

"Yeah you are," Theo said, "you kidnapped my friend and used him against me, for starters."

Nor stepped in front of Theo, as if to shield him from whatever came next. Theo's gut clenched at the gesture. He didn't need his protection. But he kept quiet, the words too sharp, too unnecessary.

"I hate to admit this," Nor said, his tone quiet but firm, "but he's right. They're not the ones we should be worried about."

Theo blinked and snapped his gaze back to Nor.

"What do you mean?" Scarlett voiced his thoughts, her face tight with confusion.

"Remember the Yak that attacked the hospital?" Nor said, his voice low.

"Yeah, my source told me '*Damian*' sent it," Scarlett said, "but he died a long time ago. It can't be him."

Nor sighed, his expression hardening.

"Well, hate to break it to you, honey. But he's very much alive." Morgana clicked forward on her heels, her eyes locking onto Theo's with a knowing glint. "And he wants Theodore."

What?

The pieces snapped into place with a sickening clarity.

"So that monster was after me, not just killing people?" The words left his mouth before he could stop them, and a cold shiver ran down his spine. What the hell did this *Damian* want with him?

"It was my fault." His voice was small in the middle of the room.

"Yeah, you're a—" Morgana started, but before she could finish, John cut her off with a sharp gesture.

Scarlett's gaze locked with Nor's, her face pale as she processed the gravity of the situation. "Don't tell me...Damian wants to put his brother—"

Nor gave a stiff nod, confirming what apparently no one wanted to say out loud.

Theo's stomach twisted into knots, panic creeping up his throat. What did he want with him?

"What does he want?" his voice was strained with frustration and fear. Why couldn't anyone just tell him? "Who's Damian?"

Scarlett caught his hand, the touch grounding him, though the storm of questions inside him raged on.

"I'll tell you when we get home, okay?" she whispered, dragging him with her toward the door.

He couldn't bring himself to pull away, too shocked to resist her grip or even speak. He hated being kept in the dark. Like with Kai. His brother had always shut him out, leaving him with unanswered questions. Theo clenched his jaw, trying to tamp down the frustration bubbling inside him.

Nor followed them toward the door, his steps firm but purposeful.

"Come on, Peter," he said, his voice low.

Theo kept his focus straight ahead, forcing himself not to glance back. He didn't want to see the blank expressions on Morgana's and John's faces—didn't want to feel the weight of their stares on his back. He could almost feel them watching, cold and unblinking. But he kept moving, the air thick with everything unsaid.

10
ADRIFT

Theo lunged toward Scarlett. Shadows blinked under the harsh glare of the bunker's buzzing fluorescent lights. One of the light fixtures had been flickering for week. He'd started timing his moves to its rhythm in his training sessions with Scarlett.

But maybe that wasn't such a good idea.

Theo's hand shot out to catch Scarlett's punch, but she was already several moves ahead. Instead of a left hook, she grabbed onto his forearm and jerked down sharply. He stumbled backward until he hit the wall behind him, teetering on one foot and crashing onto the wood floor below.

"That's five wins in a week." Scarlett smirked, wiping sweat from her brow. "You're slipping."

"I'm still injured, remember?" Theo squeezed his eyes shut and leaned on the wall as he staggered to his feet.

"Sure, sure." Scarlett extended a hand to him. "Come on. Enough for today."

Scarlett flopped onto the large couch and sighed. "So…John and Morgana seem to have let us go."

"Yeah," Theo chuckled, sitting beside her. "I bet they got fired."

"Listen." Scarlett crossed her legs and opened a bottle of water. "I know you're wondering why I was so stressed out about the whole Infernales thing."

Theo watched her twist the bottle cap with one hand in a flash. "Oh, it's okay, you don't have to—"

"I want to." She took a sip and cleared her throat. "I trust you."

Theo blinked at the strange words he had never heard said to him before.

"Thank you." A smile he tried to stifle found its way to his lips.

Scarlett nodded and exhaled a sharp breath, letting her back fall against the couch. "I've been to Infernales before, like, I was an actual prisoner there." she shifted uncomfortably as if she was sitting on a rock. "But I escaped, eventually."

A prisoner?

Theo turned his body toward her, preparing himself for the rest of story. "Why, was it a mistake?"

"No," Scarlett sighed. "I don't wanna get into the details, but I can tell you it was during the lowest years of my life. Around the time when I lost that someone I told you about before, remember?" She uncrossed her legs and glanced at the ceiling, "Gosh, I think almost forty-seven years ago, now?"

Theo nodded, his heart skipping a beat. She did tell him about the loss of someone dear to her that almost pushed her to darkness.

"Hey," Nor walked in from the kitchen, startling them both back to reality. A bottle of Scotch and three glasses were clanking in his hands. "So, we've got Damian breathing down our necks. What're we gonna do, now?"

"Listen." Theo nodded as he remembered what was awaiting them. He sat on a wooden chair in front of his friends. "Now that we're all here, we need to talk about what happened."

There was a moment of silence before Scarlett broke it. "Wait, where'd Peter go? Didn't he come back with us?"

They'd been in the bunker for five hours and Theo hadn't thought about Peter once. The realization came flat and cold. He pushed it aside and pulled it back. He should have noticed Peter's absence.

"He said something about finding a better location to work." Nor shrugged as he poured the drinks in the glasses, the ice cubes swimming around the liquid.

"Yeah," Scarlett smirked, "I guess the prison break was too much for him."

"Anyway, it's been over a month and we still can't find Kai, too." Nor clicked his teeth, taking a sip of his drink. "He's our only available ticket to the hunters' organization."

"We don't need him," Theo said. Involving Kai wasn't right.

"Why? How are we doing it, then?"

"You heard Morgana and John," Theo muttered, rubbing his temples. "The hunters aren't the only problem anymore."

The room fell into silence again. Scarlett stood and walked to the window, her arms crossed tightly. Nor swirled his drink, the ice clinking against the glass. They exchanged glances over his head. That silent communication had always made him feel like an outsider.

"Come on, guys," he rose from his chair, running a hand through his hair. "What does Daniel want?"

Nor's hand stilled on his glass. "His name is actually Damian." He set the drink down with deliberate care, the sound echoing in the quiet room. "And we're still not sure."

"I have a suspicion. But if I'm right, he is more of a threat than ever." Scarlett turned from the window, her arms dropping to her sides as she faced them. Her expression unreadable.

"Look, if you could just tell me what he wants, maybe we could give it to him and go our separate ways." Theo shrugged, tapping his foot on the floor. If only it had been simple.

"If Scarlett's right." Nor took a sip of his drink and crossed his legs. "I don't think it's possible to give it to him."

"I think he believes you're some sort of vessel possessed by his older brother. There'd been a lot of those over the centuries." Scarlett set down her glass, the sound sharp in the quiet room. She seemed to know a lot about that stuff. Exactly how long had she lived?

Nor nodded, wearing a grim look on his face. "I heard that's what everyone assumed when Casimir disappeared. He didn't die, but found a host. You're just…where he ended up." Nor's jaw clenched, and he turned his gaze away from Theo to Scarlett.

"Casimir wasn't just powerful," she said, "he was influential. The last time he was fully present, a war almost started."

"So, this Damian dude, who everybody knows except me, wants his brother back?" Theo frowned, feeling ridiculous even saying it.

A host. A cage. A vessel. No. That wasn't it. They were wrong.

"Yeah, looks that way." Scarlett shrugged as she moved closer, perching on the arm of the couch as she studied Theo's face. Her fingers drummed against her knee as she spoke. "But, why would he be inside you in the first place?"

"Right." Theo sighed, rubbing his forehead. "How the hell are we gonna find that out?" He really should have continued studying to at least add something to the team. He had been nothing but a nuisance, always asking questions. He'd dropped out of his third year of psychology because he'd started becoming the patient more than the shrink. Nobody had told him self-diagnosis was a terrible idea.

"When we face him," Nor said, turning to Scarlett. "We ask, head-on."

"Are you serious?" Theo scoffed. "Good luck with that." He pushed back from the table, the chair scraping against the floor. He grabbed his jacket and headed to the door.

"Where are you going?" Nor caught him, his nails digging into his arm, stinging.

"He's gonna look for his brother," Scarlett said, putting her empty glass back on the table. Always snooping in his head.

"I need to see him. Don't even try to stop me." Theo pulled his arm away with more force than he intended.

"We're not going to." Nor stood and turned his gaze to Scarlett…again. She wasn't even speaking. "Let's go."

Outside the bunker, Theo stopped, Nor and Scarlett trailing behind him.

"Where do we begin?" he said.

"You tell us." Scarlett looked offended. "It's your idea."

"How about we find Morgana?" Nor put his hand on Scarlett's shoulder. "She was the one who sent Kai to bring me to her."

"Yeah, but how do we find her?" Scarlett looked up at him and removed his hand. It was a good move.

"Well, I heard she's not the warden anymore. So, I don't think she's at Infernales."

Of course not. Why would he state the obvious?

"We go to my dad," Nor said after a moment of hesitation. He didn't want to see him since he obviously hated him. "They seemed close." Why did he sound hurt? Or maybe jealous?

"Are you sure?" Scarlett said, putting a hand on his shoulder.

Here they went again. Theo was invisible.

Nor nodded and put his hand on top of Scarlett's. What the hell was happening?

"Okay." Theo cleared his throat. He had to interrupt them somehow. "Do you know where your dad is?"

"I know where he might be," Nor hesitated again. When Theo looked over his shoulder, Nor was deep in thought. "John will be at my mother's grave." He nodded and moved to his truck. "Get in. It's gonna be a long drive."

***

Nor's car wasn't as fast as Theo thought it would be. He wasn't lying when he said it was going to be a long ride.

"Are we there yet?" Theo sighed, resting his head on the window glass. It wasn't possible for him to be patient.

"No, but we'll be there soon. You can sleep to pass the time," Nor said.

Theo relaxed his head and closed his eyes. "Fine. Don't forget to wake me." If he could sleep; ever since the massacre at the hospital, he could not do so.

"Hey," Scarlett said, leaning forward in her seat as soon as Theo closed his eyes, obviously thinking he was already asleep. She thought wrong.

"I got a message from the high priestess," she continued, her tone leaking with excitement.

"What'd she say?" Nor's eyes flicked to the rearview mirror to check on Theo.

"She wants to meet Theo." Scarlett kept her voice low, but audible enough.

"What?" Nor's knuckles whitened as he tightened his grip on the steering wheel. "How'd she know about him?"

"You know her. She's very resourceful."

"More importantly, what does she know about what John said?"

"I don't know. She didn't mention it." Scarlett rolled her eyes. "But we can expect anything from that manipulative bitch."

Nor chuckled. "Ooh, careful Scarlett. Not everyone thinks she's manipulative or a bitch." He looked around him, smiled, and whispered. "In fact, they could be watching us right now."

Scarlett let out a faint laugh. "Oh yeah? Who would that be?"

"Why, her sources, of course," Nor said like he was stating the obvious.

Scarlett laughed. But her face tightened and her smile vanished as she looked at Theo, still asleep. "Should I tell him?"

Nor sighed. "You should. We can't protect him from everything. Besides, no one can refuse an invitation from the queen herself."

Scarlett peered at Nor. The corner of her mouth quirked up. Nor was already staring at her, a wide, dumb smile on his face.

"What?" She chuckled, looking away. It was awkward.

"You have a beautiful smile," he said, "shame you don't use it much," his voice was softer now, almost vulnerable.

"Well, I don't smile at anyone." Scarlett's cheeks flushed pink, and she turned to the window.

"Ah," Theo said, putting his hand on his chest. "That's so sweet."

"Shut up." Scarlett punched him in the shoulder.

"Knock it off, you two." Nor shook his head and stopped the car. "We're here."

Theo let out a breath and released his aching body from the small, uncomfortable vehicle. "Finally. You seriously need a new car."

"Well, we don't have the money, do we?" Nor put the keys in his pocket.

"Why don't you learn how to drive, Theo?" Scarlett moved beside them. "That way, you save to get a new car, and we get rid of your pointless complaints."

"That's what I call a win-win-win," Nor said.

Theo forced a smile. The dull weight of what was lay dormant inside him hadn't dissipated, even now, with his boots scraping the cracked sidewalk of the cemetery. He'd never told anyone that cemeteries didn't bother him. He found their quiet relaxing. Unlike the living, headstones didn't judge him.

"I'll think about it," Theo nodded. Assholes.

Scarlett narrowed her eyes. "Please do. And let's move, already."

The graveyard stretched out in eerie perfection, rows of polished white tombstones standing like sentinels over the frost-kissed grass. A bitter wind carried the scent of decaying leaves and wet earth, whispering through the bare branches overhead. Their footsteps were muffled, as if the very ground was swallowing the noise. Theo pulled his jacket tighter around himself, the cold seeping through the thin fabric.

The silhouette of Nor's father stood at a distance. Theo and Scarlett stayed behind as Nor walked over to his mother's tombstone, under the name Ingrid Wade, was an engraving, *"Beloved mother and wife."*

"You remembered," Nor said. Theo was far, but heard every word.

"Of course I remembered, son." John crouched and rested his palm on the stone. "She was the love of my life." His voice cracked slightly, and he traced the letters of her name with his finger.

"Just making sure," Nor sighed, his face contorting with disappointment and disdain. He shoved his hands into his pockets, shoulders hunched in defensiveness.

"Come on. Let's talk inside." John extended his arm around his son but Nor moved away from him and it landed in the air. Theo winced as Scarlett followed behind him.

As soon as Theo stepped into the cabin, a wave of electrical air hit him in the face, making him fall backward, but John grabbed him and pulled him straight. He had amazing physical force for a human. Almost too amazing.

"Careful," he said, "it's warded."

"Theo, you idiot. You could've died." The next thing Theo knew, he was getting slapped in the back of the head.

Out of reflex, He hit her hand. He backed away and turned to John. "Why would you put up a warding? We're in— " his mouth was stuck open and his eyes moved around on their own. "Where are we, again?"

"Northern cemetery. Just outside of New York," John grinned. Honestly, his face was too old for grinning. "It's actually close to where the Hive lives."

Hive? Theo sighed and turned to Scarlett. "Is there anything else you forgot to tell me?"

Scarlett raised both her hands. And the one Theo slapped was dripping with blood. "Well, sorry," she said, "it's totally my fault you didn't finish school."

"What's a Hive, anyway?" He had to avoid the subject, it was sensitive.

"A grand coven that has thirteen witches," Nor said, "it's powerful."

"Of course you know it, too." Theo shook his head. As usual, he was the last to know.

"I know of it. But I've never seen it before." Nor's expression was thoughtful as he shifted against the wall.

"Trust me. It's a lot better than the old ruling covens." Scarlett crossed her arms over her chest.

John arched an eyebrow at Scarlett. "I agree."

Scarlett rolled her eyes in response like she knew exactly what he was thinking. "I'm older than I look."

"They all preferred War to Peace," John nodded, his voice taking on a distant quality.

"Screw peace." The words slipped out before Theo could stop them. All eyes turned to him, he rubbed the back of his neck, hard, like he could scratch the words back. What was it he just said?

The room stayed silent for a moment.

"Look, John," Theo said, "we're here to ask you about Morgana. Do you know where she is?"

"I'm afraid she has been a ghost since the organization fired her for *failing to catch the witch.*"

"Is there anywhere she might go?" Nor said as he snapped his head toward the dark corners, his sharp eyes scanning the shadows. "Thought I heard something," His voice tight in the stillness of the air, the silence almost oppressive.

A flicker of movement caught Theo's eye. Then a low click of heels on the pavement.

"Took you long enough to notice me. I've been behind you since the bunker."

Theo turned, his breath hitching as Morgana stepped forward, a throwing knife glinting in her gloved hand. Nor and Scarlett stood like statues in front of Theo, blocking the view. He didn't even move an inch.

"Relax, people." Morgana was rolling her knife in her hand. "It's just my toy."

"How did you—" Theo said.

"Um, idiots?" Morgana chuckled. "How did you *not* notice?"

"We're looking for Theo's brother, Kai," Scarlett said. She sounded colder than usual. It was weird. Theo had never seen her cold with anyone other than him. "Have you seen him?"

"I might." Morgana narrowed her eyes and slid the knife in a sheath at her side with a slick motion, "but to tell you, you'll have to give me something first."

"Morgana—" John sighed and walked in front of Nor.

"Stay out of this, old man!" Morgana interrupted, turning to him, her eyes bloodshot and glaring.

"What do you want?" Theo said. He had to avert her attention. Clearly, there was something going on between her and Nor's dad.

"You're not the only ones with a grudge against Damian," she huffed, crossing her hands against her chest.

"What?" Theo chuckled and looked at his friends. Her condition came out of nowhere.

Morgana stepped closer, her boots crunching on the gravel. "Let's join hands." A line appeared between her brows as she glared at him.

"That's not exactly convincing. What do you really want?" Theo's insides buckled at the thought of trusting her. Morgana, a woman who had tortured them mere weeks ago, wanted to be their ally now? He didn't know whether to be relieved or furious.

"Survival." Morgana shrugged. "And right now, you're my best shot at it. Take it or leave it." Her eyes swept over him, measuring and calculating. Like a predator sizing up its prey.

He looked to Scarlett and Nor, searching their faces for some sign. Scarlett's hand had moved toward her hip, while Nor remained perfectly still, giving him nothing.

11
INTENTIONS

"No, that can't be it." Nor walked in front of her, a distrustful look on his face. "What do you *really* want?"

"Okay look. You wanna know where your brother is or not?" Morgana rolled her eyes and rested a hand on her hip. "You take me as an ally, and I'll tell you. You refuse, well...let's just say you don't want me as an enemy," she smiled, but there was something empty about it, as if she had calculated every word. But her eyes didn't match her lips.

Scarlett drew a sharp breath as if she saw right through her performance.

"That's not gonna—" Nor started but Theo held up his hand, curious to see where this would go.

"We accept." Theo arched his eyebrow at Morgana as a silent dare. "You can join us."

"You can trust her." John moved forward. "She's not who you think—"

"Stop." The word cracked in the air as Morgana's mask slipped for just a second, a flash of rawness and vulnerability crossing her eyes before she recovered. John's face crumpled as if he had been slapped. A stab of unexpected sympathy for the old man hit Theo.

"Shall we?" Morgana turned her gaze back at Nor, and took out her hand. He clicked his tongue and tightened his grip around the truck keys, his eyes locked with hers in a tense battle of wills.

As they went ahead to the truck, John caught Nor by the arm.

"Give her time," he nodded. "She has a good heart, just like you."

Nor looked at him over his shoulder for a minute, pulled his arm out of John's grasp, and walked with Theo to catch up with the others.

***

"Theo, we're here." Nor's hand on his shoulder brought him back to reality.

He was there. In front of the house, where Morgana said he would be. One thin wall was keeping Theo from seeing his brother.

He stared at the chipped wood of the door. Dread gnawed at him when he finally found Kai, not the relief he'd expected. What if Kai didn't want to see him? All the others were waiting for him to go first. He walked to the door, looking at the staring faces around him.

"Hey, wait." Morgana caught up to him from behind. "It's not like I care, but I don't think he's gonna be very pleased to see you." She shrugged. "Just a heads-up."

Did she actually think she was doing him a favor?

Everything was moving slowly until he turned the door handle. Seeing Kai, he stopped for a second, staring at his brother in longing. Feelings of guilt struck his mind. After what Morgana told him, she made him wonder what he'd done to anger his brother.

"Teddy." Kai was lying on a red couch, a beer bottle in his hand, when Theo came in. He put it on the table and straightened.

"Hey." The word came out smaller than he meant it. He took a few steps toward his brother.

"I know about your magic. I've known for a long time." Kai rose to his feet, facing him. "You thought you were keeping a secret from me. But I knew even before you the extent of it."

"You knew?" Theo said, something jamming in his throat. He wanted to shout, to scream at him for the years of silence, but all that came out was a forced whisper.

"Sit," Kai smiled, reaching his hand to him. But Theo pulled away.

Was he trying to tell him something? The look on his face sure made it seem like it. Theo settled into a wooden chair beside his brother.

"I'm gonna tell you a little story about our twisted family," Kai said, "our mother, Amarys, never loved me because I wasn't like her. She gave me to dad and told him to raise me and left. After nearly a year, she came back pregnant with you."

Something jammed in Theo's throat, hot and thick like molten lead. Amarys. The name had no weight, no memory to land on. That absence was elusive.

"Then, the day you were born, the witch took you, after having a huge fight with dad. And from that day I never saw her or you again." Kai stared at the floor between his feet, like he was reading from a script. "So, my father taught me how to fight and raised me to be a hunter so I can find her, kill her, and bring you home with me. Save you from her wickedness and magic altogether."

Theo's veins begged to jump out of his skin. His head was too fuzzy to even think. Rage that tasted bitter blinded him, yet surprisingly satisfying. The look on Kai's face was too calm.

"That's the official story, anyway," Kai sighed, his eyebrows pulling together and his eyes glistening as he turned to Theo to meet his gaze. "Amarys died in the Great War. How I hated her." He scoffed.

Theo's voice cracked. "Then, why are you doing this, now? What do you want from me?"

Kai looked away. "Because even if I hated her…I couldn't let you become her."

For a split second, Kai's face distorted into something else, someone else. Theo's arm moved. He watched it move. Then his fist was colliding with the flickering face with a sickening thud. One blink and Kai's face was back to normal. As soon as his hand made contact, a deep, biting guilt flooded his chest. This was not how it was supposed to go.

Kai fell to the ground wailing in pain and Theo tackled him, pinning his arms down by the wrists so he could not fight back.

"So, you're mad at me, because of someone else who I don't even remember?" he said, his voice cracking despite himself. Kai pushed him back with his feet and stood up.

"Wait, Theo, let me finish!" He said while Theo was still on the ground. "I said that's the official story."

As he got to his feet, Theo froze, staring at his brother, his unblinking eyes burning.

"Wha—what does that even mean?"

"Someone wiped your memories." The sentence sat there. "That's why you don't remember Amarys. But the blocks are breaking down, aren't they? The nightmares, the déjà vu moments, the way your magic sometimes acts on its own, those aren't accidents."

Theo staggered back. So he had not been just carrying Casimir. Casimir had always been there.

He shoved the thought away as Kai stepped closer, his bloody lip twitching in a slight smirk Theo thought he imagined.

"Haven't you ever wondered why some of your childhood photos look wrong? Like the shadows don't fall quite right, or the backgrounds seem blurred? Those aren't bad photography, *brother.* Those are residues, traces left behind when someone rewrote reality itself. *Your* reality."

The air in the room grew heavy with unspoken accusations. Theo's magic stirred beneath his skin, responding to his rising fury. His fingertips tingled with something dark and primal.

Across the room, Kai's eyes narrowed, clearly noting the subtle shift in atmosphere as the shadows became alive.

"Is this why you came back?" Theo's voice emerged unnaturally calm, at odds with the magic crackling through his veins. "To tell me my life is a lie?"

Kai's flinch was answer enough. The last thread of Theo's control snapped. His hand shot up, and with it, Kai's body lifted into the air as one dark tendril caught him by the throat, choking him with merciless bloodlust in the middle of the living room.

12
STRANGER

"Theo!" Scarlett pushed the door open. "Stop it, you're gonna kill him." She hurried to him and shook him with brute force.

Scarlett's voice reached him from somewhere far off. He was still. Too still. And her wrist was in his grip, a different name playing at his tongue. He didn't remember reaching for it. Violent flashes of strange faces in a pool of black filled his vision.

He should stop. A fire burned in his mind and throat, but he couldn't let go.

Right when the tendril squeezed harder at Kai's neck, a painful heavyweight crushed his chest, pushing him hard into the wall behind him. He fell to his knees, chest rising and falling with rapid breaths. As he raised his head up, Nor was standing over him, his clawed hands pulled in front of him.

Theo stood, but his surroundings blurred together and the ground came up to meet him.

Scarlett ran toward him, crouching, and turned to look back at Nor. "Did you see his eyes? What the hell has gotten into him?"

Theo registered their words, but he couldn't move. Nor's punch had been nothing more than a slight push compared to his wave of darkness. He attacked Kai.

"I don't know." Nor kneeled beside her and put his hand on Theo's chest.

"Why isn't he waking up?"

"I don't know." Nor's voice echoed in his ears like a drum. It was nothing more than a sound in a distant memory.

"Let me try something," Scarlett said as a palm hit Theo's face.

Theo pushed himself up, clutching his face. He breathed out while the fisted hand on his side pulsed to punch something. "That hurt."

"You deserved it." She pointed her finger at where Kai was supposed to have been. "You almost killed your brother."

Theo's jaw clenched, his eyes searching the room for Kai, but he was nowhere to be seen. There had to be a way to control whatever was inside him, the voice that haunted his every thought. A bell rang in his head as one person popped into his mind. Would he be able to help like he had said?

"I need to find Peter." Theo sauntered toward the door, unconcerned by his friends' reactions. There was no time to waste.

"Why?" Nor caught him by the arm. His grip was stronger than expected. "Peter left. What does he have to do with this?"

Theo pulled away from Nor's claws, that took a little of his skin with them. "He told me he knew someone who could help me get rid of the voice in my head."

"I thought it was gone." Nor stumbled back and a hint of betrayal twisted his face, tugging at Theo's heart.

"Well, it's back now." Theo put his hand over his eyes. It had never been gone.

"Even if we do find him. How do we know he wasn't lying to you?"

"He wouldn't do that. He's my friend."

"Is he?" Nor shrugged. "Since when?"

Theo opened his mouth to speak, but nothing came out. Instead, he hurried to Nor, his face inches from his, his fist itching at his side.

"Don't try to stop me," Theo said through gritted teeth.

"What now? You're gonna hit *me*?" Nor chuckled as if daring him. "All this time, you've been nothing but a naïve teenager."

"Boys, stop, for god's sake." Scarlett pushed them away from each other. "I'm sorry Nor. I think Theo is right. It might be a long shot, but we need to know what this 'voice' means."

Theo grinned. For once, she was on his side, not Nor's.

"Hey, guys," Theo jumped as Morgana called out. He had forgotten she was even there. "Kai is gone."

Theo swallowed, his gaze turning to the empty space, now stained with dark dried blood. "Great. You're a very good watch. Thank you." His jaw worked as he rubbed his forehead, glimpsing Morgana who rolled her eyes at him. "Come on."

"All of us?" Scarlett's threatening glare turned to Morgana, who was glaring back at her. What was going on with them?

"Scarlett," Theo called, ignoring her stupid question and whatever childish beef she had with Morgana. "You've known Peter longer than us. Where would he go?"

"Maybe…work for a member of the Hive?" She shrugged. "That's what he's always wanted."

The Hive? Theo blinked. The name sounded like something he had heard before, but for the life of him, he could not place it.

"What exactly is The Hive?" he asked. How did it fit in?

"A cult…If you can even call it that." Morgana raised her hands as she neared Nor's truck. "Witches who gather round in circles and pretend they're saving the world."

"I didn't ask you." Theo waved a dismissive hand at Morgana.

"Sorry, your highness." Morgana bowed mockingly and from her expression, she was as surprised as he was at his dismissal.

"They were once a ruling coven, before the war splintered them," Scarlett said as she ignored Morgana, brushing past her like she did not exist. "Now they're more of a cult with little influence and too much time on their hands."

"Exactly what I said. I'll drive, yeah?" Morgana let out an exasperated sigh as she glared at Theo while waiting for Nor to put the keys in her extended hand.

He did not.

***

The village was in the middle of the woods, hidden out of sight beneath the trees. Theo and the others had to leave the truck on the street and walk the rest. But, after seeing the place from up close, it was surely too small for a whole Hive to be living in. It was, actually, a bunch of abandoned ruins and ancient fallen buildings.

"Are you sure this is the place?" Theo looked around him as they stopped.

Scarlett blinked at him. "Yeah, I'm—"

"Shush. Did you hear that?" Morgana interrupted her. "It was a tree branch breaking. There I think." She pointed to a grove of tall trees.

"Someone's there," Nor whispered.

As soon as they prepared themselves to fight, an old man came out of hiding. He was leaning on a wooden cane. His wrinkled face peered out from under a wedge of a blue hat, which was the only thing on his otherwise bald and mottled scalp save a sparse fringe of white. His eyes were heavily lidded and weighed down with wrinkled folds.

"What do you want?" the man spoke, not with a croak of old age that Theo had expected, but with a voice like a sergeant major, strong and distinctly upper class.

"Hi, I'm Theod—" Theo put his hand on his chest.

"I know who you are, Casimir." The old man backed away. "What do you want?"

"Relax. My name is Theo," he said, keeping his voice level, trying to come off as non-threatening as possible. "I'm here for someone called Peter Darce. Do you know him?"

"If you're here about what I told you at the prison." Peter came out of hiding and walked in front of the old man, who vanished away. "Forget it. She's too dangerous. I can't tell you."

"Oh, you're not talking about the high priestess, are you?" Realization fell on Scarlett's face as she looked at Peter.

"Yeah," Peter got closer, surprised. "How did you know?"

"We have history." Scarlett turned to Nor. "We can get to her with the invitation."

Peter's jaw dropped. "She invited you to tomorrow's party?"

"Not exactly. She wants Theo there, for some reason."

"Jeez, Scarlett, Is there something else you didn't think to tell me?" Theo sighed and turned to her. He had enough of them keeping him in the dark, especially Scarlett, who was supposed to tell him everything.

"No, it's not like that. I was gonna tell you. But, I just—" she cut herself off. She must have realized that there was no excuse for what she'd done, or better yet, what she hadn't done.

"You what? Didn't find the right moment?" Theo's veins constricted. He knew that feeling. His magic was moving, flowing with his blood.

Scarlett looked away. "Well…Yeah."

"Forget it. I'm going back to the bunker." Theo rubbed the bridge of his nose as the world started to tilt. He wanted to get out of there before he did something he regretted. "I'm done with you, people." He walked past them all and headed to the truck. The others looked at each other for a minute and, as he turned around, they went after him, including Peter.

At the bunker, Theo slammed his bedroom door open and rubbed his forehead. He plunked himself down on the couch, buried his face in his hands and didn't move for a long time.

He jumped downstairs to see all the others were already there, eating and laughing. It was the first time he had seen them all getting along. Scarlett and Morgana even looked like friends.

"So." He clapped to get their attention. "Morgana and Peter, you can stay for tonight till tomorrow's party. I know you're homeless."

"Thank you, Theo, you're a good friend," Peter said as he nodded.

"What he said," Morgana murmured as she averted her gaze, but not missing the flip him off. What was her problem?

Theo's vision turned black again for a second as he glared at her.

"I guess I don't have to say make yourselves at home since you already have." He turned his face away, ignoring Morgana. Ungrateful bitch.

"Hey, what exactly is our plan for tomorrow at the party?" Peter spread his arms wide.

"Well," Theo jammed his hands in his front pockets. "We try to fit in as much as possible."

"You need to be careful of the high priestess when she talks to you." Nor leaned against the wall. "She can manipulate you into doing anything she wants."

"And don't get shocked when she tells you things about yourself, even you don't know."

"You two seem to know her well." Morgana pulled out a chair. "What'd she do to you?"

"None of your business," they said in unison.

Theo sighed and walked back to his room, closing the door behind him. He stood in front of the mirror of Kai's closet, his arms slack at his sides as the muffled downstairs noise leaked through the wood. He pulled the closet door open and found rows of black hoodies and suits. He had never liked suits. He'd always been uncomfortable wearing them. But the fancy party had a dress code. He should at least try to be elegant, to give a good impression to the high priestess. He grabbed a black, sharp-looking, and well-fitted suit and put it on and puffed his cheeks as he struggled with the tie, always coming up too loose.

"I see you're having some difficulty with the suit." He jumped as Morgana let herself in. "Want some help?" She walked toward him, a strangely friendly smile on her face. Theo turned and brushed over her figure with a quick glance. Or rather, that was what he'd intended. But she was so beautiful. He caught himself staring at the scar on her cheek, barely visible beneath a thin layer of makeup.

"Well." He blinked twice and cleared his throat. "You clean up nice."

"You're not so bad yourself." She adjusted his collar. "The suit kinda brings out your…dark side."

"Thanks, I guess." Theo held back a smile. She had no idea how ironic that was.

"I know you don't like me." She stretched her hands to his tie to remedy the disaster. "And I haven't exactly tried to be liked."

Theo frowned and forced a laugh that came out more awkward than reassuring. "Wait, you don't have to tell me—"

"I want to," she nodded, cutting him off. "Look, I'm not a bad person." Done with the tie, she sat on the couch and crossed her legs. "I do bad things that go well with my poor decision making, but I'm not bad…At least, I try not to be." she shook her head, her eyes fixed on Theo's, intense and unblinking.

"What about the knives and the people you torture?" Theo pursed his lips as soon as the words slipped. Was that too direct?

After a pause, Morgana's shoulders relaxed and she let out a soft chuckle. "Trust me, most of them deserved it."

Theo moved next to her. Up close she was almost completely unblemished except for the thin old scar running down her cheek. He drew a sharp breath, raising his fingers to his own scar.

"About why I joined you guys," She cleared her throat, tucking a lock of hair behind her ear and rose to her feet. "I lied. It's not just survival." Her hand rested on the doorknob. "I figured I could stick with you and know more about where I came from. Believe it or not, my past is a big question mark."

Theo opened his mouth but nothing came out. He smiled instead.

She returned the smile and opened the door.

"If we're being honest…" Theo let his words trail off as he leaped to his feet and caught up to her. "I'm not an entirely good person."

Morgana turned and stared at him for a minute in silence. Judging from her concerned expression, or was it shock? He hesitated to speak. Maybe he should not have said that…

Against all his expectations, her face lit up, and she gave out a soft giggle.

"Who is, these days?" She lifted her shoulders in a half shrug and jerked her head toward the door.

Theo couldn't stop smiling. He hung at the edge of the door, watching her go. The ease of it made his chest ache. The last time he'd felt like this, Mina had been sitting on his floor, writing away on that journal of hers while they teased each other about his coffee-making skills.

Maybe she could be trusted, after all.

13
MASK

Shadows stretched long and thin, merging into the growing darkness. The damp air carried the faint tang of exhaust fumes, and the road shimmered with a dull sheen. Theo sat stiffly in Nor's truck, his fingers gripping the armrest as they jostled over countless potholes.

The ride had been grueling, and they eventually abandoned the truck to walk the rest of the way. Theo didn't mind; the air out here was cooler, cleaner. Ahead, the house loomed, impossible to miss—a beacon of light and modern architecture on an otherwise desolate stretch.

The place looked too pristine, as if it was just built last week. But the windows were too tall, stretching past the roofline one second, and leveling with it the next. The massive panes revealed glimpses of elegant interiors and milling guests, their laughter and clinking glasses spilling into the night. Through one window, a couple talking together. Through another one, the same couple, from a different angle. Theo blinked. Was the house just one room?

"Alright, we split up." He shook his head and glanced at the others. "I'll find the high priestess and you figure out why she threw this party."

Theo was not just reacting anymore. He was starting to plan. And that scared him more than the voice.

"We could at least grab a drink first."Nor smirked, adjusting his fancy dark blue jacket.

Theo arched a brow and turned to Scarlett who was fighting back a smile. "Yeah, you and Nor blend in, ask questions."

"And how will we contact you?" Scarlett's tone was lighter than usual as she toyed with a strand of hair.

Theo hesitated. "Fine. I'll unblock you." She deserved another chance. Despite her deception, she had tried to protect him in her own way. Scarlett blinked in surprise but said nothing.

"What about me?" Morgana's voice cut through, sharp and expectant. She folded her arms, piercing eyes narrowing on Theo.

"You…" Theo shifted uncomfortably, beneath the weight of her gaze. His throat dried as the memory of their strangely intimate conversation flashed before him. "You go with Peter."

Morgana scoffed as her face fell.

"This loser?" She jabbed a thumb at Peter, who blinked innocently behind her. "And then what?"

"I don't know. Do your thing." Theo sighed, feigning exasperation.

Morgana frowned, her disappointment palpable, but Theo did not wait for her retort. He hurried after Nor and Scarlett, pretending not to notice her glare burning into his back.

Inside, the size of the house warred with a strange compression, as if the room where he sat was the extent of it. A woman near the bar had no shadow. Theo stared at the floor beneath her feet to make sure. Nothing.

He grabbed a glass of champagne from a passing waiter, drained it in one gulp, and set it back on the tray. It was looking to be one long night.

Theo slipped through the crowd, tracking his friends' movements. Near the bar, Scarlett sat with her legs crossed, her attempt at charming the bartender carried across the room, all tucked hair and honeyed words. But the man's contemptuous laugh changed everything.

"You're a familiar," he sneered. "I don't know what your business is, but I don't think you should be here alone."

Only Nor's steadying hand on her arm held Scarlett's rage in check. His voice carried that deadly calm that always preceded violence.

"Listen, buddy." Nor's hand shot out, catching the bartender's in what looked like a friendly shake. "None of us want any trouble here, right?"

The man's face flushed red and information spilled out of him like blood: a celebration for the High Priestess's alliance with the new coven leader. Scarlett and Nor exchanged a look.

"Damian." Scarlett's whisper carried across the room like a gunshot.

Theo backed away from the scene, his pulse quick and frantic. He needed to find the high priestess now. There was no time to figure out why the name "Damian" made his insides tighten.

As he turned, scanning the crowd with new urgency, Theo nearly collided with a woman who had not been there a second before. She leaned closer, laughing softly.

"Casimir." her voice was a raspy melody, carried by an accent he could not place. "Looking for me?" Theo stiffened, his heart skipping a beat.

"That's not my name," he frowned.

"Oh?" Her smile deepened and her eyes widened slightly. "Well, I think it suits you."

"Are you the high priestess?"

"Hmm. Come." Her smile did not waver as she gestured toward an isolated corner where a low couch sat in shadow, apart from the bustling crowd. "Let's talk."

Hesitating only a moment, Theo followed. He sat on the edge of the couch, rigid, as she sank into it with feline grace. With a snap of her fingers, a cigarette appeared in her hand.

"Smoke?" She extended it to him.

Theo shook his head quickly, the acrid scent already curling into his nose. He hated cigarettes. Their smell had always made his stomach churn. She shrugged and lit it herself, the orange ember flaring briefly in the dim light.

"So," she said, exhaling a plume of smoke that spread between them like a barrier. "What brings you to me?"

"You invited me," Theo said, shifting uncomfortably.

"Right." Her lips curved into a sly smile. "I wanted to see it for myself—that Casimir is back, But…" she trailed off and took another drag of her poison stick.

"What?" Theo frowned, squirming.

"It's a curious thing. Your face is the same, but you're different." the intensity of her gaze almost bored a hole through his forehead as he kept averting his eyes away to every corner of the cramped space she had lured him to. "That crazy old woman has really done it." Smoke blew from her nostrils as she huffed out a breath. Theo squeezed the arm of the chair until it squeaked.

He was not Casimir. Just a vessel, wasn't he? What kind of nonsense was she spewing?

As he was about to ask, she waved him off as if sensing it, her eyes blinking for the first time since they had sat down.

"You need something. What is it?" She crushed the tip of the cigarette between two fingers and flicked it to the small trashcan propped against the far wall.

"There's…" Theo hesitated, the weight of his secret suddenly pressing against his chest. The voice was louder. Pushing. "There's a voice in my head. It tells me to do things. Horrible things."

A flicker of amusement sparked in her gaze. "And, let me guess, you want to get rid of it?"

"Yes. That's why I'm here." Theo's throat dried.

Her smile vanished. "I can't help you." She stuffed another cigarette into her mouth and stood, brushing invisible dust from her dress. "What you're asking is impossible."

"Wait." Theo sprang to his feet, his voice sharper and more desperate that he would have wanted. "I was told you could. Why are you lying to me?"

The air thickened as she turned, her eyes narrowing like blades. "Watch your tone, boy."

Theo lowered his gaze, the words catching in his throat. "I'm sorry…ma'am?"

She mouthed it back as she studied him for a long moment and sighed. "This Family had always lacked in the manners department."

"What?" Theo blinked. What did she know about his family? The woman was growing more and more mysterious and confusing with each word coming out of her mouth.

"Sit," she gestured back to the couch.

Theo complied, his mind racing. There was no telling where this was leading, but the voice was relentless now, pounding in his skull, making him feel like a puppet on a string.

"Now," Her tone was softer but no less commanding, "I will tell you about your mother."

"My mother?"

"Yes," she said, a glint of melancholy playing in her eyes. "Amarys has always been a scheming, calculating one, since we were children."

"What did she do to me?" the question came out barely above a whisper.

"The better question is what she took from you." Her eyes drifted somewhere past him.

Theo leaned forward in his seat, his heart thumping at the last phrase. Finally someone, other than Damian, knew the past. But, what was her relation to Amarys?

Before he could respond, Morgana appeared, running, at the edge of his vision.

"Hey, there's—" She cut herself off, her face stark white as her eyes landed on the high priestess whose amused lightness from earlier completely fell from her face as she mirrored Morgana's expression, except her quivering lips and soft gaze.

Theo opened his mouth to speak, but a scream tore through the room. It was not human, too high-pitched and guttural. The sound vibrated through his chest, sharp as shattered glass.

When the scream faded, he opened his eyes. The priestess was gone. And so was Morgana.

Theo stood frozen, the bitter tang of smoke still clinging to the air.

Scarlett's voice rang in his mind with three catastrophic words: *Damian is here.*

Don't give him what he wants. The voice in his head interrupted, louder, turning Scarlett's voice into faint background noise.

His knees buckled, but he forced himself upright. His friends were in danger. He couldn't let them fight his battles for him.

With a steely resolve, Theo followed the trail of bodies Damian left in his wake.

14
BLOOD

Theo's senses sharpened amidst the chaos. Bloodied bodies, scattered like forgotten dolls, blocked the exits. The stench of death was pungent, mingling with the distant sounds of struggle—shouts, snarls, and the sharp crack of combat.

He had to find Scarlett. Nor's voice cut through from somewhere, calling to her. The words barely reached Theo as the sounds turned into a cacophony of echoes.

Theo's grip tightened on the knife in his hand, vision swimming. The shadows urged him forward. Every step he took brought him closer to Damian.

When he stopped, three Yaks blocked his way. Damian was protecting himself, or rather, making it hard for Theo to come near him. But it was neither; the creatures moved aside, opening a path for Damian to get by.

Without saying a word, he closed in on him thumped Theo in the stomach, throwing him backward.

The burning pain on his side was unimaginable. With a ragged breath, he leaned against the wall, trying to support his own body weight. The grin on Damian's face was so clear despite his blurry vision.

Theo desperately tried to get up but, with no hope, he slumped to the floor, coughing and choking.

"What a disappointment." Damian slithered a flat grin through his crooked lips and let out a cruel mocking laugh. "You're weaker than I thought."

Theo crawled over, grabbing a chair beside him, and hauled himself upright. Everything blurred for a moment before coming back into focus. Knife in hand, he charged at Damian with a speed he hadn't known he possessed. He swung the weapon in every direction. But as soon as he saw Damian effortlessly blocking his blows, Theo threw the knife aside and released all his energy. Magic pulsed through his body, and a colossal wave of colored energy swirled around him as he drew in a long breath.

Damian stared at Theo, his brows arched in surprise and spread his arms wide open as if he was waiting for a hug.

"Come at me, Casimir." He let out hysterical laugh that sounded like destruction and chaos.

Theo's face was stiff as ice as he jumped in front of Damian in less than a second. The magic sank into his hands as he pummeled Damian's face, not giving him a chance to attack. But Damian caught his fist and shoved him into the wall. Theo slid across the slippery floor but instantly gained his footing, and lunged back into the attack. Damian clenched his fist, a toothy grin stretching across his face, and a wave of energy slapped Theo's face.

With a silent scream, Theo fell forward, his throat and mouth bubbling with blood. He inched his arms under himself and pushed his body up on his hands and knees with his head hanging. He grasped at the floor and scraped the ground with his bloody nails, gritting his teeth through the pain.

"I won't let you touch them."

Theo spat a glob of blood and saliva as he burned all over.

Damian stepped closer, wiping the blood off his face with a handkerchief he pulled out from his suit pocket.

"Your friends don't concern me," he said, jerking Theo's head up. "But you do."

His twisted face stared at him. He placed a chilly hand on his jawbone and pushed it to the side. It was such a soft touch for a horrible being. Theo looked at Damian out of the side of his eye and realized that he was looking at the scar on his cheek. "You're Casimir. My brother."

Theo pulled away from Damian's hand and gulped down a breath.

No. That wasn't right. He wasn't Casimir. But, the voice in his head laughed, and it sounded an awful lot like him.

"What the hell are you talking about?" Theo staggered backward.

"Of course you wouldn't know." Damian stood, towering over Theo. "Ovidia did some irreversible, complicated shit to you." He sighed, narrowing his eyes, dead eyes that sparkled like clouds of gray and blue. Like Theo's.

He crouched near him and brushed his finger through the blood he spat out. "I almost feel sorry for you." He paused. "Amarys on the other hand, she would've been happy her sons finally reunited."

With a quick movement, Theo raised his head. "*Re*united?" he said in a low voice. He was pretty sure he had never seen him before.

Damian waved his hand. "Oh, you wouldn't remember that." He shook his head. "You've been erased."

The words hung in the air. Kai had told him the same thing. Theo dragged himself to the nearest wall and leaned against it, resting his hand on his side. The ground beneath him wasn't solid anymore.

Damian stood and let out his hand for Theo to catch it. "Whatever you think of me, I'm here to help, brother."

"Then, why did you kill all those people?" Theo looked straight at the bloody scene before him.

"Because it bothers you and I need it to not do that." The way he said that, emphasizing the words. It was personal.

What did Theo have to do with it?

"You looked like you enjoyed it," Theo said, "the pain of other people." the words coming out of his own mouth were like knives, as if he was stabbing himself.

"You were right all those years ago." Damian smirked. "We're the same, you and I, Casimir. That's why I need you to open the gate. You're the only who can."

"Stop calling me that." Theo shook his head and swallowed his own vomit.

"It's your name," Damian said, his eyes glinting.

"You were the voice in my head all along, weren't you?"

"Ah, as much as I'd love to get credit for that." Damian crouched again. "It was all you. You weren't possessed. You were rewritten."

"W-what do you mean?" Theo stopped moving. Rewritten. Not possessed. Rewritten. That meant there had been a first version, someone else with his face, someone who knew things Theo couldn't remember.

A sudden yell echoed through the room and he realized his friends were still on the other side of the house.

Damian looked over his shoulder and back at Theo.

"A story for another day." He caught him by the collar and punched him in the face, knocking him sideways Damian let go of his collar and was gone before Theo hit the floor.

Theo tasted blood as a sharp pain throbbed in his head and his consciousness slipped away.

The pain in his body had vanished. He raised his hands and stared at them. They faded in an out of existence like a mirage.

A figure in the dark whispered to him by a different name that was truth: "*Casimir, the first son of Mortifer.*"

Images rushed past him; war, blood, screaming men in hordes. Then a woman's voice, ancient and filled with warmth curled in his chest. "*I have wronged you. Forgive me.*"

"Who's there?" He whirled.

"*I thought I was saving you, protecting you,*" the voice said.

"I don't know who you are. What the hell are you talking about?"

'But I erased you."

"*Theo Theo…!*" Someone from a distance was calling out to him through the darkness, as a striking light blinded his vision. Then, covering his eyes with his hand, he walked toward it.

His eyes flew open, burning as he rubbed them with his shaky fingers. He found himself in the same place, leaning against the same wall, but Scarlett was there and not Damian. He couldn't tell how long he'd been out.

"Theo, wake up." Scarlett held out her hand.

"Where's Nor?" Theo said as she helped him up.

"I left him fighting the Yaks." She grabbed his arm and put it around her. "He'll be back."

"Alone?" Theo paused.

"Don't worry, he can handle them."

Theo's breathing was heavy; his chest was tightening, and he was short of breath. "We have to help him." He tried to move away from Scarlett, but she caught him again and held him on her back like an empty bag. "No, you're the one who needs help." She sighed and started walking past the destruction. "I'm sorry."

"Save Nor," he said in a very low voice that sounded like a whisper. But she ignored him and kept walking.

She positioned him on a small bed in the closest room. Though Theo couldn't move, he remained conscious enough to hear the disturbing roars of the Yaks and the agonized cries of the few people left in the house. One of those voices could've been Nor's.

Scarlett's huge protective aura flowed around Theo as her hand held his. Her heartbeats were so overwhelming that they kept him from focusing on anything else. Quickening footsteps were coming his way. As they got closer, they faded.

15
KIN

"Your boyfriend is a real asshole." Morgana thrust her chin at Scarlett. The fresh blood on her face was still glinting, and dark locks of her damp hair were plastered to her sweaty neck.

Morgana ducked into the room with Peter trailing behind her and Nor hanging on her shoulder. There were deep cuts all over his face and his right eye was red and busted.

"You look dead," Scarlett said as she touched his cheek.

"Not quite," Nor whispered as he looked up, forcing a smile on his busted lips.

"Not *yet*," Morgana corrected. "Next time I won't help him."

"Wow, gee thanks," Scarlett said, flat and monotone.

Nor gasped as she threw him on a bed opposite from Theo. "That hurt."

"That's what happens when you don't listen to me."

"At least you got to save Theo."

"Yeah, isn't he your precious master?" Morgana ripped a piece of cloth from her dress and put it on the hole in her arm. "Or do you love this mage more?"

"Ugh, shut up." Scarlett glared at her.

"We'll both shut up at the end of this, anyway." Morgana gave a bitter laugh.

"Wow, that's very optimistic of you." Scarlett sat beside Nor and shoved her hair away from her face.

"Okay, Stop." Theo opened his eyes, leaving his head on the pillow, and turned to Scarlett. "She saved Nor. Like it or not, Morgana is with us now. So try to get along."

"Theo." Scarlett hurried toward him. "You were almost dead minutes ago. How are you even talking?"

"He heals faster than us," Nor answered in Theo's place. Why would he do that? He was assuming. Nobody knew anything. "Because of some hidden power he doesn't even know about."

"How did you know that?" Theo forced his heavy head up. It was interesting how Nor knew things he shouldn't.

"I need some air." Morgana stood abruptly, leaning against the wall with her arms crossed. Her gaze was fixated on the ground, not meeting anyone's eyes. Before anyone could respond, she was gone.

"Wait guys. Sorry, I don't mean to interrupt." Peter walked forward, his hands in the air. "But I'm gonna be heading back, now." He rubbed a cloth over the dried blood on his face and chuckled. "I came here to help with the voice in Theo's head, that's all."

"I understand." Theo struggled to smile as he glanced at Scarlett and Nor who were nodding. "Thanks for trying to help."

Peter flashed a full-toothed grin as he waved at them and headed to the door.

"Yeah, good luck, Peter," Scarlett called after him with a half wave.

"Okay, there's something you need to know," Nor sighed and sat straight, his gaze not leaving Theo's face. Ever since he met him, Nor didn't always say everything. He had always kept stuff hidden until their right time to be said. "All of you."

"What is it?" Theo straightened on the bed and put his hand on his head.

"A couple of years ago, the high priestess—Iliana. She was a seer." He cleared his throat. "She told me I would befriend a witch with powers like I've never seen before."

"Wait, I've heard that name before," Scarlett interrupted. "It's Amarys's sister's name, right?"

"Amarys, my mother?" Theo opened his mouth. How did they always know about that stuff?

Scarlett nodded and rested her hand on the bed.

"So my aunt and the high priestess are the same person?" Theo caught a cloth that Morgana threw at him and pressed it to the wound right above his eye.

"Probably." Scarlett shrugged. "I mean, no one knows where she went after the war."

The door opened quietly and Morgana slipped back in, her face pale and conflicted.

"I have a confession to make." She closed the door behind her as atmosphere, suddenly, became uncomfortable. Everyone fell into silence and turned to look at her.

Morgana sighed and dropped herself back on the bed, crossing her arms over her chest.

Theo removed the bandages Scarlett used on his wounds and put his shirt back on. "We're listening."

"I wasn't going to say anything. But after what happened…you deserve to know." she turned to Nor, her voice wavering. "I'm your sister."

Nor blinked. "Huh?"

"Well, sort of. Your father raised me." She shifted, pulling at a rogue piece of fabric in the pillow.

Theo's mouth fell open. It was *Morgana.* The woman who tortured him and his friends in the prison, and who also worked for the hunters. He struggled to believe it, given the facts in front of him.

"I know it's hard to believe," she said, as if reading his mind. "But, it's true. You could ask your father."

Nor let out a long breath, eyes dropping to the floor.

"I believe you," he said in a low but clear voice.

Theo laid his head back on the pillow and turned a blind eye to their conversation, finding Scarlett doing the same.

Morgana hesitated "You do?" She sounded disappointed, more than surprised.

"Before we left John's place…" Nor lifted his head and, to Theo's surprise, he was smiling. "He told me to trust you and believe what you have to say to me. I didn't understand what he meant, then. But, now I get it. And I can't see any reason you would lie to me about something like this."

Morgana nodded and blinked slowly. "Okay. Now that I cleared that, I can tell you what I know about Iliana." She drew in a long breath and started. "Before John, she was the one who found me; a little girl on the street looking for food. I never knew where I came from and who my parents were."

"At first, Iliana took me in temporarily and took care of me, until she could find my parents. She looked and looked. But, there was no sign of them. Not alive or even dead. Naturally, she gave up and kept me with her. She taught me everything about magic, even though I didn't have it. Then, she went away and told me to stay inside and wait for her. I did till the war ended but she never showed. And like the dumb kid that I was, I went looking for her. Didn't even pack, just went out the door. Found myself in the middle of one of the war zones. The whole place was just…death. And no sign of Iliana. Then, John came and raised me as his daughter." Morgana turned away and cleared her throat. "Basically, John and Iliana are the only parents I've ever had."

After Morgana finished telling her story, there was silence for a long while. The atmosphere changed.

"Come on." Morgana clapped her hands together and got to her feet. "I don't need your pity," she said it in a low voice. She even sounded offended that they pitied her.

"But." Theo stood and crossed his arms around his chest, mesmerized. "That was kinda rough." If he'd know her story earlier…

"It was," Morgana nodded. "But it doesn't matter, now."

"What matters is that if both Ilianas are the same woman or not." Nor put his hand in his pocket threw the truck keys to Morgana whose eyes widened in surprise. "That's why we need to talk to the only Iliana we know."

"That's obviously gonna be hard since she ran away in the middle of her own home's invasion." Scarlett perched on the arm of Nor's chair, crossing her arms.

"We'll find her." He was tired of finding other people. He needed to find out what he really was. "Seems to be what we're good at these days."

"I'll go check if any Yaks are still here." Nor went through the door, and Scarlett flew behind him.

Feeling her gaze on him, Theo turned his head slowly to Morgana. He looked at her with the best reassuring smile he could make at that moment and put his hand on her shoulder. He was taller than her.

"I'm—we're here if you need us."His voice came out as a whisper.

Morgana chuckled, as if noticing his stutter.

"Thanks." She nodded and went to join the others.

Theo couldn't help but turn and look at her as she walked away.

16
POSSESSION

The next day, rain hammered against the truck windows as they approached the building, the city's neon lights casting sharp reflections on the wet streets. The structure loomed ahead, blending into the storm's dark backdrop.

Up close, the stone looked ancient, its sheer size pressing down on Theo's chest, making each breath shorter than the last. Leaving the bodies piled in the high priestess's house gnawed at him.

The building was unremarkable; gray, utilitarian. There was nothing comforting about it, only cold stone and the certainty that whatever waited inside was far from ordinary.

"Hey, is it really okay that we left the house like that?" Scarlett stood abruptly as she closed the truck door.

"The hunters are gonna be all over the place, anyway. It's not our problem," Morgana said before Nor could answer.

"She's right." Nor buried the keys in his pockets and walked forward. "If they found the place clean, they'll suspect and find us, eventually."

"But they can't know we were there without a guest list. And there isn't one." Theo shrugged.

"Iliana has one, and they will make her give it up unless we find her first." Morgana leaned against the truck.

"You're not coming?" Theo stopped and turned. Morgana was getting comfortable on the hood of the car.

"Are you kidding? I'm an ex-hunter and widely known for my violent 'interrogations'." She chuckled, dangling her feet in the air.

"It's okay. You're not that person anymore, right?"

"They call me 'the blinder'. What do you think?"

Theo snorted. "Oh, okay." He lowered his voice to a whisper as a grin pulled at his lips. "If you get bored, there's a bunch of knives in the trunk. Just don't kill anyone."

Morgana tensed for a second, her heartbeat quickening. But she laughed.

"Go." She nodded toward Scarlett and Nor who were already halfway to the building. "I'll see you later." She gave him a mock salute.

Theo shook his head and sprinted to catch up to them.

"So, how do we get in?" Scarlett looked between Nor and the building. "Front door?"

Nor rolled his eyes and said nothing.

The rain pounded against their backs as they followed him up a long stone path. The building stretched on endlessly, the tall oak doors ahead standing like an impenetrable wall.

Nor's steps were steady, confident, as he reached the door and knocked three times. A pair of eyes appeared through a crack in the door.

"Who is it?" a voice asked, muffled behind the door.

"It's Norman," Nor said, pulling something from beneath his shirt. A necklace, with a strange symbol etched into the metal. He showed it to the eyes.

The door creaked open. They stepped inside, and the warmth hit him like a wave, sharp against the cold he had just come from. The shadows recoiled from the light, retreating deeper into darkness.

Inside, a man hurried toward them, his face lighting up when he saw Nor. "Welcome back, Wade."

"Looks like a hotel in here." Theo's voice sounded distant, as if he were underwater. He shook his head and scanned the area, avoiding its corners. Hallways, elevators, doors opening and closing—agents going about their business surrounded them.

"Yeah." Nor's tone was flat, his focus on the smiling man hurrying toward him. "In-training agents, unassigned ones. All sorts."

"Welcome back, Wade." The man shook his hand and walked past him.

"So." Theo followed him with his eyes and he could have sworn the man was almost skipping. "How we gonna find Iliana in here?" He shoved his hands in his pockets as he returned his gaze to Nor.

"We're gonna talk to my boss. He's the best tracker there is."

"Wait, aren't you in the outs with him because you told Theo your big secret?" Scarlett asked.

This was the first time Theo had heard of that. He didn't know that Nor and his boss were fighting because of him. But why the hell wouldn't he tell him about it? And more importantly, why does Scarlett know?

"Yeah, but if we go in together, I'm hoping he won't do anything." Nor knocked on the door three times before the man behind it told him to come in. "He's very understanding."

The voice coming out of the room was gruff, oddly musical. As Nor pushed the door open, the man sat in a chair that looked like a throne, his back turned to them as he gazed at an incredible view of New York City through a vast window. It was the best view Theo had ever seen.

"Norman." The man's Scottish accent was thick. "I see ye brought some company." He turned the chair around and stood to face them. Though he was no taller than an average fourteen-year-old, there was no mistaking his age. Muscle packed his compact frame.

He wore official-looking clothes, the kind a boss would wear. He was holding a short cane and wore black sunglasses obscured his eyes. It did not take a genius to figure out he was blind.

"Hello, sir. I'm Theod—"

"Yes, yes, I know." The man interrupted and turned his head to the left. "Welcome back, Wade."

"Thanks, boss." Nor put his hands behind his back and lowered his head a little. "But, I'm not staying."

Behind the glasses, Theo couldn't tell if the boss was angry. But it was clear he wasn't when he laughed and shook his head. "Of course you're not, son." He spread his arms wide. "Come here."

Nor smiled and went to hug him.

"Um, excuse me," Theo interrupted as he remembered what they came here for. "We're looking for someone."

"Oh." the man turned to him. "Who might that be?"

"It's Iliana. She's missing."

"That's a hard one. She's always been the best at covering her tracks."

"It's okay; we have nothing else to do." Scarlett walked forward and took a sip from a bottle of scotch on his table after sniffing it. "And we're pretty desperate."

"Great." The boss paused, surprised. "Let's get started, then."

"Hmm." Scarlett smiled and threw the bottle to Theo, who caught it out of reflex and put it in his bag. How in the hell did they come to stealing scotch bottles?

They followed every step the old man showed. Theo expected him to use some kind of device or power for the tracking, but he just kept tracing what little *Ashé* Iliana left behind. Theo could sense it too, but it was floating all around him in no specific direction. And when, out of curiosity, he asked him how he could do it, he just said. "It's one of my many talents". The guy was creepy as hell.

"She's in some cemetery just outside the city." The boss spoke. Hints of sadness and hesitation wavered in his voice.

"Yeah, that makes sense." Nor plopped down on a bench beside Morgana in a park where they stopped to rest as the sun was halfway down the sky. "This week is the anniversary of the Great War's victims. She's gotta be visiting someone's grave."

"If she's who we suspect she is, she could be at my mother's. If we catch her there, she can't lie about it."

Scarlett looked at Theo in surprise and softly punched his shoulder. "Good on you, Jensen. Taking the initiative."

"Well, I gotta do something sometime."

The old man sighed and stood up. "I think my part here is done." He put his hand on Nor's shoulder. "I hope you find what you're looking for, Wade." He smiled and vanished in an instant.

Morgana looked up from where she sat on the truck's hood as they approached. There was something different in her expression, more troubled or conflicted than when they had left her. She pushed off from the truck as she turned to Theo and opened her mouth like she wanted to say something then closed it. He was too tired to ask what was wrong. He blinked at her once and managed a smile. They had bigger problems to worry about now.

As night fell, Theo told the others to wait for him in the truck. He needed a few minutes alone, though they didn't have that kind of time.

Every decision and mistake that led them here replayed in his mind. Two months ago, he had been just a guy with a secret. But time had turned into a puppeteer, dragging him along like a useless doll.

It wasn't the danger he dreaded, but the nameless ache inside him. Deep down he knew he was not made to save anything. Damian was never the real threat. *He* was.

Theo snorted and looked up. The sky offered nothing. The stars were nonexistent, streams of gray the color of ash and soot stretched instead. They blanketed the sky, hiding the full moon in its powerful light behind them. Theo thought of it as a good thing, because the moon irritated him when it was full. He sighed and went back to the truck.

Theo was halfway to the car when the first spatter of rain prompted him to pick up the pace. The night was strangely quiet except for the relaxing sound of the faint water drops on the roof of the truck as they drove through the empty streets. A soft touch on his shoulder startled him as he buried his face in his hands.

"Hey, you okay?" Scarlett's voice was so low it was hard to make out the words.

He was tired of that question.

"Yeah, why wouldn't I be?" Another day, same lie.

"I don't know. You just seemed off these past weeks, and you've been blocking me."

"No, really." He forced a chuckle. "I'm fine."

Nor stared at him from the rearview mirror as he drove.

Were they both suspecting something?

***

The cemetery was the kind that pretended to be maintained. Gravel paths between stones, a few plastic flowers in wire holders. But the older graves at the back had sunk into the ground, some tilted forward as if bowing, others listed sideways.

"Theo," Morgana's voice strained as she fell into step beside him. "I should have told you before, but…" She swallowed hard. "I saw Iliana yesterday. After the fight. We talked." The weight of her words settled over him like the dampness in the air.

"What?" Theo halted as he turned to her, fists shaking at his sides. "Why didn't you say anything?"

Morgana averted her eyes, picking at her nails. "Because I…she was practically my mother. She said she looked for me." She paused. "We talked for so long. She told me she sent John to take me because she couldn't come back." Blood pooled at her fingertip as she pulled out a hangnail. "She said she would fix it. She even gave me how to contact her. But I don't—"

Before she could say anything else, Theo spotted a distant, blurred silhouette. Smoky fog rose from behind it and slid along, moving between the tombstones; creating a blinding screen.

"Did you see that?" He pointed at nothing.

Morgana blinked at the sudden change of subject, not knowing that it was deliberate because he hated seeing her stripped of her usual confidence.

"What?" Nor narrowed his eyes ran from behind them. "I can't see a thing."

Scarlett shifted and flew her way past the thick fog.

Theo followed her with his eyes and started running toward the figure. As he stopped, he dashed his hand through his wet hair as the rain swept it over his forehead. The scene in front of him was clearer now. Theo's eyes flew open. He covered his mouth, nausea surging. The body lay against his mother's tombstone, drenched in blood. Eyes and mouth wide. Throat slit open. Iliana, the high priestess, the woman they've been looking for all day.

Morgana stumbled past him, her face white as death. "That's not—" A strangled sound escaped her throat, stopping her mid-sentence. "I should have stayed with her." She fell to her knees beside the body. "She raised me. She was my…" Her forehead creased as her voice cracked, cutting the sentence short.

Theo's heart broke like he'd lost a part of his soul. She *was* his aunt. She was alive this morning.

He froze in place, eyes burning at the edges. Somber fog floated around him like a protective shield as his hands balled into fists.

A switch flipped, shutting off everything that made him human. All the good memories flashed before him, fading one after the other. The void consumed him—suffocating, locking him away, and suppressing the light as the darkness took over.

17
INTERLUDE: KAI
MORTAL WEAPON

The mansion creaked under Kai's weight as he moved through shadow-filled halls. A door ahead, marked with bullet holes and deep scratches, stood ajar. As he stepped forward, the oppressive silence broke with the rhythmic drip of water from the ceiling. He froze.

"Crow." A rough voice rang out from behind him, in the dark.

Kai whipped around, flashlight flickering before breaking, plunging him into darkness. He tossed the useless light away, straining to sense the man's presence.

"Are you one of them?" Kai croaked, throat dry. "The guardians?"

"What do you know about us?" the man's growl was directionless, making Kai whirl around in his place.

Mid spin, a grip closed around his throat, lifting him off the ground.

"I…I know about the weapon," Kai choked out, the words barely making it past the pressure on his windpipe. The grip loosened as the lights flickered back on. Kai used the moment and shoved the giant hand away and leaped backward, massaging his neck. As he looked up, the man stood, tense fists on his side, and his gaze unreadable.

"No one talks about it anymore," he said between gritted teeth as he thudded closer toward Kai.

"But it exists, right?" Kai straightened, trying to put on a confident front, while his throat dried and his head spun from the choke. "Where are the other guardians?"

"Few people know of it. But yes, it exists." The man sighed and sank to the floor, his eyes drooped and tired. "Why do you want to know?" He tilted his head down staring at his scar-studded hands, the hands of a warrior. His eyes held a familiar glimmer of regret.

"A war's coming." Kai dropped beside him. "And the weapon is the only thing that can stop Damian." The man looked up at him and Kai wanted to give him a hug, but he settled for a light touch on the shoulder. "You should know that."

After a beat, the guardian broke out in a series of low, ground rumbling laughs "A war is always coming, as long as Damian is alive." He shook his head and his frown deepened, creasing his forehead. "What makes you think the *weapon* is enough to stop him?"

"It's a risk I'm willing to take." Kai exhaled sharply and jumped back on his feet as Theo's face flashing behind his eyes, reminding him what he was fighting for. "My brother shouldn't suffer for Amarys or anyone else's mistakes."

"Your brother?" The man scowled and a deprecating chuckle escaped him as a flash of recognition crossed his eyes.

"Yes." Kai's mind's landed on the memory of Theo punching him, and his mouth stretched into a smile. "Even if he hates me."

"Then you don't know him very well," the man whispered, "this *brother* of yours." He pushed against wall behind him to get to his feet. Kai followed suit and helped him up.

"I hope you know what you're doing." The man crouched to pick up a cane. "For me, there's no point in fighting. I'm a guardian with nothing left to protect."

Kai's eyes narrowed and he swallowed. "Did the weapon kill the others?"

"What?" The man staggered back in bafflement. His gaze drifted to a distance Kai was not privy to. "She never killed anyone."

"She?" So it was a human weapon, just as he suspected. "Do you remember who she was?"

"It has been almost thirty years, son." The guardian's jaw worked. For a moment, the shadow of something broken muddled the man's face stood abruptly. "I'm sorry, but you need to leave now."

"Please." Kai grabbed his wrist, regretting it immediately as the man sent him a deadly glare. He let go and softened his voice. "Tell me what happened to her, and You'll never see me again." This weapon was his last chance to save Theo, his last hope before he…

"She was so small," The man said in a hesitant whisper. "The hunter carried her on his shoulder like a doll." He paused. "Unconscious, covered in blood."

"Who was this hunter?" Kai did his best to stifle a smile. He was so close.

"He went by Shikari at the time." The man scoffed. "I'm sure you've heard of him. He was infamous in witch circles."

"Wait." Kai staggered at the familiar name taking him back to his early training years. "He was my mentor." He ran a hand through his sweaty hair and let out a sharp breath. His own mentor had the information the whole time, and he kept it from him, even knowing his desperation.

"Yes," the man nodded, snapping Kai from his spiral. "He is the one you want to find."

Kai sent him a half nod and printed out the door, feeling bile rising in his throat.

The B&B walls closed in on him as his mind raced. His mentor, Shikari, involved in stealing the first human weapon? He had to speak with him, confront him.

Kai pulled on his Crow clothes and left, moving swiftly through Brooklyn's quiet streets. Near the bridge, the headlights of passing cars illuminated the road, leading him toward his bunker, now commandeered by his own brother.

The place was too quiet, too still. No one was home. Kai rifled through the drawers, searching for anything useful. He froze at the sound of Nor's truck pulling over. Panic made his hand tremble, and he scrambled for a hiding spot, but it was too late. Nor and Scarlett's voices came first, sounding like they were in the middle of intense conversation when they saw him. They halted, Scarlett falling silent mid-sentence.

"You're here?" Scarlett's voice was incredulous. "What are you doing here?"

Kai steadied his breathing and glanced behind them, hoping to see Theo. "I'm looking for my brother."

"He's not here." Nor crossed his arms and moved toward Kai, towering over him like a threat.

"Don't worry, I'm not gonna hurt him." Kai forced a smile and raised his hands in surrender. "I just wanna talk."

"He's gone." Scarlett blurted, as her expression turned somber. "We lost him."

"What do you mean, you *lost him*?"

What if it had already happened? What if it was too late? "How?"

"We were looking for Iliana. We found her in the cemetery," Nor said, his voice heavy as his arms fell to his sides, all defensiveness gone. "Theo…he didn't take it well, and we lost track of him in the fog."

"His eyes. Were his eyes black?" Bile rose in Kai's throat. No, it could not have already happened. There was still time. He still had time to make it right.

Scarlett and Nor nodded, exchanging uneasy looks. They had no idea what they were dealing with or who their friend truly was.

"Damn it," Kai muttered, unable to hide the quiver in his voice as he paced the bunker from wall to wall. "I'm afraid he's already gone."

"Kai, stop," Scarlett shouted, grabbing his head to force him to look at her. "What are you talking about?"

Kai's vision blurred and his limbs went numb. Another attack was coming. One of the last ones. "I can't do this anymore." His breathing labored as he rested his hands on his knees. "I can't die and leave him like that."

"Wait." Scarlett stepped back, mouth agape. "You mean you're…dying?"

Kai could not manage anything but a slight nod. It was out now and there was no going back.

"Why?" Nor's voice was flat. "What's wrong with you?"

"It doesn't matter." Kai wiped sweat from his forehead. "I just wanted to help Theo. But it's too late now."

"Then what do you want to do? Just let him go?"

She understood nothing, and yet she still fought for him. Maybe he would be in good, capable hands after all, after Kai was gone.

"I'm pretty sure Damian is behind his disappearance." Nor leaned forward.

Scarlett frowned. "Why would he listen to us?"

"Because I know what he wants," Nor said, "and I know how to get it."

"What are you talking about?" Kai asked.

Nor turned to him. "Damian's always wanted one thing…his brother."

"You want to give him Theo?" Kai's eyes widened.

Nor shook his head. "Not Theo. Just Casimir. We just need to separate them."

"No, that's impossible." Kai stomped closer to Nor. But there was no point; they would not hear anything else. "We'll lose him, anyway. You don't understand—"

"We're going to see my father," Nor interrupted him and turned to leave. "He knows more about Damian's history. And when Theo comes back, we don't tell him any of this. We tell him we're killing Damian."

Kai stood still for a moment as a sigh escaped him. "I hope you know what you're doing," he muttered. "I'll come with."

"Are you sure you—" Scarlett started.

"Yes, I'm fine." Kai stood straight. There was no way he would have missed a chance to save Theo. Not while he was still alive.

"Good." Nor smirked as fished his truck keys out of his pocket. "Let's go."

Kai shifted on his feet, glancing at Nor, whose hand hovered over the door, fingers twitching as if knocking was beneath him. There was something unspoken between them, a familiarity with how Nor braced himself before the door opened. Kai couldn't tell if it was impatience or reluctant resignation. Finally, he knocked. The sound echoed, sharp and final.

John stood in the doorway, wary but not surprised. He eyed them with unsettling knowing.

"John," Nor and Kai said in unison.

Kai swallowed. He hadn't expected to feel small in the presence of a man who once had so much power over him. He sank into the couch, stiff, as though the weight of secrets would crush him.

Kai slid the paper across the table. "This is part of the blueprints for the weapon's creation."

John's face went pale. "You shouldn't have that. You shouldn't even know about it!"

"I went to the orphanage," Kai said, voice tight. "Alix told me everything. About what you did to her."

Scarlett's voice cut through. "Wait…the mortal weapon?"

Kai and John turned to her, startled.

"You know about her?" Kai asked.

"Of course," Scarlett replied, voice edged with bitterness. "I was a guardian."

"But Alix told me they were all dead." Kai's lips twitched as frustration piled up inside him. "Why would he lie?"

Scarlett's eyes flashed with something Kai could not place, and she glanced away. "After the incident, we were the only ones left. I told Alix to swear he'd tell no one about me being one of them."

"Wait, you know who she is, then." Maybe Scarlett was more useful than he had thought.

"I don't know what she looks like now." Voice low, Scarlett shrugged. "The last time I saw her, she was a child with no identity."

Nor shifted, leaning forward. "Isn't there someone who could recognize her?"

Scarlett murmured. "Maybe…Alix? He was closest to her. If he sees her again, he might know."

"We need her." Kai was on his feet. "She's the only one who can kill Damian and bring Theo back." It was finally happening. Damian would be gone, one less threat to Theo's existence.

John's eyes narrowed. "You think she would kill Damian?"

Kai met his gaze. "I believe she can." Even if she, whoever she was, wouldn't want to, he would make her. There was nothing for him to lose at this point.

"Theo's not our only problem anymore." Nor stood abruptly. "We need to move fast."

Kai closed his eyes. "We'll need to find her. And then we'll have to make sure she's willing to do what we need."

18
FAMILY

Theo rose from oblivion with a grunt, rolled over and curled around himself, trembling from the cold. With a gasp, his eyes flew open to darkness. Not pitch black, but some greenish darkness that barely allowed shapes to form. The tang of seaweed and the distant breaking of waves roamed the air.

What happened? How did he get here?

Theo pressed his palms into the ground, slipped on something slick, and fell back into the wet sand. He raised his slick hands, trying to see what it was. Under the faint light, it looked like sticky black goo.

"Back to your boring old self already?" a voice echoed behind him, low and familiar.

The person now stood before him, holding a torch in front of his face, covering his face. But Theo didn't need to see his face to know who it was. Damian.

"Where am I?" Theo rose, standing on wobbly feet as he kept the shadow, threatening his resolve at bay.

"Some beach." A grin pulled at Damian's lips before he tossed the only source of light into the deep sea, pulling them back into darkness. Theo squeezed his eyes shut, resisting the urge to lunge at Damian and give him a reason to never smile again.

"How the hell did I get here?" His tight fists trembled. The last thing he remembered was standing in the cemetery over Iliana's dead body.

There was no answer, but the sound of heavy boots crunching the sand beneath them.

"I brought you here. Found you passed out with Iliana." Damian's voice was too close, his warm breath brushing Theo's face, making him recoil.

"Is everything a joke to you?" Theo clenched his jaw, teeth grinding together as he shoved Damian's shoulder. "Get the hell away from me, bastard."

"That's not very polite, Teddy." Damian feigned offence as a dramatic gasp escaped him. "Didn't the hunter teach you some manners?"

"You don't get to fucking call me that." Theo managed between labored breaths as he wrapped his wet jacket around him. "Only my brother can call me that."

"But I *am* your brother." Damian placed a warm hand on his shoulder.

"No, you're not." Theo shrugged his hand off, immediately missing the warmth of the contact. "I don't know you."

"Sure, you do." Damian's footsteps retreated. "You just need another little push to remember who you are first."

"W-what do you mean, another push?"

It was getting harder and harder to speak as his teeth chattered against each other. Theo wanted to kill him, but he had never killed before.

Or had he? He looked down at his hands again. The black goo—whose blood was that?

"Damian, what on earth are you doing? I thought I told you to get me when he wakes up."

The man held a flashlight in his hand. The glare blinded Theo.

"Seth. I was just having some fun with our guest." Damian put his hands behind his back as he gestured his chin toward the guy, who sighed and rolled his eyes. "Of course, you're welcome to join."

"Yeah." Seth nodded and as soon as he turned to Theo, he froze. Clicking his fingers together, Theo started moving toward the man, and halted as he faced Seth, hanging by his shirt in the man's grip.

Seth's eyes were those of a true killer; cold, empty. Deep scars webbed his yellow skin. His long silver hair hung around his twisted face.

"Did you see my mother?" Seth said.

His mother?

Theo blinked, turning back to face him. "I don't even know who you are, let alone your mother."

"Right." Seth sighed and let go of him. "She's the high priestess. I assumed you met her."

Theo clenched his jaw as the horrifying image flashed before him again; Iliana's bloodied body, leaning against his mother's grave.

"She's dead." The words barely came out.

Seth's eyes widened and he turned away.

"I see."

"Oh, no." Damian ran in front of them and twisted Seth's hands, who gave an agonizing scream. "Don't tell me you're gonna get all sad and broody."

Seth's jaw worked as he glared at Damian, a look promising death. "My mother is gone."

"So?" Damian shrugged and released him. "It doesn't matter, now."

"You're right." Seth twisted his hands, every little bone cracking back into its place. "Let's enlighten Cas, shall we?"

Numbness enveloped Theo. What kind of people was he dealing with?

An extended pale hand startled Theo, whose owner was smiling at him, dimples at both sides of his cheeks. The face was...*familiar*. He'd never seen this person before. He knew that. But the shape of the jaw, the slight crookedness of smile.

"I'm Seth," he said, "your cousin."

Theo's tongue went dry. The familiarity was Casimir's.

"See? It's a nice family we have here." Damian moved closer, his hands on his hips as he shook his head. "What a beautiful little reunion."

"My mother is no longer with us, remember? And neither is yours."

"Speaking of family." Damian's grin widened as he turned to Theo. "You really thought our little fight was random? That I just happened to attack you?" He chuckled. "I wanted to force you to use your magic. I needed Cas back, not weakling Theo."

"You...you planned it?" Theo took a second to understand, but the understanding was worse than not knowing.

Damian nodded. "Though our pathetic hunter brother keeps being a pain in the ass, wanting to *save you*. But you don't need saving."

“What are you even talking about, you manipulative little shi—” Theo started forward, but Damian cut him off as he raised his hand.

“Now, now. No need for that.” He snapped his fingers.

The sound was loud and daunting as Theo’s neck twisted and he thumped onto the wet sand, his vision going dark.

19
REVELATION

The numbness of sleep slowly faded from Theo's limbs. Dead grass poked into his back, like tiny needles. He gasped, choking on his dry tongue.

Damian and Seth were a blur, but their voices carried.

"What did you do?" Seth backed away and put his hands on his head. "Did you kill him?"

"Of course not. Relax." Damian raised his hands and closed his eyes. "It's just something I invented—slows the body down a bit, makes you think you're dead."

"Well, did you consider what would happen to your grand plan when he's seriously dead?" Seth's voice rose in frustration. "Of course you didn't, because you *never* do."

"Oh, shut up, look." Damian gestured toward Theo. "He's already awake. Plan intact."

Theo's muscles were like stone, but he managed to turn his head. Damian's finger was pointing at him, and Seth was slapping his forehead repeatedly, muttering under his breath.

In desperation, he sucked in another breath, burning his lungs, like he was on the edge of disappearing. But his mind was clear; it was like his brain was the only thing alive inside of him.

"You'll be fine, brother." Damian's tone didn't match his words.

"Let's hope he's still the same old Casimir." Seth sighed.

Theo pushed Damian and threw him on the ground as he tried to place his hand on his shoulder. His knees screamed as he stood.

Theo walked, his unblinking eyes fixed on Damian, who was still struggling on the ground. He caught him by his hair and pulled him up. For the first time, unmasked pain and inconsolable fear consumed Damian's face. The expression filled Theo with satisfaction; he couldn't hold back a smile. Then, as Damian was screaming in agony, he spat on his face and threw him into Seth like garbage.

The two fell on each other. Seth lost consciousness as he hit his head on a piece of wood. But Damian got up fast and ran, barefoot, to the crescent. Theo moved to follow, then collapsed to his knees, coughing black blood that poured from his eyes, nose, and ears. He slipped against the solid wall. The headache was back, infinite whispers overwhelming him until he hit his head repeatedly on the ship's body.

He struggled to breathe, struggled to move as he trembled. The only thing keeping him conscious were the images of Scarlett every time he closed his eyes; she looked in pain too, screaming, hands on her head.

Let *him in, let him in.* One voice spoke, louder than the rest. The old woman from the dream, except deeper, harder to hear.

Theo couldn't think straight. So, he let it all out in a deafening scream that shook the earth, and everything went black.

***

Theo was not in a white room. No, this time. It was a dark stormy forest where everything burned and got kicked around by the wind. In a distance, he spotted it for the second time, the entrance, the exit, sealed for as long as he could remember. It was now gaping wide. Beckoning him into the world he was afraid to see.

His footsteps echoed despite the loud whistling of the wind and the wild growling of the flames. The gate closed with every step he took. So he ran faster, gasping, panting and coughing, and jumped to the other side without thinking.

Theo opened his eyes and, as he drew in a sharp breath, life came back to him. He looked around him; he was back in the bunker. Nor leaned against a wall, Scarlett paced, Kai sat rigid on a small table, Morgana beside him. Their faces were turned away, except Morgana who held his hand and stared at him with watery eyes.

"What is it?" Theo broke the depressing silence. "What did I do?"

But there was no appropriate reaction to his questions. They just shook their heads and looked away. Theo had just started imagining the worst, and Morgana sighed and stood up. "Cut it out, already," she growled. "He needs to know that we know."

"I'm sorry, Teddy," Kai said, his voice beginning to break. "I tried to save you so many times, but you wouldn't let me."

Kai must have told them while Theo was with Damian. Their eyes said everything, sadness and resignation. Mourning him before he was even gone.

"Why the hell didn't you tell us that Casimir is part of you?" Nor snapped and moved closer. "We could've helped you."

As if.

Theo scratched his hair and turned his gaze away. There was no helping him.

"You know what? Fuck you." Scarlett glared at him.

"Scarlett—" Nor started.

"No, no, let me speak." She raised her hand, shutting him up. "You block me from your head for months, and tell me that nothing was wrong." She turned to Theo. "I'm your familiar. Why do you think we can do telepathy, huh? My sole and only purpose in this shitty life is to support you, to help you! Why can't you see that?"

She was right; even if he didn't want to tell anyone else, he should've told *her*.

"I'm sorry." Those were the only words he could form, knowing they could never be enough.

"Did you know you unblocked me earlier?" Scarlett's voice was back to normal, but her exhaustion was painfully obvious. "Or you just slipped, I don't know. But you attacked me." Tears fell on her face. "Your mind is…messy. I actually feel guilty and I hate myself for it." She wiped her face with the back of her hand. "Look at me, I'm crying and they're not even my emotions."

"Hey, come on," Nor's voice saved Theo from having to answer Scarlett. "What's done is done. It's all in the past now. We need to focus on what's coming."

"You *can* say it, you know?" Morgana nodded. "*War* is coming."

What war?

"Well, we all agreed to the plan except Teddy." Kai jumped from the table and removed the hood. "I'll fill him in."

Theo looked around, and everyone was nodding their heads in silence.

"I haven't forgiven you, you know?" He grunted as he pushed off the bed.

"I don't expect you to. But I just need you to know that everything I did and will do is for you. Please, never doubt that."

Theo sighed, feeling guilty. He stomped on that guilt, but it sat inside his heart like an unscratched itch. Every person in the room was avoiding eye contact with him, and that was worse than staring.

He turned his gaze to the ceiling. "What's this plan you were talking about?"

"I know you don't like introductions." Kai pulled Theo with him to the bed and sat beside him. "So, I'm gonna get straight to the point. We're gonna kill Damian."

A murderous glee jolted Theo to his feet, but he sat back down, trying to tune it down.

"How?" He shook his head as his veins shifted under his burning skin. "Did you find a way? I heard he was unkillable."

"Well," Kai nodded. "We're gonna use a human weapon to destroy him."

"I can do it. I think I'm more powerful than him. *Casimir* is more powerful," Theo said. Who could do it other than him? It had to be him.

"No, you can't control Casimir." Kai shook his head. "Even if you succeed, we'll lose you forever."

"I don't care. He has to be stopped by *my* hands." Theo took a deep breath. He wanted to shout, let it out. It was just so easy to be cruel at that moment.

Scarlett reached out to him. "Theo, we're just trying to protect you—"

"Stop saying that. I'm not a fucking baby!" There it was. Like a veil lifting off him.

"He's right, it isn't always about protection." Morgana joined and glanced at Kai. "You have to let each other make your own decisions. So, it's up to Theo; we move with the plan or we let him handle it."

"What happens if I fail?"

Morgana's mouth quirked up. "We die heroes." She raised her hands. "Look, I'm not gonna lie to you, it *will* be your fault."

"No," Scarlett interrupted. "We find another way like we always do."

"Settle your feathers," Morgana scoffed. "That kind of wishful thinking never got anyone anywhere except into an early grave. But, if you're into that…" She shrugged.

"It's called hope. Something I'm sure you've never heard of." Scarlett looked her up and down.

Theo stared at the floor, his hands shaking at his sides. The silence pressed down on him, suffocating. He had to make a choice and it wasn't just about him, not this time. There were lives at stake. But he didn't believe in hope anymore. Their belief would have to be enough.

"Fine. I'll do it." He looked up, steadying his voice, and glanced at Morgana. "But if it fails…" He let the threat hang in the air.

"We're confident it won't. The girl has so much power," Kai breathed out.

"Okay, so we'll be looking for the weapon." Nor grabbed the keys and threw them to Morgana. "While Damian is not haunting us."

"Hey, can I talk to him for a second?" Morgana said, pointing at Theo.

"We'll be waiting in the car." Nor nodded and went as the others followed him.

Theo kept his gaze on Morgana as she got closer to him.

"Are you sure about this?" she asked as she caressed his cheek. Her touch was warm, soft; it sent shivers down his whole body with every stroke of her finger. Morgana had a way of calming him he couldn't pinpoint.

"Are you worried about me?" A corner of his mouth lifted.

"Don't be ridiculous." A flush crept up her face as she quickly removed her hand. "I just wanted to make sure that you weren't gonna chicken out at the last minute."

"Hmm." Theo narrowed his eyes, still smiling. "Why are you doing this?"

"What?" She brightened.

"Treating me like a person. That doesn't seem like you."

Morgana chuckled and swallowed again, her heart beating like a drum. "Umm, I mean…that's an excellent question. Do you think we should find out?"

Theo nodded and gulped down a breath.

"Well." He stood and leaned over her, holding her face in his hands. Her skin was soft. "I guess we should if the plan works out."

"You mean *when* the plan works out."

"Is that wishful thinking I'm hearing?" Theo chuckled. "Guess you're the one who's into an early grave."

Theo put his finger on Morgana's lips and planted a light kiss on her forehead as she opened her mouth to speak. He kept his expression steady while his insides trembled.

"It's not a crime to have hope," he said. Although he didn't believe in it, it needed to be said. He had to say it to *her*. Theo stared into her eyes, into her soul; it was one of a little girl in a corner, just as broken as he was, hiding behind a wall of glass, a mask, afraid to face herself.

"What happened with Iliana? Before we—" He softened his voice, his hands still framing her face. "Before we found her. When you saw her yesterday, what did you talk about?" He paused, searching her face for a reaction. "You've been different since you got back."

"She said she didn't do it." Morgana's eyes flickered, and for a moment her mask slipped, her eyes filling with tears that she refused to let fall. "She didn't abandon me." Her voice caught as she pulled back. "John threatened her to leave, and he…he took me from her." She turned her gaze away and wiped at her eye as a single tear emerged. "We said we were gonna be in each other's lives again, we…" The self-deprecating laugh that followed was harder to hear than anything she'd said.

He bit the inside of his cheek and pulled at her chin, making her look at him. "You'll be okay," he nodded, not sure he meant it. "You're the strongest person I know." Theo let go of her face and walked past the door without looking back, his heart in his throat.

20
SHADOW

Nor's truck stopped in front of the building where they were supposed to find Alix. Theo got out, closing his eyes against the darkening sky. A tingle crawled up the base of his skull as he stepped inside. Quiet. Creepy.

Scarlett flew past them. Kai and Morgana stayed close. Theo raised his hand. A small ball of light bloomed into his palm, bright enough to fill the mansion.

"Are you sure this is the place?" Morgana picked up one of the broken dolls from the floor.

"Of course, I would never forget this orphanage." Kai snatched the puppet from her hand and threw it away.

Theo shook his head as the chaos overwhelmed him; violence, sadness, grief, pain…even happiness. Kai's hand on his shoulder was reassurance enough.

"Are you okay?" he said.

"Sure, I can handle it," Theo mumbled, unconvinced, watching as Kai's uncertain nod sent him toward Nor.

"Well, it's just you and me. So…"

"Yeah, we are…alone." Theo didn't know what to tell her.

"Oh! Did you see that?" Morgana yelled, breaking the awkward silence. "Something black just passed by us."

"Maybe it's him, the guardian." Theo raised his head. As soon as he started running, Morgana fell behind him, choking.

"Hey, what's wrong?" He grabbed her. She tried to speak, but blood choked her answer. Casimir pushed at edges of him. For the first time, he wanted him through.

"Theo," Morgana choked up his name. "Your eyes, they're black." She stood, gripping his face. "Whatever you're doing, don't. I'm okay, look at me." She smiled, even as blood trickled the corners of her mouth.

He was back. Morgana pulled him back. He didn't know how, but she did.

"Yeah, yeah. I'm good." He backed away, and suddenly the light went on and a man appeared.

"You're Casimir." He bowed his head. "A true honor."

"Did you do this to her?" Theo walked closer to him.

"I didn't know you were Casimir." He bowed again. "Forgive me."

The way he spoke was strange to Theo. His tone and words had a fair amount of respect in them. It was the first time Theo had met someone who has heard of Casimir beside Damian. Someone who didn't hate him.

"Are you Alix?" He certainly looked like an Alix with his brown hero hair and the round-shaped face.

"I am, yes."

Theo needed to know more, and clearly Alix knew him better than he knew himself. "What do you know about me?"

But the man wasn't able to answer him as Scarlett interrupted. "Alix," she called. "Long time no see."

He turned to her and went to hug her. "Scarr? What are you doing here?" His gaze went frantic, shifting from her to Theo.

“Scar?” Theo repeated under his breath, but Scarlett heard him and rolled her eyes, pointing at him.

“I’m this dumbass’s familiar, believe it or not.”

“Really? Wow.” Alix sounded unenthused, and he looked like he was about to burst as he forced a chuckle.

“Yeah, well.” Scarlett shrugged. Her face shifted when she said it. A flicker of something like recognition Theo almost missed. “He’s a pain in the ass most of the time.”

“Oh, okay.” He nodded at the uncalled for insult, not able to shake the unsettling feeling in his chest. “Thanks for letting me know.”

Met with silence, Theo turned to Alix’s wide eyes fixed on something over his shoulder.

“Birdie,” he muttered under his breath as his face blanched, looking like he’d seen a ghost. Theo frowned and followed his gaze all the way to Morgana, who glanced at her sides as her upper lip stretched in annoyance.

“What?” She shrugged, but Alix ignored her and moved closer with careful steps, the way one would approach a child. Without thinking, Theo shifted slightly, putting himself between her and Alix.

“You found her, Scarr.” He blinked, eyes never budging from Morgana’s face. “Why didn’t you tell me?”

“Do I know you?” Morgana frowned and crossed her arms.

“What are you—” Scarlett cut herself off as her mouth fell open and she went very still for a moment. “You sure?”

She pointed her finger at Morgana and turned to Alix, who nodded at her with a smile.

“What? What is it?” Theo didn’t understand what was going on, but he could tell from Scarlett’s expression that she realized something important and she was stupid not to see it.

"It's her." Scarlett turned back to Theo after she spared a glance at Morgana. "This bitch is the goddamn weapon."

Scarlett stared at her feet with her mouth fully agape.

Morgana moved closer to Theo, not quite touching, but close enough that he felt it. It was subtle, probably unnoticeable to the others, but after she had confided in him last night, something had changed between them.

Morgana stiffened slightly. Her lips pressed together, eyes momentarily clouding with something unreadable.

"You didn't know?" Alix broke the silence that stretched uncomfortably more than it should have.

"You're wrong. She can't—she can't be the weapon."

If she were, Theo would have to break his promise to protect her.

"What are you even saying?" Scarlett shook her head in disbelief and pointed her finger at Morgana. "You need to stop protecting her. Don't you remember our little rescue mission when she kidnapped and tortured Nor *Just for fun*? Did you?"

"That's all in the past. She's changed now."

"Since when?" Scarlett scoffed. "Since she came to us begging to be our friend? Or—"

"Careful there." Morgana moved to face Scarlett with a furious look on her face and a dagger in her hand. "Just because I'm here doesn't mean I have to like you." Morgana gritted her teeth. "Push me, and I'll pluck your feathers and shove them down your throat."

Theo could have sworn Scarlett flinched for a second.

"As for you." Morgana turned to him. "I didn't ask you to defend me." She sighed. "And if I'm the weapon, how the hell are we gonna use me?"

Theo pursed his lips. Her walls were back up.

"Well, look at you. Still up for it, huh?" Scarlett shrugged. "Guess I stirred the pot for nothing. My bad."

"Just stop." Morgana rolled her eyes to the ceiling and groaned.

"No, you don't have to do it. We have the other plan, remember?" Theo said. He wanted at any cost to free Morgana from that responsibility and take it himself, like he had planned.

"We started with this plan, we go on with this plan." She nodded. "I'm up for it. I'm not scared."

"You say that now." He held her gaze. "But you've never confronted Damian before, have you? You don't really know what he is. You've just heard of him, right?"

"I don't need to *really know what he is* if I have the means to kill him." She shrugged like it was nothing.

She was confident. Theo could smell it on her, too strong to shake with fear. In the first place, wasn't the weapon built to "destroy" Damian?

"Fine." He raised his hands is surrender despite the swirling in his stomach. "Do what you want. I'm not gonna stop you. But I'm not gonna help you either." Against his expectations, she smiled and put a hand on his cheek.

"Suit yourself." She walked past them, heading to the exit. But, as she neared the door, something stopped her from moving as if she were in the confines of an invisible cage.

"What the fuck?" She pushed at thin air.

"It's a barrier," Alix spoke as he emerged from a distance. Theo could have sworn he had just seen him standing next to them. He turned to Theo, kindness replaced by disgust. "I'm sorry, Scarlett. I didn't know you'd be with *him*."

"Remove it, right now." Morgana cracked her fingers as she reached for the dagger in her belt.

"I'm afraid I can't do that, my dear." He took a few steps back and raised his hand, making it into a fist. "It was something I had to do." With one last glance at Scarlett, he vanished into thin air.

"No!" Theo stumbled over, hitting the invisible wall. "Why would he do this?"

"Someone got to him," Scarlett sighed, rubbing the bridge of her nose and looked around. "Where the hell are Nor and Kai?"

"Well, something must have happened to them while we were distracted by that asshole." Morgana flumped to the ground. "I can't believe we fell for it. He's obviously one of Damian's lapdogs."

"So now we're stuck here." Theo sat beside her. "And it's your fault." He pointed at Morgana and Scarlett, who were crossing their arms, averting his gaze, feigning innocence. Theo rolled his eyes. "Great. Let's wait for the rescue."

Hours passed and they were still trapped.

Morgana tried to slash air with her daggers, Scarlett with her beak and talons. But nothing worked, like the barrier was not even there. It was too powerful and more ancient than any of them.

Alix really knew what he was doing.

"God, I can't sit here and do nothing," Scarlett said as she got up and turned, then started hitting the air with her beak.

"Hey genius, that guy was *your* friend." Morgana rolled her eyes. "You're the reason we're here in the first place," she mumbled to herself.

"Say that again." Scarlett turned back and rushed toward Morgana.

"Look where we are. " she sighed. "Your *friend* betrayed us. Who knows, maybe you're next. Just shut up and sit down." She waved a dismissive hand and turned to Theo. "Hey man, you're the witch here. Do some witchy stuff."

Theo froze. Her voice was far away. He was there but not, surrounded not by walls, but by images and words. He was lost in himself. In the past. Casimir's past.

His fingertips tingled—but steady, not the frantic tremors he had known. A slow exhale. Shadows flowing like waves instead of prickling thorns. Tendrils bending around his arms, calm, obedient. The sensation of dipping a hand in warm water, vast but welcoming. Breathing in rhythm with the shadows. He *was* the shadows.

"Theo?" Morgana called, but there was no answer either. Then, the look of realization fell on her face and she clicked her tongue. "Casimir?"

At that moment, Theo drew in a sharp breath as his eyes burned and his vision darkened. He stood and walked to the barrier, barely touching it with his hands. He inhaled and, as his bones rattled, the barrier disintegrated.

Theo gasped and took a step back as Morgana and Scarlett watched in silence. He looked up, a smile pulling at his face.

"I actually did it." His eyes darted between his hands and his friends. "That was me."

Except it wasn't. Not really. There was a difference, the shadows he'd grown used to versus what had moved through him a moment ago. It had a foreign edge to it, effortless, unrestrained.

"Sure it wasn't Casimir?" Morgana narrowed her eyes and pushed herself to her feet, dusting off her clothes.

"No, I was in control. I think." Theo frowned. Was he?

"Don't do that again." Scarlett caught him by the shoulders. "We can't risk it."

"Let's find the others and get the hell out," Theo sighed as he slammed his arms at his sides. *Bullshit. What did she know about risk?*

Morgana and Scarlett nodded, but skepticism crossed their faces. They weren't sure they were talking to Theo, who wasn't even sure he was himself. His skin was on fire and his eyes were going to pop out. Casimir's energy still flowed through him. Too much. Too alive.

21
WARNING

The sun streamed through the cracked window glass, yet Theo's mind was clouded with gray. They had already found his brother and Nor locked in a room. It was obviously Alix's doing. But, as they were leaving the building, everyone was on their guard and they were all glaring at Theo.

"What?" He walked past them with his head down.

"There is something seriously wrong with your face." Scarlett shook her head and looked away, her eyes glistening for a reason he didn't know. She knew something and she wasn't going to say it.

Theo pushed out a nervous chuckle and headed toward a mirror propped on the wall. It had that patina of age over its bronze frame, and likewise, the surface of the glass was splotched black in places. Theo stood before the mirror, his reflection distorted, showing the face the world saw, Casimir's. A webbing of dark veins was creeping across his skin. They beat around his eyes and neck as if alive, like snakes.

Breathing hurt. He kept moving anyway. But every step cost him. The darkness swallowed his vision, and he began to wonder if things could ever get better. The voices in his head started calling, but he never said a word.

Theo stared at himself in the mirror, at the sad, broken look in his eyes. Did nobody care? Had no one noticed?

Two gentle arms grabbed him by the shoulders and forced him to raise his head. Theo was ready to put on that usual fake smile.

"Don't," Nor's voice was a comforting sound. Theo looked up, his drooping eyes as gray as the ash in the dying fire. "You don't have to pretend with us." And behind him, his friends were smiling.

"But I have to." Theo fell to his knees and wiped his face. "You can't help me, no one can."

"Yes, we *can* help you," Scarlett said, reaching a hand towards her broken master.

"Were you not listening?" Theo shouted, swatting her outstretched limb as he stood. "Help doesn't—" he was silenced by a larger figure pulling him into a gentle yet firm hug.

"We're your family. We always want to help. And we will climb down into that pit ourselves to get you out if needed. I want you to smile for real again and I will not take no for an answer. You think you're alone in this, but it's the opposite. You've had me at your back since before you knew it."

There was a sweet moment of silence that Theo hoped would last forever, but—

"Don't mean to interrupt." Morgana got closer, her hand fanning her face. "But, we don't have time for this."

A chuckle escaped Theo as the other turned to her with a matching glare.

"What, I'm serious," she nodded. "We need to get out of this place before Axel finds out we escaped."

"I'm sure his name was Alix," Theo chuckled as he straightened.

"Oh great, he speaks." Morgana crossed her arms.

"Yes, he does." A strange rush jolted through him as he clenched his fists, a smile pulling at his lips. "Let's get out of here."

An instant later, there was a blinding flash coming from the outside, a ball of flame and a fist of gray smoke.6

Theo and the others hurried outside to find Nor's truck bursting into flames.

"What the fuck!" Nor raised his hands to his head and stumbled toward his once beloved vehicle, straight into the burning wrecks. "My car."

Theo stared at the fire. The warmth. The joy. His mouth quirked up on its own and a chuckle escaped him. He lowered his head and covered his mouth to keep himself from bursting with laughter.

"Dude, seriously?" Scarlett hit him on the back of the head.

"It's Casimir," he said between the laughs. "He won't stop."

"I've got the perfect cure." With a smile, she stepped on his foot without warning.

The world shook around Theo, and he almost fell on his back.

He and Scarlett ran beside Nor to get him away from the vehicle that was going to explode at any second. The smoke spread through the area like fog, so thick it was impossible for Theo to open his eyes, let alone see anything.

Then he stumbled on something. Something that shouldn't be there—something big—it moved. Theo hit the ground and fell on his face, but he turned around and it was there. A man, a body, a corpse.

"Nor," Scarlett called from somewhere. "I can't find you."

Was it Nor? Was it Kai?

Theo got back on his feet and stumbled toward the corpse.

There at last, but the face wasn't clear. He dropped to his knees and started pressing his palms on the person's chest. It was no use; he didn't move an inch.

Was he already dead? Theo put his hand on his head and focused all his energy on staring. He finally saw it as the smoke cleared. But, it wasn't at all what he expected; the body was faceless. It had a head, but no eyes, no ears, no mouth, no nose, and not even hair.

Theo flinched and backed away, but the faceless body got closer. As long as he kept backing away, it got even closer.

Was it a nightmare? A hallucination?

Theo stumbled, his hand moving on its own to the faceless body closing in, his hand stretched to its neck, and sliced through soft skin. Black goo—or was it red?—gushed from the wound as Theo frowned. This wasn't happening. He was seeing things.

Like a great rush of water, memories surged. Memories of Casimir. The images were from a different time, an older time. Damian was there, Iliana was there, and someone he recognized as his mother, Amarys.

Not evil. The thought pushed through like something foreign.

Theo crawled, with no clear direction of where he was. The smoke slapped him in the face as he ran. It was warm like a body, yet cold as a disease. It smelled like death, like the darkness that floated around him. Someone lay in front of him, motionless.

The smoke started to dissipate. The blind running was over and the burning truck was back in sight.

But something was wrong; Scarlett and Nor weren't there, and Morgana was nowhere to be seen.

Theo looked down at his hand. His fingertips were stained red.

A few feet away, a person was still unmoving, a pool of red gushing from his neck. Theo slid over to him.

Theo couldn't see his face, but his chest rose and fell as he let out a hissing sound, choking on blood.

The hissing got closer, closer, and right into his eardrums then turned into a shrill whisper.

The smoke cleared and Kai's face emerged beneath it, tears glistening on his cheeks.

This wasn't real. It couldn't have been.

"*Kate...*" Kai breathed out, his hand reaching into thin air.

Theo didn't know who Kate was. He knew next to nothing about his own brother, other than the small things. How he took his coffee, what his favorite shirt was. It was the one he wore right now; stained with blood, gushing out of the slash in his neck as Theo held its collar, while Kai bled out. He didn't know Kate. Kai's chest stopped moving. Theo stayed on the ground, the blood hot against his fingers. The truck still burned somewhere behind him. The smoke enveloped him and Kai in a cloud, separate from anything else. His brother was dead, Theo's hands were red, and he'd been calling Kai's name.

Kai hadn't been afraid. He'd looked at him with warmth he'd never shown before. In his last moments, he'd been at peace and not because of Theo. No, he hadn't looked at him.

He'd called someone else. He'd wanted someone else beside him. Someone that wasn't Theo. Wasn't even anyone Theo knew. That was the last thing his brother did.

Theo lifted his hand to Kai's face and closed his eyes that had stopped on warmth not meant for him.

22
NUMB

The numb pounding in Theo's skull threatened to engulf him entirely when Alix's shadow fell over him. He wasn't sure how long he'd been on the ground. The skin of his arm had gone gray, thick, as if all the blood had leeched into his core. Every movement he made was crisper than the last, almost robotic, like something vital had gone with it.

"Casimir." Alix's voice. "Killing your brother then crying about it is a new kind of psychopathy."

Theo stood, vision blurring with unshed tears. He didn't want to stand. There was nothing up there. He just wanted any reason to stop feeling this numb kind of grief. And Alix just gave him one.

Everything went fuzzy. His mouth twitched. He wiped his face and his hand came away wet. He was crying, wasn't he? That made sense. He clicked his tongue and looked up.

"Alix." The name left his mouth before he'd thought it. "Disrespectful as ever."

Alix's face fell. His mouth hung with lips slightly parted and his eyes froze, wide open.

The air turned into black fog around Theo. Everything he touched simply changed to dust…or ash. With abrupt motion, darkness fell, and clouds shifted into black little voids that assembled together in the sky.

"Ca-Casimir?" Alix fell backward, looking above with the same expression on his face.

Theo turned to him with an empty face. There was a whooshing sound coming from behind where the guardian sat.

Damian.

The whooshing stopped, and black footsteps appeared as if his feet were swimming in disgusting Yak goo.

Theo stood there, waiting to see what Damian had in mind.

Mid-thought, Alix's head flew across the street; blood splashed from his neck in a thick spray.

Damian stood behind him. His hand, red from the clean-cut, was still hanging in the air. Somewhere in the distance, Scarlett made a noise that wasn't a word.

Something was wrong with Damian's face. He had black bags under his eyes, and his grimace extended all the way to his cheeks.

"Brother, finally." He walked closer, feet sliding on the ground, splashing blood to his sides. The red liquid was mixed with goo and dirt, turning it black. "Remember the promise I made you?"

"How could I forget? You were almost convincing." Theo raised his head to his face. "But I'm Theodore now. Are you sure you can hurt this innocent face?"

Damian's smile vanished as he turned his gaze away, keeping silent.

"Don't worry." As Theo approached, a mocking laugh escaping his lips and his gaze fixed on Damian who relentlessly retreated, looking like a dejected pup. "I know what you did to get through to me. I saw everything. Worse than anything I ever did."

"No, you would've done the same." Damian suddenly stopped and turned. "He means nothing to me and he's a nuisance—"

"He's me." Theo appeared in front of Damian's face; his eyes staring directly at him…without blinking. "So you want to destroy him, too." He caught Damian's face between his fingers. "Never worked, did it?"

Damian's heartbeat thundered.

"Go on, tell me." Theo dipped his nails into Damian's cheeks, ready to crush his face. "What your plan is for me?"

"Stop," Damian's voice cracked and watery liquid fell out of his eyes. "Stop—"

Theo let go of Damian as the hot tears dripped all the way to his hand.

Damian clenched his jaw and wiped the tears from his eyes. "I don't think you'll be able to speak for much longer."

"You mean our cousin hiding away somewhere will do something to me?" Theo shook his head, and with a movement of his hand, Alix's headless body ate into itself and disappeared along with all the unclean blood, revealing Seth's presence. "I doubt that."

Damian closed his mouth and nodded for Seth to come out.

"I'll be at the base," he said and sprinted away instead, eliciting a soft chuckle out of Theo.

There was absolute stillness. No air stirred the grass or leaves. No clouds still drifting in the sky above. Theo let out a longing breath, but even his own breath died as soon as it left his mouth.

The silence stretched thin until a violent blow of wind broke it completely. A wave of darkness. It swallowed Theo's laugh in its unending expansion.

He dropped to his knees, head jerking violently, and agonized screams came out of him.

"What's happening?" Damian's voice faded, but the wave of wind made it echo all the way to Theo's ears.

Violent shivers traveled through Theo, his limbs numb and heavy. His eyes were glued shut, he struggled to open them. Where there should have been memories was a blank space. But at least he knew who he was.

What was he doing? Why was Damian there?

Yes. He'd wanted to *kill* Damian, but he didn't at the same time. He was going to split in two any minute.

Theo rose, his feet leading him to Damian, who was mumbling something, his head bouncing left and right, and his mouth as dry as the desert air. "This'll end when you die."

Nothing was stopping him from finishing Damian right there.

"Theo, stop," a familiar voice called to him from where he was running. It was Morgana, no doubt; her gentle yet loud voice reached into his heart, and he froze in place as she came in his sight.

She was standing in front of Damian and Seth, who looked dazed and had a confused expression on their faces Theo had never seen before.

"Morga—what are you doing?" Theo's vision blurred as his eyes burned.

"I'm not gonna let you do this." Morgana shook her head and an intense look controlled her eyes. "You're not a killer. At least Theo isn't."

"You don't know what you're talking about. *I* killed Iliana. It was me. I can still feel it."

She scoffed. "We both know that was Casimir. I can't believe I'm saying this, but you can resist him. I've seen it."

"He's too strong. Kai is dead. We're the same." Theo raised his head, holding back a sob as tears welled at his eyes.

Morgana's mouth fell open, but she quickly covered it with her palm.

"We'll find the others and get through this together, okay?" Theo could swear her eyes watered. "Come on, we need you…" She stuttered like she was about to say something else, but thought against it.

The words reached him late, like he'd had to travel a distance only to meet them halfway.

What could he say? He'd never been in that kind of situation before. He wasn't feeling anything else except his loathing towards Damian. How could he express something he didn't feel?

Theo stayed quiet for a moment. "Get out of my way, Morgana!" The best thing he could think of was not answering—at least not now.

The world tilted sideways as a clawed hand lashed out, spinning his world and slamming his head against the rough ground. When black dots quit covering his vision, he was standing in the middle of the street with Nor clasping his arms behind his back, the pain of his hold causing Theo to let out a startled little gasp of pain.

"That's no way to reject a girl." Scarlett's hands were on her hips as she shook her head.

"Ugh, fuck you, guys." Morgana ran in their direction, gasping for air. "What the hell took you so long?"

"Oh, it's nothing." Nor shrugged, still holding Theo's arms, who was looking at them, perplexed. "We were a little busy not getting sucked into a wave of darkness."

"Very funny." Morgana rolled her eyes. "What do we do with him?" She pointed to where Damian was standing, but he was no longer there.

"Ugh." Scarlett shook her head. "What a coward."

"I don't understand," Theo said as he found his way back to reality. "Where were you?"

"We were here the whole time." Nor let go of him. "Casimir did something…we could see you, but I think you're the one who couldn't."

"Oh, I—"

"Do you remember anything from…the last half-hour or so?" Scarlett put her hand on his shoulder and spoke to him in a very gentle tone. It reminded him of when they first met.

"Half-hour?" He jumped. "No, I don't think I do…"

"What about the last ten minutes?" Scarlett smiled and turned her gaze to Morgana, who cleared her throat.

"I think…I'm gonna go…check the area," she said and disappeared.

Scarlett snorted.

For a moment, they felt like family. The only one he had left. Mina was gone. Kai was gone. And somehow what remained of him was supposed to be enough reason to keep going.

23
REMEMBRANCE

The pain in Theo's mind spread through every vein in his body. He looked down at his arms—blackness covered them. He had consumed the darkness Nor had warned about.

Though they couldn't see Damian, his presence hadn't vanished. Could he be hiding, waiting for the right moment to strike?

"He's still here," Theo said. He was already walking before he'd decided to. "We have to find—"

"No need," came a voice from the wreck of Nor's truck. Damian emerged, his usual smirk firmly in place. "Unlike Seth, I wouldn't leave with unfinished business."

Scarlett stepped in front of Theo, her stance unyielding.

"What do you want from Theo?" she asked, stretching her arm to block Damian's path.

Damian chuckled, mockery dripping from every word. "Theo?" His grin widened. "What I want is Casimir. Your Theo means nothing to me."

"Same thing," Morgana interjected, returning from behind. "What do you want with Casimir?"

"You must be Morgana." Damian spread his arms wide as he approached her, disappointment etched on his face. "I just want my brother back." He leaned in close, his whisper as loud as thunder, making Morgana tense up in her place. "You know family. We just never can let go."

Scarlett tossed a glare over her shoulder, her lips tight, as Damian slid into Morgana's personal space. "You don't know the first thing about her."

Morgana was about to swipe her dagger out of her back pocket when, before he realized it, Theo was suddenly standing before Damian.

"Stay away from her." He shoved Damian with intense force, almost toppling him.

"Oh, you're being protective. How adorable," Damian taunted, raising his eyebrows in mock surprise.

Theo's vision blurred, a strange darkness pressing at the edges. A voice, low and foreign, whispered from within.

"Give it up, brother. You can never reach Eirene." The words spilled from Theo's mouth without his consent, and Damian's smile vanished, replaced by shock. "No one can survive there a week, let alone two centuries."

"What did you say?"

"What? I didn't say anything." Theo glanced at his friends. Confusion and shock flickered in their expressions. Did he say something?

"I'm done with your lies." Damian lunged forward, grabbing Theo by the neck.

But as Damian's hand touched him, an invisible wave surged outward, flinging Damian away. His hand burned, the skin charred and smoking.

"Son of a bitch." Damian recoiled, his face red.

Scarlett stepped forward, arms crossed, her tone biting. "Move away, Damian."

Damian laughed darkly, his astonishment almost genuine. "Who are you again? Oh, that's right—the thousand-year-old alcoholic."

Scarlett's glare could have cut steel. Theo spotted Morgana smirking from the side of his vision.

Nor stepped forward, fists clenched. "You won't get to Theo unless you get past us."

Damian ignored him, locking eyes with Theo. "Come on, you coward."

But Theo wasn't himself anymore. His voice changed—deeper, colder. "Brother, I'm always here."

His legs moved without his consent, carrying him toward Damian. "Theo is Casimir, Casimir is Theo."

His arm shot out, grabbing Damian's throat with inhuman strength. Theo tried to pull back, but his body wouldn't obey.

Nor moved to intervene, but Morgana grabbed his arm, her voice low. "Leave him."

"What are you doing?" Nor hissed. "He needs to be stopped."

Scarlett put a hand on Nor's shoulder, her expression grim. "I don't think that's possible."

Damian's struggle only intensified, but Theo's grip tightened. With a surge of desperate strength, Damian broke free, stumbling backward, his face all red and bruised, gasping for air.

"Give me my sister back." He screamed, his voice cracking. He jumped at Theo, red wavy energy crackling around his fingers as he sliced across Theo's shoulder, blowing his left arm off into the distance.

A searing pain shot through Theo's shoulder and up into his skull. His mouth opened to scream, but his jaw snapped shut before any sound escaped.

Crying out was weakness.

Blood gushed out of his mouth as he coughed, while Damian ran at him again, landing a punch on his cheek, sending dark droplets of blood out of his mouth.

"You may have invented new tricks," Theo's distorted voice chuckled as he spat a molar and looked down at his amputated arm. "But you're still a weakling." He placed his palm on his severed shoulder lone shadow tendril swirled around it, consuming all the blood and closing the wound.

Damian's defiance crumbled, replaced by desperate grief. "Just get her out of there," he begged, voice cracking. "Why won't you do it?"

Theo sighed, his jaw cracking as he spoke without meaning to. "You know why. The world is full of her and the likes of her. Too much of something is sickening. Besides, she's completely changed from when you remember her. That is if she's still alive."

"She's not something. She's your sister." Damian stumbled, his balance failing.

"She isn't." Theo smirked.

Damian fell silent, his body trembling as he turned his gaze away.

"I'll get her out myself," Damian growled. With a snap of his fingers, he vanished, leaving behind a pile of ash floating in the air.

Theo collapsed as he quashed Casimir's will, making him retreat into the depths of his being like he was never there. He was left alone with the aftermath of actions that were both his and not his. The world spun around him. A single speck of ash fell, soundless, to the ground before everything went dark.

***

Small pellets of water spat on Theo's hands. The cold seeped through his skin, sending chills throughout his entire body. He blinked against the rain and saw the moon, radiant against the night sky. His friends scattered around him, sitting on the wet ground, all wearing tired but relieved smiles.

He groaned and tried to sit up, his brain still commanding his left hand to push against the ground. The wound didn't hurt, but the glaring absence. A signal his body couldn't answer, his shoulder searching for weight that did not exist. He nearly toppled over, but Scarlett caught him just in time, her grip firm.

"Does it…grow back?" she said.

"No, not this time." Theo shook his head as he examined the stump. The wound was clean and bloodless, sealed like a pipe with cement. His mind kept reaching for the missing limb, expecting to flex fingers that were not there. The constant sensation was worse than pain. He sat with it for a moment.

"How did this happen?" he said before it consumed him.

"You don't remember?" Nor asked, stepping closer.

"No, not that." Theo gestured to his stump. "How did the wound heal, but the arm's still gone?"

Morgana stretched as she got to her feet. "You can heal, but your body still has normal human cells. It can't regenerate. John gave me a bunch of horrifying books about Casimir—'Ruler of Darkness,' or whatever." Her voice tightened at the mention of his name, but the casual way she glossed over it did not fool him. He remembered her tears, her confession about Iliana.

"I'm surprised you remember anything about books, of all things." Theo released a faint chuckle as he debated reaching for her hand.

"It's because of how *boring* they were," Morgana shot back. "The really dull stuff sticks, you know?"

"Wait." Theo sat up straighter, realization dawning on him. "Do you still have them?"

"Actually, *you* do." Morgana gestured at him with her chin. "I gave them to Kai—God rest his soul—to put in the bunker. Had to get them out of my sight."

"Ah." Nor tossed the truck keys to Morgana. "At least something's on our side."

Morgana twirled the keys around her finger, her lips curling into a smirk. "Car's dead, remember?"

"Truck keys without a truck," Theo said, catching the keys and tossing them aside with a laugh. "Kinda reminds me of Alix."

The group fell silent, staring at him, faces confused. Cold air breezed through.

Scarlett cleared her throat, her tone cutting the heaviness of air. "I'm gonna fly ahead. See you there."

She didn't wait for a response, launching into the air and disappearing into the darkness. Theo frowned.

Had something happened?

The bunker hadn't changed much. Dust blanketed every surface, but the familiarity of it all was oddly comforting.

Theo ran a finger across the dusty glass table. "Feels like I haven't been here in ages."

"It's been a while." Morgana skipped, heading straight for the knife shelf. "Hello, beauties," she said with a smile, brushing the shiny rows with her hand as she passed them.

"Hey, guys," Scarlett's voice echoed from the library, drawing their attention. "You gotta see this."

Theo was the last to enter, coughing as dust swirled into the air with every step. Books were strewn across the floor, their pages yellowed with age. Spider webs hung loosely from the shelves, and dirt covered nearly every surface.

"You find something?" Theo asked, his voice muffled by a cough.

Scarlett held up an old, leather-bound book. "I think this is Casimir's," she said, flipping through its pages. "But there's only one entry in the entire thing—from 1862." She chuckled. "Our guy wasn't much of a diarist."

Theo froze, his gaze locking onto the date. It was as if a black hole opened in his chest, sucking away his breath. Memories he'd buried deep began to surface, fragments piecing together into a haunting clarity.

His vision darkened. Snippets of a life he had long forgotten played out like brief, but searing flashes of lightning. A name echoed in his mind, over and over again, pulling at the edges of his sanity.

24
MORTIFER

June 19th-20th, 1862
Bucharest, Romanian United Principalities

The manor loomed before him, decayed beyond recognition. Withered vines snaked across the crumbling brick façade, their black tendrils gripping the stone like desperate hands. Through grimy windows, dying light cast sickly reflections across the overgrown ruins of the garden.

Boarded windows and mildew crept across panes. The once-prized gardens were strangled by weeds.

Casimir walked to the front door, which, at least, was still intact. It squeaked open with one touch. The stairs twisted upward in their familiar spiral, each step marked with a thick layer of undisturbed dust. Dirt and black smuts had coated the antique cream interior.

The silence pressed against his ears. No footsteps, no voices—had everyone turned to dust while he was away?

He let his hand fall onto the black iron rail, rough in its rustic charm, and placed his weight on the first step. There was no creak or sign of rot; they were as solid as the day they were made. He walked swiftly to the top, leaving his shoe prints behind.

"Casimir, my son!" Amarys came running his way as soon as he reached the peak of the stairs. She wore a black gown that set off her pale skin and pitch-dark eyes and hair. "I have news," she whispered, putting her hands on his shoulders; they were cold as a corpse.

"Mother." He pushed her hands down. "No 'welcome home, son'?"

She sighed. "The prime minister awaits you."

"Are you certain it's not you he seeks?" He chuckled and moved past her to find an old bearded man sitting on one of the surviving chairs, sipping red liquid from a fancy glass.

"Catargiu, from conservative lawyer to Prime Minister," Casimir laughed as he strode toward the man. "The world does enjoy its little jokes."

"Is this how you address your superior, Casimir?"

"Oh, forgive me. I forgot I serve in your cabinet now," he chuckled and bowed in mockery. "Shall I call you Lord Barbu instead?"

"That's enough." Catargiu's face went red as his voice hardened, an ugly scowl painting his face. "Learn some manners, or you'll never work in my cabinet."

Casimir's lip twitched. He should not get riled up by an arrogant fool who had never known his place.

He drew a sharp breath and opened his mouth. "Perhaps I should—"

"He shall behave more appropriately in the future," Amarys said, her cool voice cutting through the tension as she placed a restraining hand on Casimir's arm.

"Don't count on it," Casimir murmured, earning a sharp squeeze from his mother's icy fingers.

Catargiu stepped closer, his eyes now hard with barely contained hostility. "I'm not here for your amusement, Mr. Mortifer." He turned to Amarys, who maintained her placid smile. "Do not make light of your position. Are you prepared to proceed?"

Casimir tilted his head, enough to hide the smirk tugging at his lips. "As you say, Lord Barbu."

Catargiu remained silent. His glare lingered for a moment before he retrieved his hat. "I'll expect you tomorrow," he offered Amarys a curt nod before striding from the room.

As Catargiu's footsteps faded down the corridor, Casimir threw himself onto the chair and rested his head on a soft pillow, supporting his sore neck from recent exertions.

"Mother," he closed his eyes, "I specifically requested you avoid Catargiu during my absence."

"I know, and I did." Her fingers traced patterns on his arm, still cold as death. "It was Cuza's command. I had no choice."

"Lies. You've never heeded the Domnitor's wishes. You barely acknowledge him as ruler."

"Well…" A smile played at her lips. "Perhaps I wished to make his acquaintance. A harmless gesture, nothing more."

A scoff escaped Casimir before he could think. "Nothing about you is harmless, Mother." He opened one eye and turned to her with a raised eyebrow. "What did he promise you?"

Amarys smoothed her skirts, her expression neutral. "A position in his cabinet. Minister of Internal Affairs."

"Internal Affairs?" Casimir shifted and turned his head to the wall, an uncalculating, bland opponent. "How delightfully vague. And what does Cuza expect me to accomplish in this…honorable role?"

"He has concerns about certain…undesirable players in the principalities." He couldn't see her, but the giddiness in her voice told him all he needed to know. "You keep doing what you have always done. He believes your…particular talents are a flourishing asset to maintaining stability."

"Ah." Casimir nodded as he draped his wrist over his forehead, staring at the extravagant chandelier swinging from the ceiling. "He wants a lapdog." Cuza had always rubbed him the wrong way, but he was a useful tool in the fate of this family. But patience would go a long way. The bastard was a means to an end.

"He wants results. Your discretion always delivers."

"And in return?" Casimir said on a sigh. He knew that whatever the prince had promised them would not be enough. An attempt at control disguised as a gift.

"Legitimacy. The Mortifer name spoken in parliament halls rather than whispered in dark corners." She paused, her cold fingers tracing the edge of a dusty table. "Power, my son. The kind that comes with official sanction." And there it was. *Official sanction. Another cog in the system.*

He stood, throwing his hat on the armchair, and stretched. The soft sound of his bones cracking tickled his ears. "I'm exhausted."

"Of course," She lingered at his side. "How was business in the United Kingdom?"

"Smooth like always." Casimir nodded. "Much like France."

"You are your father's son." Her hand found his cheek unexpectedly warm. "I am so proud of you."

The familiar question rose to his lips, the one she'd never answer. "Who is my father?"

Silence stretched between them, heavy with unspoken secrets. As usual.

"Never mind." Casimir recoiled, running his fingers through his hair. "Where's Damian?"

"In the back gardens. Or what's left of them," she muttered the last part and strutted away.

Casimir ambled his way outside, the weight of the house's stifling atmosphere lifting slightly with each step. Noticing the laid flowers on the ground, he walked slowly along, following the colorful path that lit up the dark, rotten corners.

As he turned beyond the wall, an overly loud voice and shrill cries, unmistakably Eirene's, shattered the quiet. Her voice grated on his nerves—sharp, insistent. He stopped, plastered a smile on his face as his gaze fell on Damian and Eirene. His brother was squatting down in the flowerbed, his hands diligently pulling weeds. Eirene stood nearby, her arms crossed and her dark eyes fixed on Casimir with barely concealed disdain.

Damian looked up first.

"Brother, you've returned." He rose, brushing dirt from his hands as he walked toward Casimir and pulled him into a tight hug. "We've missed you."

Casimir allowed the embrace, though his attention lingered on Eirene. Her sharp gaze hadn't wavered. Something about her unnerved him. Her hostility had never made sense to him. He hadn't done anything. Not to her. Not yet.

Casimir waved at her with mock cheer. "Eirene. Still keeping Damian company in the dirt, I see."

"Better the dirt than your company," she scoffed.

Casimir nodded, refusing to acknowledge her further.

"How was the trip?" Damian cleared his throat, cutting through the tension.

"Look what mother did," Casimir ignored his useless question as he pulled the signed contract from his coat and waved it for emphasis. "I'm officially a member of Catargiu's cabinet."

Damian's expression shifted immediately, his posture stiffening. "Has she finally lost her mind?" he asked, stepping back with a frown. "Our family cannot involve itself in politics."

"So I said, but…" Casimir caught his brother's arm, drawing him a few steps away from Eirene's piercing gaze.

He hated the way her eyes followed him. Like she could see through the mask he had perfected over years of carefully curated indifference. Casimir ignored the discomfort it stirred in him, keeping his tone casual.

"We might turn this to our advantage," he lowered his voice.

"What madness are you suggesting?" Damian's nervous laughter didn't quite mask the unease beneath it. "People despise us, call us a curse. It cannot worsen beyond that."

"It matters not," Casimir said, shaking his head and smiling faintly. "They shall learn to fear us."

"And how do you propose that?" Damian's voice dropped into a near whisper as his eyes darted to the side.

"You know how." Casimir leaned closer. "The Mortifer way."

Damian hesitated, his humor fading entirely. "And what will that cost us this time?"

Casimir smiled faintly, ignoring the edge in Damian's voice. "Everything worth having has a cost, brother."

As he spoke, Eirene's presence burned at his back.

"What scheme are you plotting now, behind Mother's back?" Of course, she would slip into the conversation now, unwelcome but predictable.

Casimir turned, his smile tightening at the sight of her standing just close enough to make her disapproval known, hands on her hips. She tilted her head slightly, her expression a mix of innocence and accusation, her timing - as always - impeccable.

"It is none of your concern, sister mine," he said, unable to prevent his eyes from rolling.

"Wasn't talking to you, *netrebnic*," she bit back. The venom in her voice was sharp enough to cut through steel.

The nickname gave him pause, though he managed to keep his expression neutral. Had she overheard something about his business in France? No, that was impossible. And yet, the unease lingered.

"How creative," he said dryly.

He hated how she could make even the smallest victory feel monumental, her sharp tongue always finding its mark.

"Mind you, don't trip over your ambitions." Her smile was razor sharp as she turned away with deliberate slowness, as though daring him to respond.

"She needs to go," Casimir muttered as soon as she was out of earshot.

Damian's hand connected firmly with the back of his head. "She's family!"

"She isn't." Casimir rubbed his scalp and shrugged.

Even as he dismissed her, he couldn't quite shake the feeling she left behind. Her parting words, her watchful gaze—they lingered like shadows in the corners of his mind, waiting to resurface when he least expected.

No matter. It would be over soon.

"Come," Damian shook his head in disbelief, gesturing toward the manor. "Let's talk to Mother."

Damian's muttered complaints filled the quiet walk back. Casimir barely heard them, preoccupied with Eirene's words, turning them over in his mind. They always found a way of slipping into the cracks he didn't realize he had.

"She doesn't mean half the things she says, you know," Damian said suddenly as they approached the door.

"No, she does. She means every word."

Damian hesitated, his hand hovering near the door handle. "She's just…She's not like us."

"No, she's not." His voice, clipped and cold, left no room for misinterpretation.

Damian opened the door without another word, letting Casimir's response hang in the air.

The piano room was as desolate as the rest of the manor. Dust coated every surface, and the heavy air smelled faintly of decay. The mismatched chairs and sofa, covered in white sheets, stood like forgotten monuments to a past they no longer spoke of.

Amarys sat at the grand black piano, her pallid fingers hovering like spider silk over the tarnished keys. The discordant notes she played filled the room with an eerie, fractured melody.

Casimir lingered in the doorway, studying her in silence. She gave no sign of noticing him—though with Amarys, that meant nothing.

"Mother?" he said, landing a soft knock on the door before stepping inside. Damian remained in the doorway, his reluctance palpable. She always spoke more freely to Casimir alone, and they both knew it.

She didn't look up. Her fingers stilled briefly on the keys before resuming their haunting melody.

"About our previous discussion," Casimir began, his tone measured. He stepped closer, resting one hand on the piano and the other lightly on her shoulder. "We should claim our rightful place in society. The Mortifers could reshape the world. Do with it as. We. Please."

Her reaction was swift. Her hand shot out, twisting his wrist backward as her nails raked across his cheek. Casimir winced but didn't pull away. Her strength always took him by surprise, a sharp reminder of the power she still held even now.

"Cuza already gave you what you want." her voice crackled with fury. "I arranged this position, I opened these doors. Why can't you take his kindness without always wanting more?"

Behind the fury, there was a glimpse of hesitation. Was she afraid he was growing beyond her control?

Just as quickly, her expression softened as she reached her hand to his face. Gently, she swiped her thumb over the blood streaking his cheek. "Remember that I made you what you are." her tone was eerily calm. "Now leave and never interrupt me here again."

Casimir stepped back, his jaw tightening. Without another word, he turned and left the room. Her discordant notes chased him down the hallway, each jarring chord scraping against his nerves.

Damian stood outside, fingers twisting together in that nervous habit he'd never outgrown.

"Well? What did she say?"

"Nothing of consequence." Casimir flexed his fingers, wincing at the fresh bruises from his mother's grip, before cracking them back into place. "She made her displeasure quite clear." He gestured to the open wound on his face.

"Then forget her." Damian's words carried an edge Casimir had never heard before. "We'll do this ourselves—just us. Why share our glory?"

"Brother, you surprise me." His mouth fell open. "A year is indeed a long time to be away."

Hours later, as dusk settled over the house, the familiar solitude of the parlor called to Casimir. The place he would go with the possibilities of future calculations keeping him company.

That evening, the fire in the parlor crackled softly, its warmth barely reaching Casimir as he stood near the window. The glass was cold beneath his fingers as he traced a lazy pattern, his gaze fixed on the overgrown gardens outside.

Twisted vines and blackened flowers swayed faintly in the wind, their decay a fitting mirror to the house's slow unraveling. Casimir swirled the glass of dark wine in his hand, watching the moonlight catch the liquid's surface.

"You always did like the view from here," Damian's voice cut through the quiet. Casimir didn't turn.

"It's better than the company."

"You're insufferable." Damian's footsteps drew closer, his voice carrying an edge Casimir hadn't heard in years. "Why do you always have to destroy everything?"

Casimir glanced over his shoulder, his lips curving with faint amusement. "A dramatic accusation. Care to elaborate?"

Damian's hands clenched into fists at his sides. "Eirene is gone. Mother banished her to Tartarus. Because of you."

Casimir turned fully now, a warm satisfaction unfurling in his chest as he pointed at himself. At last, the constant thorn in his side had been removed. "You give me far too much credit. Mother made her decision. I wasn't even in the room."

"She wouldn't have done it if you hadn't poisoned her mind," Damian's voice rose with raw frustration. "You've been manipulating her for years—manipulating all of us. Twisting everything to suit your selfish ambitions."

Casimir savored the moment, letting it wash over him. Eirene's sharp tongue, her calculating stares, her ability to see through his carefully constructed facades. All of it silenced without him moving a hair. The house was already lighter without her.

"If Mother decided Eirene was a threat, that's on her. Not me." He swirled the wine in his glass, watching the red liquid almost glow in the firelight.

Damian's teeth ground audibly. "She wasn't a threat. She was our sister."

"No." Casimir set the glass on the small table. "She was a bug. Constantly interfering, questioning every decision, undermining my plans." He swaggered toward Damian. "What Mother did was what I would call housekeeping."

Damian's fist shot out before he could stop himself, connecting with Casimir's jaw. The force of the blow sent him stumbling back a step, his glass slipping from his hand and shattering on the floor.

The room fell into a tense silence. Casimir straightened slowly, rubbing his jaw as a faint smile spread across his face.

Damian's hands were trembling. Casimir couldn't tell if it was anger or regret.

"You don't care about this family," Damian said finally, his voice breaking. "You never have. You love power, manipulation, destruction…You love being a killer."

"Love?" Casimir's smile widened at the clueless creature before him. "Such a simple word for such complicated necessities."

Damian's fists clenched again, but he didn't strike. His lips trembled as he stepped closer, eyes glassy with rage and something weaker. Fear, perhaps.

Casimir let out a quiet, pitying laugh, the sound cut through the low crackle of the fire, sharp like a blade. "Regret has never served me."

"We're nothing alike." Damian shook his head, his expression twisted with disgust and sorrow. "You're not my brother."

Casimir held his breath as a grin pulled at his lips. "No, we're not. And that's why you'll always be in my shadow."

Damian's mouth opened as if to respond, but he closed it again, shaking his head one last time. Without another word, he stormed out of the room, the door slamming shut behind him.

His brother's words didn't linger. Casimir stood in the silence that followed, his gaze drifting back to the shattered glass on the floor. Beyond the window, the vines swayed again, their shadows lengthening under the moonlight.

25
CORRUPT

Theo rubbed his temples, the faint echoes of the past still clinging to his mind like cobwebs. The decayed Mortifer manor, Amarys's icy grip, Eirene's sharp tongue—it was all so real. He had walked those halls. But it wasn't him. It was Casimir.

His head throbbed with a dull ache that pulsed in rhythm with his racing thoughts. "Unbelievable," he closed the book and threw it back on Scarlett's lap. His remaining hand trembled slightly as he pressed it against his forehead. "This doesn't even help us right now. It was a colossal waste of time."

"I wouldn't say that." Scarlett opened the book again to where the story stopped and put her finger on what remained of what seemed like a missing paper. "Casimir must've shredded it a while back. So that whatever is written on it won't get in the wrong hands."

"What, you think he hid it from the one person who has the most chance of finding it?" Nor stood and dusted his clothes. "Seems way too easy."

He was right. What was Damian's plan?

"In that case, there must be something we missed here." Scarlett went back to the pages and read them again. "Here; Eirene." She pointed out.

"I think we've heard that name before," Nor scratched his hair. "Something about the fact she's no longer here."

"Eirene is our sister," Theo whispered, the words falling from his lips like a confession. His heartbeat pounded in his ears as the memory surfaced—Eirene standing in the overgrown garden, her sharp eyes cutting into him with disdain. "…Half-sister," he corrected, his voice faltering. These weren't his memories—were they?

"Wh—how do you know that?" Nor's face was too close.

Theo wanted to slap him, but he just shook his head. "I don't know, I just…know, you know?"

"Pff, okay," Morgana chuckled as she sat on a piece of wood and crossed her legs. "Can you tell us more?"

"Uh," Every time Theo tried to remember something from Casimir's memory, his head burned as if he had entered a forbidden part of it. "Wait…Casimir hated her, and she—" he closed his eyes and repeatedly rubbed his forehead. "I knew she was a bastard and used it against mother, forcing her hand to banishment."

"Hey, hey," firm hands caught Theo by the shoulders, shaking him. His body was numb and rigid, like a corpse.

"It wasn't you, remember? It was Casimir." As soft and comforting as Morgana's voice was, it couldn't open his eyes and get him out of the darkness. It just wasn't what he needed. Back when he used Casimir's magic, none of that had happened to him.

What brought him back to light was a painful hot spot on his cheek made by one of Scarlett's slaps. It was one of those that made him dizzy.

"Thank you." He put his hand on it and smiled.

"So, this Eirene, where was she banished?" Scarlett had in her hand the bottle of scotch they stole from Nor's boss's office, her fingers white-knuckled around its neck.

"I—I don't—" It was too much. Too much pressure.

"Okay, pause. Think." Scarlett set the bottle down with a soft thud. "Give me something real."

"Someplace called Tarus or Tororus?" He knew very well what it was; the nightmare of the Mortifer family, Casimir's family. Tartarus. He'd said the word once in his head and didn't try again.

"Tartarus." Nor's face drained of color as he got on his knees and put a hand on Theo's shoulder. His usually steady hands trembled slightly. "Are you sure?" Coming from Nor, who typically maintains his composure like it was armor, the reaction made Theo's stomach twist.

"Yeah, that's the one. Why?" From Nor's reaction—and Nor was not much for reactions—he was no stranger to it either. The weight of unspoken horror hung in the air.

"Oh God. That hell," Scarlett swallowed. "Scotch's not gonna do it. I need whiskey." Her voice cracked on the last word.

"What's in Tartarus?" Morgana uncrossed her legs and moved forward in her seat. For the first time, she looked interested, though her expression suggested she might regret asking.

"A place where people banish people," Scarlett put the bottle back in the bag and rested her head on her palm, her fingers massaging her temple. "The less you know, the better."

The tremor in her voice made it clear she herself wished she knew less.

"What, you mean regular people or magic people?" Morgana's question was ridiculous, even for Theo. But she had a point. Did humans know of its existence?

"Both, I think." Theo's mouth fell open, and he jumped to his feet, the realization hitting him like a physical blow. "It's full of half witches and bastards, like Kai."

"Kai?" Morgana shook her head and tapped her finger on the table beside her. "But he wasn't—" she cut herself off and a look of realization clouded her face. "His death was mysterious."

"It was instant," Theo sighed and lowered his eyes, the words coming out smaller than he intended. His fingers absently traced the edge of his missing arm, a phantom pain throbbing where flesh used to be. "And I didn't understand what was happening."

Talking about him was supposed to make him feel the longing and grief. It didn't. The guilt of this truth settled in his chest like a stone.

"I'm sorry I brought him up," Morgana pressed her fingers to her collarbone. "I can't imagine what you're feeling—"

"It's fine," he sniffled, trying to keep the tears at bay, but the salt of them burned in his throat. "We'll find out what really happened. We always do." The words didn't land, even as he said them.

"Well, how the hell do we use this to solve our problems?" Morgana sighed and slapped her palm on the book, releasing a cloud of dust. "How?"

"It may solve one of them. Damian." Coughing, Theo grabbed it and put it on the shelf. "We promise him Eirene, as long as he helps us get rid of Casimir."

"It's nice, except we can't get him his sister—" Morgana rolled her eyes and looked at him like a crazy person. Was he crazy? The line between desperation and madness had gone thin.

"And we won't. When Casimir is gone, we cut him loose," Theo said, too easily. The thought scared him, but not as much as it should have.

"You mean kill him." Nor narrowed his eyes. An expression of suspicion and doubt covered his face, as if he was seeing Theo—really seeing him—for the first time.

"Yeah…" Theo's voice caught, and he forced himself to meet Nor's gaze. "Yeah, that's what I meant."

"He won't believe we have the power to get her back unless he's stupid and naïve like Scarlett, and that's not possible," Morgana said and no one answered. The library was like a ghost town and they were the outsiders.

Dizzy, Theo massaged his temples. "We just have to assume he will."

The question echoed in the silence, unanswered and unanswerable.

"Okay," Theo sighed and got up. "I'm gonna change. I'll be right back." He looked down at his shirt as he walked. The blood had already dried up.

"And then what?" Scarlett said, as she followed Theo all the way to the bathroom door. From the look on her face, she was worried and possibly doubting him.

"Then we find my brother," Theo struggled to unbutton his shirt. It was going to take a lot of time for him to get used to being one-handed. "Then we make the deal. Let's hope it'll work out."

"What if it doesn't?" Nor leaned against the wall in front of the bathroom and Morgana stood behind him with her arms crossed. "We're depending too much on our luck. And we don't seem to have a lot of it lately."

They all doubted the plan. But Theo would make it work.

"Who said anything about luck?" Theo released a breath and smiled as he finally unbuttoned the shirt. It removed itself and flew to the washing machine. All eyes followed it and turned back to Theo in perfect sync.

"All we need is a good poker face." He stepped barefoot into the bathroom. "And I happen to have that talent. Let's say one benefit of having a previous life." And by previous life, he meant Casimir, who was involved in politics and many other 'businesses'. Theo waved his hand in the air at the faces staring at him in shock, or awe, as he'd like to believe.

"Now, do you mind? I'm gonna take a shower." He pushed the door shut.

Theo stepped into the shower, toes flinching as they touched the chilled ceramic floor. He turned the dial, old and metallic, releasing thousands of lukewarm drops. The water poured down, darkening his hair and trickling down his back, as his mind faded into dullness and everything was a foggy illusion. The sensation of the steamy water calmed him; it took his mind off things. But he could never get those pictures out of his mind. His eyes fell closed over and over, each time showing him the images like photographs. Images of Casimir's life.

Theo turned the water off, put on a towel, and headed to his room upstairs. A milk crate on top of the nightstand doubled as lamp. Mina's journal sat on beside it. He plopped down on his bed and listened to the muffled voices coming from the living room. His head spun and the stump of his arm stung. That was the worst thing about losing a body part; it was there, but it wasn't, exactly like losing a loved one, and he knew a lot about that.

He remembered Kai's death. He still couldn't grasp it. Was he feeling what they called denial? He didn't even get to bury his body. He just left it there, lying on the ground in the middle of nowhere, alone.

As he was, the door hissed open, louder than usual. He lifted his head to find Morgana standing there, her hand on the knob.

"Hey," she rested her head against the wall and smiled. "Can I come in?"

"Um, sure." He wasn't even dressed yet. "What's up?"

"Nothing." Already walking, she shrugged and sat beside him. "Just checking if you're okay."

She sighed and moved closer to him. Too close.

Theo looked down. This wasn't very…Morgana of her.

"I," he stuttered like an idiot. "I'm great." He forced a chuckle.

"Hmm." She just stared at him, at his eyes with her mouth ajar. Was she actually listening to him?

"Right," She shook her head, still staring. She looked disappointed. "Does that mean you are at peace with your inner conflicts?"

Theo didn't know what to say. What kind of question was that? He just sat, looking at her, at her neck that was throbbing, and he listened to her heartbeat.

"Okay," Clearing her throat, she swallowed and stepped away from him to the door, gasping as if she was coming back from the dead. Her face was redder than blood, looking confused herself.

"I'll see you later." She nodded and closed the door with a thud.

Clearly, he wasn't the only one with "inner conflicts".

26
FALSE PROMISE

"I know a place we can start," Theo descended the stairs, his mind still tangled in the strange conversation with Morgana. He sank into a chair.

"Damian has a ship," he muttered, "The Crescent." The name came to him easier than he expected.

He couldn't shake the feeling that Morgana was avoiding him, slipping into the shadows like a ghost.

"How do you even know that?" Scarlett said. She was relaxed on a sofa while Nor tugged her to her feet. She was drinking again. They didn't seem to notice Morgana's disappearance.

"After we found Iliana's body," Theo sighed. Somehow, it became easier to talk about her. "I blacked out and found myself there." He frowned as the familiar sense of that specific beach surfaced. "I feel like I could find my way there again."

"Oh?" Morgana came from the kitchen and she was holding a sandwich. Theo jumped. She didn't disappear. "But you don't black out anymore, right?" She was right. Casimir had started doing things while Theo was conscious.

What changed?

"Yeah, I guess." Theo was not thinking. His empty stomach clenched, demanding action. Without hesitation, he snatched the sandwich from Morgana's hands, stuffing it into his mouth before she could protest.

Morgana froze, eyes widening in disbelief. "Hey!" She raised her hands in mock outrage.

Theo mumbled an apology through a mouthful.

"Alright, do you actually know where it is?" Nor finally got Scarlett to her feet, walked her near a table, and poured her glass of water.

"I have an idea," Theo said, trying to keep his voice steady despite the gnawing discomfort inside him. The beach…he shouldn't remember it, but the image was as clear as if it had just happened yesterday. He knew what that place meant to Damian. He couldn't share that with Nor, though. Not yet. Nor would see it as a sign that Theo had finally given in to Casimir. Maybe he had…

Scarlett let out a small grunt as she stumbled into the chair beside the table, her fingers closing around the glass of water like a lifeline. She drank it in one go, then pushed the empty glass back into Nor's hands without a word.

"I'm good." Her movements were sluggish, eyes half-lidded, but she straightened herself up, still trying to seem more in control than she was.

"The crescent you said?" She slurred.

"Um, yeah." Theo wasn't sure if he could rely on Scarlett in her current state. She could be a liability in their already risky plan. But, being his familiar, he couldn't exactly kick her out, could he? "You sure you're good?"

"Just a little tipsy." she raised her hands and slapped them on her side. Her words lacked conviction.

"*I'm* good to go." Morgana shrugged, grabbing her jacket from the back of the chair she was sitting on, and tossed it over her shoulder, holding a dagger in her other hand. Where the hell did it come from? She was sitting there the whole time.

Morgana turned toward Nor, a grin playing at her features. "Norman is too, aren't you, bro?" Theo couldn't help but chuckle, watching Nor's expression shift between disbelief and confusion. His half-nod was priceless, the look on his face as if he was questioning his own sanity.

Theo almost cracked up, but Morgana laughed in his stead, the sound warm and unsettling in the tense atmosphere. "Theodore, lead the way." She bowed playfully and let him go before her.

Theo went outside hoping to find Nor's truck, but it struck him that it blew up along with everything in it.

"We don't have a choice; we're gonna have to walk." Theo sighed. The last person who would want to walk long miles on foot was definitely him.

"Or we could take a cab?" Nor shrugged, crossing his arms around his chest. He *had* to be joking. Theo shook his head and pretended he didn't hear that.

"Let's move." There was no way they would put an innocent in danger. Nor, of all people, should've known that. He *had* been acting weird since they got to the bunker.

Theo was almost out of breath from walking on foot the whole day. He hadn't walked that long since his last year of college when Mina forced him to go look for her lost necklace. He was a witch; getting tired should not have been possible.

"We're close." The path had changed beneath his feet. Cracked asphalt gave way to pale gravel, then to sand that found its way into his shoes before he saw it. A familiar scent of salt and rust hit him, soft waves slapping sand.

"I can't do this anymore," Morgana gasped, dragging her feet. "I'm done fucking walking." Theo never expected to find someone lazier than himself. It was a joy.

As he was about to make a joke, his words died in his throat. Without warning, a hulking figure materialized in front of them, its large form blocking the path. The air thickened, heavy with the Yak's presence.

Theo's heart skipped a beat. This wasn't just any Yak—it was a guard for Damian's ship. His brother may have been many things, but stupid wasn't one of them.

Backing away, Theo moved beside Morgana. "Well, I hope you're not done with fighting," he muttered, tension coiling in his muscles.

"No need for that. No one needs to die." Damian's voice rang out as he emerged from behind the creature, slapping its large arm with casual familiarity. "This thing can kill you all in less than ten minutes…well, maybe not you," he pointed at Theo with his usual grin.

Theo's eyes narrowed as he stepped forward, every muscle tense. "I want to make a deal," he said, his voice cutting through the tension like a knife. He gestured for the others to back away, unsure whether they would like what he was about to offer.

"I hate to admit it, but we need you, Damian." The words tasted bitter on his tongue, but he kept his gaze locked on his brother's, waiting for the shift.

Damian's laughter stretched on, a mocking sound.

"A deal," he said, amusement in his eyes. "I hate to disappoint, but there is absolutely nothing in the world that an insect like you could give me."

"Insect?" Theo's smile spread across his face, a plan forming. "You need to work on your insults, little brother."

The effect was immediate. Damian drew in a sudden breath and backed away, looking as if he'd seen a ghost.

"You know I can open Tartarus for you and get your precious sister back." Theo loomed closer to Damian.

Theo exhaled a long, weary sigh. The exhaustion in his body wasn't just his own. Something older weighed on him. He swept his eyes over the beach, lingering on the wrecked remains of the ship—Damian's ship.

Then, without thinking, he crouched, his fingers sinking into the sand, and an unfamiliar, possessive urge gripped him. His mind raced with a mix of confusion and clarity.

He brought a handful to his nose and inhaled deeply. The scent of salt and age overwhelmed him, almost intoxicating.

"I remember this place," he murmured, his voice deeper and more resonant. "Wyckoff's Hotel, 1842." A bitter smile curled his lips. He shook his head and looked up at the sky. "That was so much fun wasn't it, brother?"

The surrounding beach warped slightly. Past and present blended together in a disorienting dance.

He stood slowly, the weight of another's memories pressing down on him. Theo fought back a laugh at Damian's shocked expression. He had to keep acting, though he wasn't sure if it was an act anymore. A fleeting thought crossed his mind: at least Nor was not listening and judging.

"Oh, and remember Johnny? John Vanderbilt?" Theo clicked his tongue. "Poor man. Such an untimely death, so much left to do in his life. Oh, I mean the father, of course. His son died thirty-five years later…that was also something."

"Shut up!" Damian shook himself out of the trance, his eyes suddenly dark with rage. His gaze shifted, not demon-like, but still full of venom. His posture—defensive, almost familiar—reminded Theo of the kid who once looked up to him with blind adoration. But there was no innocence left now, just a raw, vengeful hunger.

"You were with me that day. In fact, it was your idea." Damian's veins relaxed and he held out his arms. "I mean, that's what you do, isn't it? Get rid of 'bad people' and 'eliminate' dirty politicians. No one was dirtier than Johnny. You walked me through the whole thing."

Theo remembered the hotel, but not the rest. What had he walked him through? What 'dirty politicians' was he talking about? What exactly did Casimir do?

"I want you to help me get rid of Casimir. And I'll open Tartarus for you." Theo raised his head, smiling, confident about the plan, but not confident enough; Casimir's memory was like an unfinished maze that could not be trusted.

"Are you taking the deal or not?" Was everything falling into place?

Damian's smile widened, the flicker of amusement in his eyes sending a chill down Theo's spine. He leaned in, his voice dropping to a near-whisper. "You're dumber than I thought, *Theo.*" He turned, his coat billowing behind him as he sauntered away.

Theo swallowed the doubt and dread creeping back in. Was that him accepting? What if Damian could fail to deliver and Theo might have to. He pushed the thought away.

The plan had to work. He couldn't possibly afford another failure.

27
INTERLUDE: DAMIAN DOUBLECROSS

An hour after watching Theo walk away from the beach, Damian drew a sharp breath as he found Seth waiting by the old pier. He replayed Theo's proposal in his mind, nothing but silence and night darkness surrounding him.

Damian would never consider Theo's deal. But he had to trick him into believing he took it. The opening of the portal would happen on his terms alone.

Besides that…the hotel story, anybody could have known that; it wasn't a secret that the Mortifers had friends and enemies from high places back in the day, and without a doubt, those 'rumors' about them resolving 'problems' by literally eliminating them. Theo was faking it. He didn't have Casimir's presence.

"You're absolutely useless," Damian said, as he grabbed Seth by the collar and threw him onto the sand. "How could you run away like that? You were supposed to distract them while I—"

"I don't want to see Casimir." Seth stood, shaking his head. "Besides, your plan already failed." He smiled. "You got what you wanted, Cas fully present, and you chickened out at the end."

"I don't believe this," Damian laughed and rested his forehead on his hand as he let himself fall to the ground. "How could I be so fucking stupid?" His voice was low and quiet. He didn't have it in him to yell.

"Hey, don't beat yourself up. You'll still have other opportunities." Seth's smug face and the shrug he gave were done on purpose. He was provoking him. But, no. He wouldn't be stupid enough to fall for it.

"I don't know, you seem distant lately. Your heart isn't really in it." Sometimes, the best tactic is to play the victim. "What did I ever do to you?"

"Where do I start?" Except for Theo, the hatred on Seth's face was like nothing Damian had ever seen before. How long had he been hiding it? How long had he waited to show that ugly side of him?

"You're nothing but a child with anger issues," Seth said, "you're hung up on something big brother Cas did to you over a century ago. Your mother was a slut." He let out a long breath. "I'm about done with you and your lunatic family involving me in your problems," he wasn't wrong. "Look where my mother ended up. I don't remember why I even tagged along with your stupid revenge fantasy in the first place."

"I'm gonna kill you." That was it. Damian's veins started moving and his magic wanted to get out. His darkness wanted to eat Seth whole.

"You see?" Seth had an expression of pity on his face and he was pretending he wasn't afraid of death. "Killing is the solution to all your problems. You're even willing to kill your own family, the thing you cherish most."

"Jeez, relax. I get it." Damian got to his feet and moved closer to Seth, keeping his fists at bay. "If you want to leave, fine. But there's one last thing I want you to do for me." He had no choice but to do what Damian wanted, or else he would find himself a corpse before morning. He was sure Seth knew that.

"I want you to talk to Ovidia and get her to talk to me." He had a new plan. The ancient witch obsessed with Casimir.

"You know I can't do that." Seth's lips twitched, making Damian smirk at the sight. He had known full well the effect the mention of his godmother would have on him. "You're the last person she'd want to talk to."

"Not when I have something for her." Damian's mouth curled up. "Casimir's location. She's been hunting him almost as long as I have."

Seth's face fell. Damian chuckled at the sight.

"Go relay the message." Damian pushed Seth's shoulder. The look on his pathetic face was priceless.

"I hope you know what you are doing," Seth nodded, staggering backward at the impact. "Otherwise, it's your funeral."

"That old woman can't touch me," Damian scoffed. If Seth had not left the minute he did, he would have shredded him to pieces.

***

Three hours of waiting and walking, Damian arrived at the dark narrow alley Seth appointed as the unnecessarily creepy meeting place and leaned against a wall away from people. But people seemed to not get the hint; it was still full of human scum, especially those who live in alleys like the one he was in. Who knew, Maybe it *was* someone's home.

Damian had never actually waited for someone, except for Casimir. People always waited for him.

Seth cleared his throat to announce himself as he came down the stairs, near where Damian stood. Was Seth the scumbag who lived there? "Not sorry to keep you waiting."

"Is it done?" That asshole seriously wanted to die; he never stops provoking him. "Did she accept?"

"Unfortunately, yes." Seth buried his hands in his jacket pockets and had the audacity to let his body slide against the wall near Damian. "She said she will get him. But don't get me wrong; she still hates you, but as much as her obsession with Casimir."

"Whatever. You're of no use to me now." Damian stood straight and made his hands into fists covered with black goo. "Ready to die?"

To his surprise, Seth scuffed and shook his head. He was too confident of a guy who was about to die. "You can't hurt me." Come again? "I'm not here."

Damian tried to punch him in the face, but the fist went right through him and he landed at the feet of the stairs and the fake figure of Seth disappeared right after.

A chuckle rumbled from Damian's chest. "Projection. Smart."

"Not really," one last echo of Seth's voice rang in his ears. "You're just that stupid."

All that Damian ever wanted was to get his little sister back, and he ended up chasing Casimir for a hundred years instead. Was he finally getting what he wanted? Of course not. Nothing was ever that simple for him, not the way it was for

Casimir. Always the golden boy, Amarys's favorite son. Could he really, for once in his life, beat him? Even if he couldn't save Eirene, at least he wouldn't die in Casimir's shadow.

Damian sat there at the stairs for a long while. Then, he stood abruptly after realizing the risk he was going to take with Casimir and Ovidia, the most powerful beings he knew. He took a deep breath, then raised his arms to the air and held his head to the sky with his eyes closed. He had to get it out. Before he could process it, he opened his mouth and screamed.

28
FALSE HOPE

"Damian must be laughing his ass off right now." Theo sat on a wooden bench, automatically reaching to steady himself with both hands. "Thinking he can use our deal for his advantage."

The bench was filthy. Black spots stained the white wood. No wonder the others sat on the ground.

"We've thought of everything," Scarlett said as she settled on a branch hanging from a huge olive tree. "He can't blindside us."

"Um, what exactly are you guys talking about?" Morgana was eating an ice cream cone, cross-legged on the grass. It wasn't his decision to keep Morgana out of the plan, and he didn't understand why they wanted her excluded.

"Guys, are you keeping me out of the loop…again?" She rolled her eyes as she stretched her legs before her.

Theo couldn't just sit there and lie to her face. She was part of the team and she deserved to know. "I'm sorry, we—"

"We don't trust you," Nor said, interrupting Theo.

"Great, you should've said that." Morgana shrugged, still licking her ice cream.

"It's weird, though." Yes, Nor had been weird for a while. "I thought I've proven myself enough." Morgana stood and looked only at Theo, glaring at him. "Guess I was wrong." She walked over and let the cone fall on his head.

It was cold. And she was pissed.

"Wait." Theo pulled the cone from his hair, sticky chocolate dripping down his neck.

He couldn't just let her walk away. "I don't know why we're not letting you in on the plan. But I don't care, I'm gonna tell you."

Morgana stopped and turned around with a faint smile. "Awesome." she folded her arms and waited. But Theo had no clue what to say. What was he going to do? What would Kai do in his situation?

"I'll tell her," Nor jumped to his feet. Theo's shoulders sagged with a profound release, the tension draining from his body. But Nor's rigid posture told him he wouldn't like it. "We're gonna use you, the weapon, to triple-cross Damian after he double-crosses us. The thing is, we don't know how to activate you yet."

"Are you kidding me?" Theo was on his feet before his brain caught up. "You can't do that to her. She's a fucking person, Nor."

"Theo, stop." Morgana's hand touched his burning chest and somehow relieved his pain. "It's okay," Her soft whisper reached into his mind, convincing him it was okay. "There's nothing I want more than to bury that bastard."

"See?" Nor moved closer to Theo, and Scarlett jumped down off the tree. "That's why we didn't tell you. You're too emotionally involved."

"What about me? Why not tell me?" Morgana's voice was lesser than a yell.

"Honestly, we thought you were gonna think that we wanted to get rid of you." Scarlett shrugged. "Though, I don't mind if we really did get rid of you."

"That's pathetic." Morgana smirked and rested her hands on her hips. "But, seriously, that's enough. What's your problem with me, huh?" Finally somebody asked that. Theo had been dying to know since he met Morgana.

"Nothing, forget it." Scarlett looked away. "I don't wanna talk about it, okay?" Theo had never seen Scarlett look like that; broken, scared, like a child left behind.

"Alright, that's enough." As much as he wanted to know, he couldn't miss Scarlett's rising level of sadness. It was crystal clear that she didn't want to talk about it…ever. "It's getting late. Let's move." As he tried to stand, the black spots glued him to the bench.

"I knew it." He shook his head and passed his finger on one spot. Slick, cold. "Shit, we walked into some kind of trap. This is Yak goo."

"Of all the places we could've stopped in," Nor ran to Theo with the others and tried to get him up, but failed. "Lucky us, huh?"

Then, an electric jolt thrust into Theo's mind and body, and he jerked without control. The last thing he saw was his friends backing away from him before his eyes swiveled towards the back of his head in a distressed sense of a headache. He tilted his head to the edge of the bench, a cold, dark substance oozed out of his eyes. His surroundings warped in blink.

His existence began to fade, and he was finding trouble hanging on to it. Pain and suffocation were all that he knew. One minute, he was there, and the next he was not.

29
GATE

“Wake up, Cas,” the voice echoed. Theo was lying on solid ground, and he had a hard time moving his legs. His remaining arm shook as he tried to push himself upright.

“Wake up.” the voice said again, forcing Theo to open his eyes. Who was it? Not many people called him by that name.

The scene before him was dark, and his vision was still not perfect. The only clear thing was four or five steel bars. Did the hunters catch him?

“Who are you?” He looked up as someone stood tall in his sight. “What do you want?” He rubbed his eyes and shook his head.

“I’m truly sorry, child. I tried to help you,” it was a feminine raspy voice reached his ears.

Theo stood against a wall and stretched his arm to one of the bars. “What—” he breathed. “What the hell are you talking about, lady?” He tried to stand but his legs failed him. “Do I know you?”

“No, not anymore.” The closer she got, the clearer her face became. She was a wrinkled woman who seemed to have one foot in the grave. Her twisted smile stood out on her pale, sagging face. A dark aura emanated from her as she flipped her thin, gray hair away and kneeled in front of him.

"What do you mean? How do you know me?" When he looked deep into her eyes, he knew there was something missing from her life. They were pitch black, but seemed as if they were once brown and got the light sucked out of them. He could sense the despair, but deep down, a hope that she didn't want to let go of.

"I—" She was about to say something, before Damian stormed in with his loud voice.

"I see you caught the biggest moth." He stopped right in front of the cage and gripped the steel bars. "Good work."

"You don't give up, do you?" Theo shook his head. "You just have to go and die in Tartarus for absolutely nothing. Eirene is dead. She's been dead from the beginning." He provoked.

"Oh, you would know." Damian's voice shook and vein popped in his forehead. He backed away from the cage and sat on the ground, cross-legged. "You think you know all about the family now," he said, shaking his head, still a smug smile on his face. "You don't know shit, *Theo.*" Wrong! It was Damian who didn't know shit. Actually, nobody knew what Theo was really going through. He sighed and moved closer to the bars. His legs shook and his hands ached. Damian should've known better than to mess with him.

"I can give control to your brother," Theo barely recognized himself. He fought every minute of every day for that control. "Let's see what happens."

His eyes were already burning. Damian took a sharp breath and jumped back. The scared expression on his face was priceless. And before he could say anything, Ovidia dragged him behind her like an empty sack and stared intently at Theo, directly at his eyes. The haunted expression on her too pale and sad face gave her eyes a despairing look as she kept opening her mouth to speak, but never saying anything.

"What? Why are you looking at me like that?" She looked like she was on the verge of tears. Damian, for once, kept his mouth shut, but the surprise in his shrunken face said everything. Theo was the only one in the dark.

"Casimir, listen to me," finally she spoke. "I know you don't remember me. My name is Ovidia." She walked closer, her fingers trembling at her sides. "There's no easy way to say this, but you're not Theodore. He doesn't really exist."

"What are you talking about?" What she said was insane, impossible. "I'm—" His throat was raw, sour. "I'm right here." His uncertain voice turned into a mutter.

"Oh stop, hag," Damian growled. "Don't sugarcoat it, he's a big boy." He walked and stumbled on a rock, almost falling. "You are Casimir, you've always been, and you're one hundred and eighty years old."

"That doesn't make sense, I don't believe you. I'm—I'm real." Theo couldn't shake the doubt in his voice as the last words came out almost unfamiliar. But, the more he mulled it over, the more it sunk in and the more his brain turned to a spinning top, finding more questions than answers. Worse, the idea was familiar. Not a memory, but an echo.

The already haunted place became uncomfortable; nobody was speaking, nobody moving. The quiet thronged the darkness. He was trapped, not only in the prison cell with the two people he didn't want anything to do with, but in his own body.

"Hey, dumbass," the stillness withered as Damian said, snapping his fingers in Theo's face. "Don't faint yet. There's more." With a half-smile, he turned to Ovidia who avoided his gaze; they both seemed to know what was going on and had the missing pieces to the holes of Theo's past.

"Enough, Damian," Ovidia said, "he doesn't have to know more. It'll destroy him."

"No, tell me." Theo held his breath. "I need to know everything."

Ovidia moved closer to Theo's cell and raised her hand; he couldn't tell if she was glaring at him or if that was her usual expression.

She snapped her fingers and the cell bars twisted enough for Theo to get out.

Still inside the prison, in his frozen state, he let out a shaky breath, closing his weary eyes. He grasped one of the twisted bars, the cold metal sending a shiver up his already quivering arm. His heart slammed against his ribs as he stepped out, slow and silent.

Could he really handle it? He shook his head, disallowing his second thoughts to get the better of him.

"Stop." Damian appeared right in front of him and pushed his shoulder back. "You let him out." He was looking at Theo, but addressing Ovidia behind him.

"You are going to open the gateway to hell for him." she ignored Damian's words and stepped away.

"Why would I do that?" That was their plan? Ask nicely?

"Because you are the one who put the girl there." She was more confident than before. What changed? "Do it."

"I-I don't," Theo had absolutely no idea how to even begin to open the stupid gate they keep mentioning. "Fine, I'll do it." if he said he couldn't, they surely would've killed him, so he might as well stall.

He kept on walking, dragging his feet on the ground. Damian was looking from afar, waiting with excitement, and he even looked happy, but Ovidia stayed beside Theo, still staring. What exactly was she waiting for? It couldn't be the gate too…could it?

"Come on." Damian clapped his hands and jumped like a kid waiting for candy. "Walk faster."

Theo kept his mouth shut, because if he spoke, walking slower than before, he raised his hand and closed his eyes, pretending to open the gate. Wherever that was. He should've done something before they realized he was lying, if they haven't already.

Where was Casimir when he needed him?

'Theo, can you hear me?'

Theo had never been happier to hear Scarlett's voice. *'I'm stuck here.'*

'Where are you? We'll come to you.' She sounded distant even in his head.

'Not sure, but I can hear waves. I think I'm back in the crescent.'

Another voice hummed in his head. It was loud, and Theo suddenly couldn't hear Scarlett anymore. In that dead silence, a snap of fingers deafened him. His eyes blanked, and he lost his balance. It was like a gunshot that sounded near his ear. He fell forward on his shoulder and glimpsed Ovidia's raised hand. It was her. She interrupted them.

Theo groaned and pushed himself up. Though his ears were still ringing, it didn't prevent Damian's loud and annoying voice from reaching them.

"What did you do?" He was addressing Ovidia. But, before she could answer, Theo raised his head and hurled himself at her, his hand seizing her throat while his brain still tried to command his missing left hand to follow.

She gulped and gasped for breath. She tried to pry his fingers away. But Theo just looked at her, a life between his hands. One more squeeze and it would be gone.

"Don't…There are things you don't know…about Mina." at the words leaving her mouth, Theo's heart thumped and his eyes widened as his grip loosened.

Mina.

He hadn't heard that name for too long. He hadn't even thought of her as much as he should have. What did she have to do with anything?

His hand slipped from Ovidia's pulsating neck and he backed away. He didn't want to, but it was the right thing to do.

"There's the Casimir I know." Damian hadn't moved an inch since Theo attacked her. He stood far away, arms crossed over his chest.

But Theo knew he had it in him. Nothing he'd done or would do will ever surprise him, and he could expect anything from himself, from Casimir.

"I don't know how to open your fucking gate, okay?" There was no point in stalling anymore. Nobody was coming to save him.

"Yes, you can." Damian didn't seem to get it; he was smiling and looked kind of confident. "You just have to push a little." Push what? What he said made no sense.

'Theo, you there?' How was she talking to him? Didn't Ovidia block her?

'Scarlett!' Theo almost yelled out loud. *'How did you—'*

'Shh, listen to me, don't make any reaction. That old lady still thinks we can't talk.' Scarlett's chuckle came through his brain. *'But we've gone incognito. It's a trick I learned a while back.'*

'You're a lifesaver. What do I do?'

'Don't worry, man, we're coming to you. Details later.'

What did she mean by details? It didn't matter, as long as they were coming. He had to wait a little longer and keep stalling in the meantime. But all he was wondering about was what they had been doing since his kidnapping.

"You know." Theo's skin stopped shivering and his chest stopped burning. His sudden calmness was too much, even for him. "I get why you want to get Eirene back." Damian didn't scare him, not anymore. "But what makes you think she wants to see you?" Theo couldn't stop himself from bursting with laughter. "I mean, seriously, what are you hoping for? A big happy reunion?" He laughed until his brain started hurting. "There are no happy reunions. Not in this family."

"Casimir, stop," Ovidia said, although it was none of her business. "Just open it." She walked up to him, smiling. Was she not afraid he would choke her again?

Theo moved his gaze to her neck, and it was still stamped with his red palm print like it was a burn scar. But, there was something else. It was a necklace she wore. Even with it half-hidden under the dress, he still recognized its unique silver chain.

"Where did you get that necklace?" He wanted to know, but he was afraid of the answer, like somehow he already knew what it was.

Ovidia backed away and sighed. "I'm sorry." Her eyes were sadder than before. "You were never supposed to find out."

Theo was too focused on her shallow, sunken look to listen to what she was saying. His shoulders shook, but he refused to look away. His hand clenched into a shaking fist, in a desperate battle against what he knew was true. A lone tear traced down his cheek.

"You're…Mina?" Not until the name tore at his throat did his determined gaze fall, to fixate, once again, on the necklace.

30
MEMORIES

The necklace. He knew that necklace. She'd been wearing it the whole time he'd known her. The night she went into a coma and all the days after that, pressed against her neck because she'd said it helped her sleep. She had been attached to it.

Theo laughed. No it wasn't him, too low. Every memory was a pillar. Every pillar now crumbling.

The coffee she'd hated but drank anyway because he made it. Was that real? The journal. He'd read every word of it. He'd grieved every word of it. Had Mina written it at all? No, this old woman had worn her face, her handwriting, made it soft and familiar so he'd believe it.

He couldn't feel his legs. He sat down on the floor. His legs made the decision without him.

Theo's lungs weren't there. He tried to bring air in, anyway. His muscles strained, his thoughts slipping into dizzy confusion.

He took a few steps back, bumping into the cold steel bars like he wasn't expecting them. His head snapped back with the impact, vision spinning. His breath was uneven as he began to gasp.

Theo's mouth smirked on its own as the last memory of Mina faded, like a passing breeze. A breeze that caressed him with warmth then left. "What do you have to tell me? I'm listening."

"What is happening?" Damian stood frozen, shaking his head.

"Oh Damian, it's so good to see you as my little brother again and not as someone I…despise with every bone in my body."

Theo's veins tightened as his arm spawned back, black like the shadows curling at his feet. He flexed the fingers. They moved faster, lighter, closing before he'd finished the thought. "Thank you, Mina. You made me realize everything cared about was a lie."

"Casimir, what do you remember?" Ovidia looked at him as if he was a broken pet, and approached him like one would approach a wounded animal.

"Who are you, really?" Theo frowned.

"I'm the high priestess who was banished ages ago," she sighed and looked over her shoulder, glaring at Damian, who had the same expression as Theo. "I'm sure you've heard of me."

"Hmm. I don't concern myself with the past." Theo said. He didn't know her, but he'd heard of her. She was a princess, besides being queen to the witches, and an enemy to the most notorious of them. He looked into her eyes, pitch black where brown used to be. "Did you know my mother?"

"I—"

"Wait, wait." Damian. His timing impeccable as always. "We're not here to chat. Open the gate." He was shaking like a leaf. "We had a deal, hag."

"I knew her," Ovidia said, as if Damian didn't even speak. "More than I would've liked." She had a look in her eyes as if she'd buried something behind them for longer than she would've wanted. "She was a snake, a manipulative viper. I suppose that's how everyone would describe her."

"What did our dear mother do to you?" Damian finally came to his senses to forget about Eirene to join the chat.

"She killed my best friend." Ovidia's voice was on the verge of breaking. Her memories hurt her too much, as if locking them away for as long as she did made the impact even more painful to remember. Just like him with Casimir's memories—being responsible for all those deaths. Maybe she understood.

"Who was it?" Damian was engaging more in the conversation and asking all the right questions. That was strange behavior for him.

"I knew you would find out. But I had hoped it wouldn't be from me." She gulped down a breath as if preparing herself to say words she hadn't spoken in years. "It was your father."

Nobody spoke. Damian's mouth opened then closed. Theo kept his face still. A door opened somewhere inside him, into a room he hadn't known was there.

"That can't be. Some banished witch killed our father—" Damian stopped. The sentence died on its own. They'd both heard Amarys say those words. They'd both believed her.

Ovidia surprised," she said, finally, shaking her head. "That woman would do anything for her children to see her as the victim," she scoffed. Tired, bitter. "I don't blame her, really. Living a life where everyone loathes you, you tend to want to be loved, eventually. Guess she must have had some humanity left in her after all."

"I don't think so. She must have thought of some scheme that would benefit her from lying to us." Theo crossed his arms. They were already poisoned by their mother. What would she gain from telling them about the past? Why wait so long? "I'm sure that woman never had any humanity."

"Wow Cas," Damian said, clapping his hands together. "Who made you soft?"

"I'll open the gate." Theo jerked his head toward the wall behind Ovidia. "What happens after is your concern, not mine."

"I don't understand." Damian couldn't hide it. He was overjoyed. "Why would you do that for me? You made it very clear that you don't care about Eirene."

"The one thing we have in common is our blood."

"No, you're supposed to be worse than that," Damian laughed, short and disbelieving. "What happened to you?" The laugh died and his face turned.

"Our misunderstanding has lasted long enough. And I'm not doing it for you." He knew full well that Damian could never get out of there, sister or not. If anything else, his perishing would be a win-win for both Theo and Casimir.

"A misunderstanding." The word came out clipped, ugly. "You'd call it that."

Damian, always so dramatic, still didn't understand anything. He was constantly thinking about Eirene, that he couldn't see the bigger picture, or better, the bigger sin, which beat anything else he had ever done. In a way, it was better that way, because Damian would always find a way to be an abomination to Casimir's plans. It was nothing short of unforgivable.

What *had* he done? What were all those blank spaces left in Theo's mind? Everything else had filled, but not them. He knew how bad it was, but he didn't know what it actually was.

He walked past Ovidia with his eyes closed.

A terrible rumble sounded from deep inside the earth as it shifted like a wave on the sea. The lights swung violently from the ceiling. Cracks appeared from the ground beneath. Damian and Ovidia stayed on their feet and never lost balance. That showed how powerful they were; to resist such power coming from energy, no one could understand.

The gate was not what Theo expected it to be. Not even close. Instead of a typical door, it was a mouth, gaped open, with sharp thorns for teeth and a dark bottomless throat.

31
ACCEPTANCE

Instead of rushing to the door, Damian backed away with an alarmed look on his face and tripped, falling on his back.

"What the fuck is this? Is this some kind of trap?"

"That's Tartarus, little brother," Theo said "What did you expect it to be, bright pearly gates?"

Damian's furrowed brow turned into a satisfied smile as soon as he stood. "Glad you haven't lost your sense of humor." As soon as he dusted himself off, he jumped into the mouth of the beast without a word or a whiff of hesitation.

He was gone.

Theo stood very still. The relief he expected didn't come. Just the image of Damian dusting himself off, smiling at him, jumping. He'd finally given him what he wanted.

Theo blinked. "That was unexpectedly fast."

He shrugged. Ovidia wore a judgment on her face, trying and failing to hide the disgust on her face. That was a first. Slightly taken aback by her expression, Theo flinched.

"What?"

"I was hoping you had changed after your life as Theodore." That was it; she knew he sent Damian to his death. "You disappoint me...you disappoint your father—"

"Enough." Theo's veins danced and shifted around on his forehead. "You didn't exactly stop him." He narrowed his eyes. "You're as much of a disappointment as I am."

Instead of firing back, she looked past him and closed her eyes slowly, like she was about to sleep.

"You're right," she murmured, her hand reaching to her neck and pulling Mina's necklace with controlled force, breaking the clasp.

Theo watched her in silence. What *was* there to say? It was clear she was out of energy and exhausted from the world—from life. He wouldn't want to add to her pain.

The beautiful silver chain dangled between her fingers. The one he'd seen attached to Mina's neck for four years and the one that had glistened in her collarbone, catching the light above her hospital bed

Ovidia extended it toward him. But, he didn't take. Not right away. His hand lay fisted against his side.

"Take it," she said. "I have no use for it anymore. Mina was yours. So is this."

He grabbed it and held it in his palm. The chain was heavier than he'd imagined. Mina wasn't real. He knew that now. He'd known it since he first laid eyes on Ovidia, the familiarity of her face striking a chord he couldn't place. The person who loved Mina had been a lie built around a lie. Just like the person who'd grieved her. But, the grief didn't seem to care about the lies. It still stung like the first day. Ovidia looked at him with pity he didn't earn and said nothing.

Theo closed his palm around the pendant.

"So." He pushed the necklace into his pocket. "What now?"

"Go back to your friends." Ovidia's smile was faint, almost nonexistent. "I'll leave here, if that's what you want."

"No. Don't go anywhere." Whether he liked it or not, she was the closest thing to family he had. "I want you to tell me more about my father. Stick around. It would be good to have you here…we *are* still in America, right?"

"We haven't even left New York." She raised her hand and swayed her index finger in the air. The place changed and went back to its familiar, miserable state as Damian's ship.

"It's a mirage, nothing complicated."

"I knew it. I smelled sea salt as soon as I got here." Theo crossed his arms and let himself fall against the wall behind him. The only thing left was to deal with Casimir.

"It's impossible, you know? You can't get rid of him," Ovidia said as if reading his mind. "He is you. You're him."

"I know, I just—" Theo broke off. "When I'm talking, I don't know if it's Theo or Casimir." He never said it out loud before, but now he was ready. "I don't know who I am." A tremendous weight came off his back, and the knife stuck in his heart pulled itself out.

"Acceptance," she said, "of your past, your sins."

She was right. He'd been Casimir more than he'd been Theo. Filling one remaining hole in his memory was all he had left to do. That unforgivable sin he had done…what could have been more unforgivable than being a fucking assassin?

His legs failed him and he slipped to the ground. He was a killer. A betrayer. He remembered their names, their faces, their screams. Barbu, Amarys, Alexandru and Adrian. All betrayed and dead at his hands.

If he let himself fall now, he could never get out.

As he fell to his knees, regret and guilt tore at his heart, ripping at his insides. His body was paralyzed, as was his brain.

Ovidia did nothing to help. She towered over him and watched, a faint smile tugging at her lips.

32
SPURNED

The world quivered, blurring at the edges. He couldn't tell up from down. He was not sure if he was breathing. Blinding light swallowed everything. He choked as he was pulled apart, as he slowly exploded from the inside out…The pain was unbearable, building, building, building—

A scream tore out of his chest. Quickly, a shadow fell, washing away the blinding sharpness of the sky. A moment of silence. Then everything shattered. The face of darkness, the face of Casimir, close…closer…too close…then nothing—

Theo gasped and opened his eyes to a blank wall staring back at him. He raised his trembling hand to his head, turned to his left, his right. More walls.

"Hello?" It was louder than he intended. "Anyone?" It echoed. Still no one, nothing. Just walls.

He was lying on a surgical bed when he jumped to his feet. The ground was so cold it sent shivers through his body. He looked down at his hands. Still the same black clothes, but no shoes. Mina's pendant was still warm in his pocket. Theo spotted a door behind him; it looked a lot like the doors in the bunker. But he couldn't remember which one. He tiptoed through it; still no one; empty hallways left and right. He was a black dot in a white room. No more doors, just walls, again.

His breathing quickened, loud in his ears. Panic climbed from his stomach to his chest—no. Anger. Casimir never panicked.

The shadows gathered around his arm, restoring it. He flexed his fingers, still startled by having it back after so long. The black arm was cold as if what ran beneath the dark skin was not warm blood.

He stopped staring as he raised it and rested his palm on the only wall within reach, to his left. As the wall shattered, he stepped over the rubble and jumped through.

He was back at the bunker. Funny how he never knew there was a space past the weapons room where he ended up.

Did the others know about it and kept it to themselves? It wouldn't surprise him in the least.

Theo turned around and drifted back through the weapons room into the central space. The map table was as they'd left it. His eyes found the coffee cup before he'd meant to look at it. It still sat on top of the African continent, exactly where it had been the first time he walked in here.

It had to have been Kai's.

He stood there for a moment staring at it. Kai had sat on the table, drinking cold coffee, tracking whatever it was that he tracked, and doing his job Theo still had no idea about.

Theo picked the cup up. Coffee remains had dried on its walls, brown smudges turned black with age. He turned it over in his restored hand, the black of it contrasting with the white of the cup. He blinked hard and set it back down in the dried-up ring it had left on the table. Right where Kai had left it.

He'd never had a meaningful conversation with his brother. Never asked about his life away. Not once.

Shaking the thought away, he reached his hand to the knife shelf and grabbed one.

"You're awake."

Theo gasped as a familiar voice spoke from behind him.

Nor was glaring at him from afar, his hands balled into fists at his sides.

"What's wrong?" Theo dropped the knife and forced a chuckle.

"Theo is dead." Nor's words spilled out in a trembling whisper. "There's no need to pretend."

"I don't understand—"

"Some old woman brought you here. You were dead, your heart stopped." Nor's forehead dripped with sweat as he took the first step forward.

"Dead?" Theo frowned. He no longer felt his connection to Scarlett.

"If you were dead before, you must've woken up as Casimir." Nor wiped the sweat and crouched, his arm extended to the knife.

"Why couldn't I have woken up as Theo?" Theo crouched, smiling, and met Nor's eyes, daring him to pick it up, and as expected, Nor hesitated enough time for Theo to click his fingers and put Nor to sleep.

Theo stood and turned slowly. The sight of Nor unconscious best friend didn't brought not even a whiff of guilt. Only a rush.

Theo slapped the smile off his face. He could not recognize himself since he woke up. Even the kitchen, where he found himself, was unfamiliar to his new eyes despite the time he used to spend there with the others.

He held his breath at the thought of seeing them again.

"Hey." the call came so suddenly and so loud as if emerging from his own ears.

"Huh?" The hair on the back of his neck stood upright as he turned.

"It's Morgana, you idiot." she was juggling a knife in her hand, as usual. "Which idiot am I talking to?" She was confident as ever. It put that stupid smile back on his face.

"You certainly look…different." She bit on her lower lip. If he didn't know any better, he'd say she was flirting.

"If you must know," Theo passed by her, brushing her neck with his breath, and stood behind her, "the better idiot," he breathed and her body tensed, the veins on her neck tightening.

"Where's Scarlett?" He jumped backwards and turned his face to the ceiling, but Morgana was still standing there like a statue. He was talking to a wall. "Do you know she's not my familiar anymore?" Maybe that would wake her up. "I can't feel her."

"What?" She turned with quick motion and rolled her eyes all the way back. "So you're *not* Theo?"

"No, I am, I'm just…not." It was the hardest thing in the world to explain, if it could even be explained. He didn't understand it himself. "Maybe you should go check on Nor," He jerked his head towards her. "Put him in a bed or something. He was gonna attack me, so I put him to sleep."

"Right, I'll get right on that." Morgana's sarcasm rolled out of her mouth as she instantly narrowed her eyes for half a second that seemed like forever.

"What?"

"It's just…Theo never hurts his friends." Morgana nodded. "I guess you *are* changed."

"Yeah," he chuckled, and started walking. "As I was saying."

"You won't like…kill the bunch of us, will you?" Morgana trusted him. He could sense it. But she was also the kind of gal who would blurt out anything on her mind. So that question was understandable. But why did it bother him so much? He would never hurt them…would he?

"Of course not. I'm still the same guy." He forced a chuckle, though there was nothing to chuckle about.

"Hmm…" Morgana was very transparent like that; if she was suspicious, she would act suspicious, and that was one of those times. "You got a black arm." She pointed at it.

"I swear I'm not gonna hurt you, okay?" Theo put his hand on his chest as his pulse spiked. "I swear on my mother's grave…wait that's not worth much, is it?"

"I guess." She shrugged. What the hell was wrong with him? Saying stuff like that would only worsen his situation. But, Morgana was very open-minded. He was sure she would let it slide.

"You go wait outside and I'll fetch Scarlett." she pointed at the ceiling and sprinted out of the kitchen. "Feel free to chain yourself to the door in the meantime." Open-minded, indeed.

"Ha ha." Theo waited for Morgana to turn at the end of the hall and followed her down there. He knew the way to the library; Scarlett must have been there. "You're following me," Morgana interrupted his thoughts and stood abruptly in front of him. He almost bumped into her. "Huh." She nodded, as if understanding something.

It was plain stupid of him to try following a trained hunter. Of course, she would discover him. "Uh, yes I am, and surprisingly, I didn't feel like chaining myself to the door." He scratched the back of his head and spotted Scarlett at the library door, sitting on the floor with his almost-journal on her lap.

Morgana sighed and stepped aside. "Go." She jerked her head toward the door, her eyes communicating something that was lost on Theo. He gave her a half nod and marched towards his familiar.

As his knuckle touched the door; she looked up at him, expressionless, unreadable. "Hey." He didn't expect her to speak to him right away, but she did, and that made him happy, at least the Theo part of him.

"Hey," he sat beside her and glanced at the page she was on. "Whatcha doing?"

"What do you want from me?" She closed the book, sending a cloud of dust to his face. He coughed and jumped to his feet; clearly she didn't want him sitting with her. "I'm not your familiar anymore; I got no business with you," she said with a cold and harsh voice that was followed by a frown. "You cut me."

"No, I didn't." Her words hurt Theo, and he did not bother hiding it. "Scarlett, don't say that!" He closed the door behind him so there wouldn't be 'ears' listening to his heartfelt speech. "You know damn well you're not just my familiar. You were my first friend. I need you." He extended her a hand and shook his head. "I didn't cut you."

"You don't get it," she ignored it and stood on her own. "I don't wanna be a familiar to Casimir; he destroyed a lot of lives, including my own." She turned her face away as if she didn't want to look at him for one more second. "I never told you this—"

“But, I don’t remember anything,” Theo had never been so confused in his life. Of all the people he could’ve ruined, did it have to be Scarlett? “What did I—”

“I’m sure you will, and when you do,” she walked past him and opened the door. “I don’t think I can forgive you.”

With nothing left to be said, Theo stood, wide eyed. His tongue felt too big for his mouth and his head spun all over the place. She spoke to him as if he were a stranger when, for the past months, they were the closest of friends. What could he have done to make her hate him?

At that moment, he just wanted to bury himself deep into the depths of the ocean and stay down under. Instead he turned and walked out of there without looking back.

He would make her forgive him.

33
AWAKENING

Ovidia had told him he would find peace and acceptance if he became whole, if he became one, but no—his whole life was falling apart bit by bit.

Theo ran up the stairs of the bunker, almost hitting his head on the lower side of the ceiling as he walked out. No one crossed his path. It was for the better. He couldn't take being there one more second. It didn't feel like home anymore.

They used to care.

***

It was dark again. It always was, when he was near. Not just night, but that silent kind of vanishing. Like even the concrete surrendered to it.

What else was there to do? For the last few months, which seemed like years, he never had a quiet day until now. Now that Damian was gone. But was here really? Maybe he could crawl out of Tartarus in one piece. Perhaps even find their sister still intact. What would it be like? To have a family.

Family.

His chest tightened. Maybe everyone really did die alone in the end.

"Give them time," a voice said.

Theo stopped walking and slowly let out a breath. Everyone kept ambushing him from behind since he woke up. Could he not feel them anymore? He turned around and there she was; wearing the same torn dress and bearing the same heavy, desperate look.

"What?" Something snapped in him. Her cryptic words, the judgment in everyone's eyes—he was done. "They already made their choice." He turned his gaze to the black sky as a white owl passed by. "You should have seen Scarlett."

Ovidia didn't have any reaction to his words, and she didn't budge even a little, as if she knew what was going to happen. If she ever did, why didn't she warn him before making him feel like he was stabbed in the back multiple times?

After a moment of uncomfortable staring into each other's eyes, she sighed and shook her head.

"I suggest you do what your instinct tells you." She extended her hand and gestured for him to follow her. "Keep hiding. Eventually, you'll find yourself choking on your own skin."

They reached the peak of the mountain.

"What do you see?" Ovidia pointed forward.

"I don't—" More cryptic questions. He was so tired of them.

But, she didn't push him to answer. She just stood there, which was worse.

He looked. The sun was coming up in the distance. It was just the slow leak of it, gray going amber. He'd stood here with

Scarlett once. When they watched the sunrise. When she promised him she would be by his side through anything.

"The last time you stood here," Ovidia said. "What did you feel?"

"Like I'd lost everything." He looked straight at the sun until his eyes watered.

"And now?"

"Different." His voice faded as the sun dipped behind the buildings, clearing the sky.

Something had shifted, had loosened inside him.

Ovidia said nothing. That was, he was starting to understand, her version of agreement.

"What you feel now," she said after a long moment, "is just a taste of what you could become. You're not yet there."

"So I'm not Casimir yet?"

She didn't answer that either. He was beginning to think she genuinely didn't know.

Theo closed his eyes and took a long, satisfying breath, as if inhaling life itself.

"Thank you." When he finally got the words out, she disappeared.

He shrugged and turned back toward the bunker, something like hope still clinging to him.

From afar, he was seeing it with a new light because someone had changed the street lamps in the area. The sun was not fully up in the sky. He'd been walking all night.

Theo pushed the door open with his shoulder, and it squeaked. The bunker was quiet; the others must have been asleep still. He climbed straight up to his room, which was just as he left it weeks ago; from the bloody shirt he threw on the bed to the open drawer where he usually stored Mina's journal that always reminded him of death.

Theo kicked the door closed and stared at the open drawer in silence and darkness.

Casimir lived for a long time. Should he not be afraid of death anymore?

He slapped off the thought from his head and let himself gently fall on the floor, his back against the bed, and his head tilted almost all the way back.

His back ached against the bed frame, cold steel pressing into his spine.

"What do you want from me?" He addressed the blank ceiling, expecting an answer…not from the ceiling, but from Casimir. There it was again, the quiet unraveling he had stopped pretending to fight. Out of the blue, his body throbbed all over, all at once; it must've been the stress of his fucked up life finally getting to him. His eyes fell closed, as his eyelids were too heavy for them to hold. His body heaved too as if the Ashé was leaving it, even his magic hand evaporated into nothing, leaving its phantom behind.

He shook his head as the light flickered like thunder. His hand twitched, and words that were not his formed on his tongue.

What if he could do that too? Evaporate and leave nothing behind? But no, that would be wrong. He couldn't keep hiding from himself, not in the state the world was in. He should destroy the world to save it. Rebuild it. Let witches rise from the ashes.

—Wait. What was that?

Theo's eyes flew open, insides twisted, head pounding as if hit by a bus. Violation and invasion flooded him. Filthy. He removed his shirt after a struggle, jumped into the shower, and let out a breath.

His skin crawled. Why did he ever ask that stupid question? The fault was nobody's but his.

"Theo!" His name echoed through the room louder than it should have.

In the middle of the night?

Theo grabbed a towel and almost slipped on the water as he looked out the window. Nope, it was day. Time seemed to pass a lot faster since the previous day. Was it because of his 'new dawn'?

"Who is it?" Theo yelled back, putting on some clothes he found in the bathroom, and ran to the door. It was weird that he didn't recognize the voice, as he knew everyone living in the bunker with him.

Shiny silver hair was the first thing that came into view. It extended all the way to his shoulder.

"Hey there." That smile begged to be punched off.

"Seth, you're not welcome here." Theo said, more aggressively than he intended. *He deserved it.* "How did you even get in?" Theo kept the door halfway open. He was on Damian's side, and all those who sided with that insect get equally loathed.

Seth's jaw tightened. "Your mage let me in." His gaze fell to Theo's foot, blocking the door.

Nor, that idiot. What was he thinking?

"And why would he let you in?" Theo removed his foot and backed away into the room, leaving plenty of space for Seth to come in. "All my friends hate you as much as I do…well, maybe more."

Seth scoffed as he entered the room and kicked the door closed behind him

"I'm not here for you. I'm here because my godmother asked. She told me what you two talked about." He stopped short and threw himself into the chair, reluctant. "She said I owe it to my mother to tell you the truth she couldn't."

Godmother?

Theo backed away until he hit the wall. "Ovidia? We didn't talk about anything, really."

Seth looked up at him from under hooded eyes. Piercing, eagle eyes.

"I know you killed my mother," he said in a steady tone no one should have when saying that sentence.

"What? How did you—it wasn't me it was Ca—" Theo stopped.

"You should listen to Ovidia." Seth interrupted "Just because she's the complete opposite of your Amarys."

Theo blinked at the abrupt change of subject, then held his breath and pulled out a chair. "You're gonna tell me everything you know."

34
CONFESSION

"Okay." Seth sat forward. "I assume you already know about Casimir's *profession*?"

"Assassin?" Theo pressed his back to the wall, about to cross his arms, then remembered he had only one.

"Not exactly. He did carry out kill order from a bunch of politicians. But, he mostly worked for Cuza, the prince of Romania."

Something in Theo's clicked into place.

"Wait, I don't understand." Theo pushed off the wall. "I thought Casimir wanted to cleanse the world from those people. Why was he working for them?"

Seth chuckled and shook his head as a flare of surprise crossed his eyes like he was not expecting Theo to know that.

"Classic Casimir move," he said. "Before anything else, he was a hypocrite. Any side he fought against 'Should have a taste of their own hypocrisy'. His exact words," Seth sighed, a faraway look in his eyes as if he had firsthand experience. "That was the ultimate weapon of betrayal to him."

Theo stiffened. Casimir was farther away, harder to recognize. "He gets off on betrayal."

"Well, I can't say that's new information." Seth shrugged and crossed his legs.

Nothing was new about Casimir, despite the gaps in his memory. But, hearing the truth for once was a satisfaction on its own.

"What about my father? Do you know anything at all?"

Seth's smile stretched all the way to his cheeks. "Lucky for you, I know everything my godmother told me, which is a lot." He adjusted himself on the chair and sat at the edge of his seat. "Are you sure you want to know? It's quite delicate."

Theo paused, pursing his lips. "I'm sure, go on."

"His name was Alistor, and he was your mother's familiar."

Theo stood and moved to the window. A romantic bond with a familiar was forbidden. "Why would they—"

"Well," Seth cut him off and continued. "He was in love with her. That was why he chose her. She would say the same too, but I don't think she ever meant it." Seth turned his face to the window. Sunlight cut across the left side of his face, turning him almost transparent.

"See, Alistor wasn't just any familiar—" Theo tuned his gaze back to Seth. "He was the rarest kind ever; a raven, a white raven. He was majestic." Seth sighed, tapping his foot over the wooden floor, an echoing rhythm haunting the silence. "I think your mother was using him to create powerful witches." He chuckled. "But, I guess it didn't work twice because the second turned out to be a world class idiot."

Theo couldn't hold back a smile. Seth was definitely growing in his eyes.

“I know she killed him in the end. Alistor.” Theo picked up his knife from the nightstand. “How did it come to that?” The words left a bad taste.

“Amarys did something…unforgivable.”

Theo scoffed. That sounded oddly familiar.

“Like the cliché she sometimes was…” Seth stared at nothing as his fingers played with some scattered motes of dust on the table. “She cheated on him with the arrogant prince, and then gave the bastard a sample of your father’s blood.”

“Why his blood?” Theo pressed his finger against the sharp edge of the knife, pulling it away before it drew blood.

“Cuza’s plan was to use the blood to *make* the same kind of familiar, because obviously Alistor was the last one of his kind. Didn’t really work out, though.” He paused, looking in the distance then shrugged. “Anyway, you know how megalomaniacs get.”

He knew too well.

“So, my father found out about it?”

“Oh, he did.” Seth nodded, snapping Theo out of his trance. “And he made the mistake of telling my godmother. She suggested they throw Amarys in Tartarus.” he sighed, looking like he had been holding it the whole time. “Later on, your mother found out about everything. No idea how, but she did, and she confronted Alistor—”

“That’s when she killed him?” Theo sank to the floor, the truth settling heavy in his chest.

“Well yeah, with tears in her eyes according to my godmother who supposedly witnessed the murder from afar,” Seth said, his smile emerging then slowly fading from his face. “Lucky for her, Amarys didn’t see her.”

"So what, she left it at that? No confrontation?" It seemed Ovidia had always been a coward, despite her position as the High Priestess at the time. How had she landed it?

"Of course there was a confrontation." Theo should have let him continue. "A few months later, right when you were born." Theo's eyes widened and he went very still.

He knew exactly what Seth was going to say next.

"You see, she was six months pregnant with you when she killed him." Seth's astonished expression told Theo that his eyes were already blackened, and his veins were bulging in his neck and face.

"Go on." He managed through clenched teeth, fearing that opening his mouth too much would let the darkness out.

"Ovidia didn't say much after that." Seth rested his back against the chair, and crossed his arm. "Amarys did some sort of manipulation magic that kept her away from you. For years," he said, grabbing a half-filled bottle of water from the table. "So she pushed you to become Theo, and her, Mina." He pursed his lips. "The end."

"But why didn't she just kill her if she was a loose end?" Theo controlled his breathing and jumped to his feet, stealing the bottle from Seth's hand and set it back where it belonged.

"Hmm, no one knows why." Seth shrugged and rose from his chair, soundless like a cat. "I guess we'll never really know why Amarys does anything, will we?"

"Right," Theo whispered more to himself than to Seth. The heaviness of the past pressed on him like a familiar weight. Thanks, I guess."

"That's everything." Seth said, his voice painfully neutral. "Everything Ovidia and my mother knew before Casimir killed her." He opened the door and glared at Theo. "I'm done with you and your brother. Don't try to find me or contact me."

Why hadn't Seth done anything to him if he knew Theo killed his mother? Why was he just…leaving?

Theo swallowed his questions and watched him disappear downstairs.

After a few minutes processing, Theo descended the stairs and the first thing he spotted was Nor and Morgana sitting on the same couch, both exhibiting a relaxed demeanor, talking and laughing.

Scarlett was nowhere to be seen.

What did he miss?

"Hey." His voice echoed through the walls. He didn't even know the bunker echoed.

"Look who finally came down with the little people." Morgana let go of the book she was holding and gave it to Nor. "What were you two doing in there?" She raised her brows…twice.

Theo rolled his eyes, hating the fact he understood her implication.

"Seth told me things." he said, hiding a trembling hand behind his back.

The atmosphere turned heavy with the stretching silence before Nor spoke.

"He wouldn't talk to us." Nor shook his head. "Tell us, was it a waste of time?"

"No. You could say he let me in on some family secrets." Theo looked around for Scarlett. "Dirty family secrets. Violent, murder-y." He chuckled, before realizing that was a terrible joke. He got a smile from Morgana.

"Anyway, where's Scarlett?" The only thing left for him to do was to patch things up with Scarlett, whatever it took.

"She went for a walk or a flight, I guess…" Morgana said. "Don't fret, she'll be back." She waved a dismissive hand.

"*Fret?*" Theo chuckled as he repeated.

"Yeah, you know, like, *don't worry*...you know?" She was flustered, and it was fun to see. "This is your father's fault," she said, pointing at Nor, and looking like she was about to attack him. He raised his arms in the air, chuckling nervously.

After some seconds, Theo realized he was smiling like an idiot. He couldn't take his eyes off of Morgana. She was suddenly, if it was even possible, prettier.

"So, Morgana," Letting himself fall on the couch beside her, he put his arm around her. "We don't really know much about you, do we?" He nodded. "Tell us about yourself."

"Umm." She chuckled. "What's gotten into you?"

"Okay. That's my cue," Nor stood faster than he ever did before and headed to the door—no, hurried to the door. "I'm gonna look for Scarlett."

And he was gone, leaving just the two of them.

"Remember when I poured my heart out and told you about my past? That's pretty much all there is to me." She didn't move away from him, that was a good sign, but she didn't get closer to him either. "Unless you know something I don't?"

Theo forced a chuckle. It got awkward way too fast.

"Okay, listen," Theo said. His uncomfortable moves were getting him nowhere. "There's something Seth told me earlier that kept bothering me—"

"He wanted my number?" Morgana straightened up, her eyes widening in obvious exaggeration.

"What? No. What?" Theo fumbled, his tongue twisting in unnatural positions. He was well aware of the fact that she was teasing him, but rose to the bait, anyway.

His accidental freak out was near-impossible to hide, and by the look on Morgana's face, she was enjoying the show. Now it was even more awkward.

"Pff, why would that bother me?" He kept digging his hole.

"Jeez, chill. Never mind." She looked up at him with exaggerated surprise. Theo sighed and shook his head; he had better change the subject.

"Anyway." It was a nightmare. "He told me something about my mother giving my father's blood to some prince who was gonna make a familiar with it." What was that train of nonsense he just spouted?

"Huh?"

Exactly.

She cleared her throat and crossed her legs. "That's not creepy at all." Her words contradicted her face that illuminated with a brief crooked grin.

"Yeah, and get this," Theo said, leaning closer, "it didn't work," the words came out in a whisper, creepier than he intended. "And this failed familiar is still somewhere out there. Probably doesn't even know what they were gonna be."

"Wow, this is…" Morgana let out a breath it seemed she'd been holding for a while. "Do you know what this means?" She smirked. "That person might be in danger and you should save them. Isn't that what you and your little gang usually do? Go. Go."

"God, don't say it like that. It sounds lame." He scratched his head until it burned. "I don't know. Maybe we should just skip this one." Theo stood, extending his hand to Morgana. "I'd like to think there's some other little gang out there doing the good work."

"That's one way to see it," she scoffed as she grabbed his hand instantly and stood beside him. On her way to the door, she shot him a look over her shoulder. "See you in the car."

"Yup." He sighed.

35
UNTANGLE

The sun beat down on Theo's face. He lay tossing and turning, paralyzed by anxious thoughts, making waking up harder than usual. What if he was back to killing people? What if his only friends would leave him? What if he couldn't get used to his hand being chopped off? Every what-if lodged like a thorn in his throat.

"Hey, you got a minute?" A soft knock accompanied by the last voice he had expected to hear penetrated the door. It was definitely Scarlett. The last time they spoke, it didn't go so well—why sugarcoat things? He just didn't know why.

Theo shoved the blanket out of his way, and as soon as his feet touched the icy cold floor, he started seeing doubles like he was about to pass out.

You know what we did to her. His own voice spoke in his head.

"Theo?" Scarlett's voice echoed, clashing with the other one. "I'm coming in." *Keep her out.*

As she opened the door, the voice vanished. After a split second, he was just sitting there, staring at Scarlett like an idiot.

"He's scared of you," he said under his breath, the words tasting like ash in his mouth. He must have been. It was the only explanation that made sense. Why else would he want him to *"keep her out"*?

"What?" Scarlett walked forward and sat on the floor against the bed. She looked like she slipped, and she didn't seem to have heard him.

"Nothing." Theo shook his head. "What's up?" She shouldn't know. Not yet. Would she even believe him? Would she think Casimir had made him lose the sanity he had left?

"Well, I need to talk to you." She turned her head to the door from where she came in and rubbed her thighs with her palms. "About what I said the other day."

Theo could read her like a book. She was nervous, and when Scarlett would get nervous, it meant she was about to apologize, which she had never ever done since he met her.

"I think I was too harsh." She chuckled. "You didn't even know what I was on about."

"But, I want to know." Theo slid down next to her. "What did I do to you?" It was clearly one of the worst things Casimir had done since he himself couldn't even remember what it was.

Theo wanted to reach for her, to see inside her head the way she did with him, but she felt distant, detached. Theo's heart clutched, the walls of the room closing in on him. He *had* to know. "Come on—"

"Don't worry. Now I know it wasn't you," she interrupted him, nodding repeatedly, aggressively. Maybe *she* was the one going crazy. "It was wrong of me to blame you in the first place. I'm sorry," she whispered the last words like she was struggling to get them out.

She stood back up, and hurried out without looking back or even leaving room for Theo to say anything…she was just gone. He didn't know what that apology meant. Were they friends again, or just friendly?

Theo sighed and touched his cold, veined forehead. He wished she was still his familiar, because maybe that was the only connection they had, and he mistook it for friendship. Either way, at least he understood her then.

"Hey man, get out of there already. I'm sure the dress looks amazing." Nor's brutal knock with his lame joke got him out of his head. Maybe he should be thankful. "Everyone's waiting." His voice faded behind the door.

Waiting? When was he appointed leader of the pack all of a sudden? Why would they even see him as *the leader* when he could barely take care of himself?

"Coming," Theo coughed as his throat jammed. He pranced to the door and practically jumped over the stairs to find them staring at him with the same expectant look on each of their faces. Copies of each other.

Theo walked past them and sat at the edge of the couch, crossing his legs. "I guess you all know about the blood thing,"

Blood thing. Smooth. Where was the Casimir side when he needed it?

"I think we should find that familiar." He raised his black arm and rested his hand on his chest, clutching his shirt. "I have a feeling we should."

"We're with you, Theo. Of course." Nor reached out his hand and patted his shoulder while the others watched in silence; Scarlett resting against a wall, Morgana next to her, with her hands crossed. "But where do we start? It was literally a century and a half ago."

"We just go back. All the way to the beginning." Theo shrugged like it was obvious, like it was easy for him to say that, when it was one thing he was afraid—no, terrified he had to do as Casimir. In a way, it was right, going back to his country, to his home. He was curious to see what has changed, what has stayed the same in a century, and hopefully or not fill out the vast gap in his memory.

"What do you say—" His own amused scoff interrupted him when Morgana shook her head and slipped ten bucks to Scarlett.

Theo released a breath of strange satisfaction and a kind of inner peace he had never felt before. "Let's go to Romania."

A second passed where he couldn't breathe.

Was it panic? Fear?

To the other it was a second. To Theo, it stretched, air gone, heart hammering. The world stilled, trapping him inside that second.

Was that what dying alone was like. He didn't want to die alone. After that momentary collision with Casimir, he thought he would finally become whole and complete, but there always remained emptiness inside, forever deepening. Maybe acceptance was a bad idea after all—

"Theo, you okay there?" Nor patted his shoulder again. They noticed.

"Hmm?" Theo raised his head, pretending to be surprised. "Sure. Why wouldn't I be?" They would not understand. They would never understand. Oh, how he missed Scarlett hanging out in his head. "What are we waiting for?"

"You, apparently." Morgana stepped forward and held his gaze as if insinuating something.

36
RETURN

Bucharest, Romania

The flight had taken all day. The air in Bucharest was thick with smog and the smell of fresh concrete poured over old cement. Memory. Theo hated how familiar it was.

The street outside the airport swarmed with people, moving as if invisible hands dragged them in different directions. Just like back in New York.

That realization slightly eased his hesitation about returning to Romania, his home country, but the self-doubt never really left him even as they made their way to what was supposed to be a rest stop in a small motel that they found on the way. Except it was fully booked.

"I know my luck." Theo shook his head as he sat on a lonely wooden bench in front of the building.

"What, you've never been to Romania?" Morgana's sarcasm broke through the noise of the cars and construction sites that were right there on each side everywhere they went.

"We need to keep moving," Theo said, rolling his eyes at that unnecessary comment.

Morgana scoffed.

"I want to leave here as soon as possible." He brushed a hand through his sweat-soaked hair as he got to his feet and started almost speed walking, He didn't want to think. Not after everything. Let the half-finished buildings distract him, scaffolding on every third one, probably the same scaffolding that had been there for ten years. A country always mid-renovation.

"Come on," his voice faded with the wind, as he said. He didn't even check if the others heard him as they started hurrying behind him. Except for Nor who caught up with him.

"I hope you're not mad." He gave a half-smile. "That I asked my dad to get us here."

"Of course not." Theo slowed down and chuckled. "It's not like we had options."

Although they were broke, Theo would have still preferred finding another way that didn't involve strangers, knowing his own trust issues. But, he also could not say no to a private jet. Which begged the question; why didn't Nor have one too?

"Been a long time since I've been here." Scarlett emerged beside him as Nor stepped back to talk to Morgana. "Might check on a few friends at some point."

Theo sighed. He really did know next to nothing about his own familiar.

"I don't think we'll have time for that." He didn't want to stay here any longer than he needed to. "We'll fly back home as soon as we're done here."

Without saying anything, Scarlett side-eyed him and picked up the pace, creating a distance between them.

After the longest walk of Theo's life, they stopped at a broken-down bar. They could have been lost for all he knew. The dilapidated joint was the only place for miles, but at least it was quieter than the city. On the way, no cab would stop for them. Some would even speed up.

Was it Casimir's dark aura? Or maybe it was Morgana's resting bitch face—her whole attire, really—that scared them off?

It didn't matter. They were outsiders and they looked like it. Something Theo was no stranger to.

The bland walls and the scratched three-legged tables gave off a wrongness only Theo felt. His hair stood on end, sweat dripping from his forehead. The flickering lamp lights didn't help either. Not to mention the enormous amount of Ashé flowing everywhere.

Theo went first and pushed—no, barely touched the piece of thin wood pretending to be a door. It collapsed, dumping dust and ash straight into his face, and just his face; death itself, crawling into his lungs.

"Gee, talk about a mass grave." Scarlett covered her nose with her elbow as she kicked a human skull that was under a disgustingly wet piece of cloth. Theo gagged.

"No touch!" Some woman's shaky, pinched voice coming from under a counter broke the eerie silence; she seemed to have been kneeling behind it. Her pale, wrinkled face, slightly illuminated by a few sunrays that entered with Theo, reflected the miserable state of the place.

Her colorless eyes mirrored the windows in the front entrance, shattered and fallen. In an unsettling way, the woman almost looked like Ovidia. Hell, she would have been her twin if she didn't resemble the skull more.

Theo turned away, but she was not looking either; she completely ignored them, all of them, like they were not even there. It made Theo feel invisible again.

"Încă o rundă!"

Theo jumped in his own skin and raised his head to a bunch of people that appeared out of nowhere, yelling for another round of drinks and banging their empty, larger-than-their-heads beer glasses against the tables, barely holding on to dear life.

Suddenly, the bar was packed with what seemed to be a bunch of gangbangers and bikers, young and old, covered in scars and tattoos. It was like a den of some sort. Were they all witches? That would certainly explain the overwhelmingly massive load of magic energy he sensed earlier.

Theo backed away against a wall, only to fall backward into the cold, bumpy ground. He could have sworn there was a wall there.

"Shit," he cried out in annoyance more than pain.

"Dude, what is with your luck today?" Scarlett extended her hand to him with a smile. He smiled back. "It's not luck, it's the country." He was sure Romania hated him and had it in for him like everybody else. "It was a mirage. I can't believe I didn't—"

Before he could finish the sentence, as he was dusting off his clothes and the others too busy making fun of him, a fist like a steel doorknob, slammed into his face faster than a bullet leaving the barrel. The impact was so powerful that he was sure he felt his mouth move to his cheek. He couldn't tell which side it hit. On top of that, he fell right back to where he was. Eyes shut tight, he rested his palm on the throbbing cheek. He could not even see who hit him until he spat out a tooth and stood back up.

The blurry image before him was of the others standing there, staring at him with fish eyes, along with some old guy whose chest was rising and falling with rapid movement. His furrowed face was red like he had just been to Tartarus and back, and his glaring eyes held an expression of clear anger and slight shock or surprise; he looked like he had just seen a ghost he wanted to murder.

With one eye barely open, Theo raised his hands in surrender and backed away with small, subtle steps, "d-do I know you?" Maybe that was the wrong thing to say. The man lowered his fists and tilted his head to the side, staring.

"I don't think." he had a rough accent, hard to understand. "I thought you someone else." He paused, drawing a sharp breath. "No, Are you—"

He stopped talking as a large hand appeared on the old man's shoulder and averted his gaze. It was a young man, almost Theo's age, if he wasn't two centuries older. "Forgive my father." His sweet voice matched his delicate, innocent features. Leaving the chair he was in, he walked closer toward Theo, facing him with a calm, empathic gaze, unlike his father's. "It's just that," he had an almost perfect English accent for a foreigner, "an important person back in his day made a promise and didn't fulfill it. And the thing is—" The guy turned to his father for a quick second with sad, teary eyes and moved his face to Theo's ear. "You look exactly like him," he said in a cracked whisper.

Theo's neck tensed and he held his breath for a long time. Trying to not let expose his stress, he started sweating and trying to keep his face neutral.

Casimir made the promise a long time ago. To free himself. To free the witches. But why didn't he do it? Why did he disappear? Why did he have to disappoint those who were waiting for him…again?

"Wh-what promise?" Theo swallowed again. The guy put his hands in his pockets and stood with a poised demeanor, unlike Theo's.

"That we'd be free," he said, like it was obvious. "That we'd escape from oppression and break the chains." He pulled his fisted hands together as if showing him those chains. Theo just watched him and his enthusiasm, flabbergasted. Even though he never did what he promised, he could still see the glow of hope in the boy's eyes.

"Why are you smiling?" he asked, as Theo chuckled, realizing that he was smirking the whole time.

"What's your name?" Theo cleared his throat, realizing what he said after he said it.

"Albescu." The guy's posture was straight, head held high as he extended his hand. "Adrian Albescu." Elegant.

"I'm Theo." He raised his head, smiling and shook his hand "Theodore Jensen…From New York," he said, regretting it immediately.

***

In an attempt at an apology, Adrian, despite the protest of his father, invited them to spend the night at their house, which turned out to be upstairs, in the same building as the god-forsaken bar.

"Great, we're never leaving this place," Theo murmurs, not wanting to be heard, but the echo of the stairwell they were climbing along with the quiet made that impossible.

"Don't worry," Adrian laughed elegantly, "it's not as bad as it looks." Then, as he was leading the way, he stopped and looked up at the very high ceiling, and with a snap of his fingers, another cleaner, longer, larger stairwell fell before them. He smiled and stepped aside. "After you," he gestured at Theo, who cleared his throat and walked with hesitant steps that he hopes would not be too obvious. Theo could not just give them his trust, like he had done many times in the past. They had to need that type of security to keep something out or in their house. Who knew what could have been waiting for them up there?

As soon as they reached the door, Theo sensed a faint imprint of Ashé he had never encountered before. "Turn the doorknob," The sweet, friendly Adrian was starting to act suspicious; he put his hands behind his back, a smile on his face, and waited for Theo. "It's okay, it's just to see the kind of Ashé you have," Adrian nodded. "To be safe."

Theo swallowed. Anyone here would recognize his Ashé.

He raised his hand slowly, side-eying Adrian. He was a stranger. How could he trust them enough to bring them to his house?

Something grabbed Theo's wrist, squeezing so hard his blood vessels could have exploded.

"What's wrong with your arm?" Theo's stomach turned to water. Adrian took hold of the wrong arm. The black arm. The fake arm.

"Um…I…" Theo stumbled and Adrian leaned forward, his eyes narrowing. "My—"

"It's black tar!" Scarlett swooped in and grabbed Adrian's hand, aggressively shoving it away from Theo. Adrian almost fell. "You know…from cars." She shrugged and laughed nervously. "He fell on the way, and we haven't had time to clean up." Her defensiveness was too apparent. He could not have possibly believed her.

"I see." Adrian chuckled, then went serious as he caressed his wrist. "Come in."

He grabbed the knob with a quick, clumsy gesture and pushed the door open.

What made him open the door himself? How was he convinced so fast with that pathetic explanation? Adrian grew more suspicious with every move.

Theo stumbled at the entrance before going in. A stained glass door that he fell against blocked his fall. Strange, hand-painted black symbols that looked like carvings in a Stone Age cave covered its every corner.

As soon as they entered, the place was more spacious than it should have been. Theo found himself suddenly separated from the others and stuck alone with Adrian, who kept looking straight ahead as he walked. Before he could utter a word to break another one of those awkward silences, Theo caught a pungent smell that he could feel in his bones.

"What the hell is that?" He covered his nose with the palm of his hand. "Smells like rotten eggs."

"Oh," Adrian burst out laughing and pointed at something sitting alone on the table. An artichoke. Or it was shaped like one. "It's coming from there. I'm surprised you don't recognize it."

"Guess it doesn't grow in New York." Theo shrugged and walked forward, his eyes narrowed to get a better look at the thing, almost crouching. "What does it do?"

"It's from a place called Tartarus." Theo flinched at the name.

"It absorbs negativity and such," Adrian continued, "It's called a *carceris tenebris,* a prison of darkness." He walked beside Theo and grabbed the object with one hand. It could not have absorbed much dark if it was *that* light. "And this foul stench is the smell of darkness."

"Why can I smell darkness?"

"I'm surprised myself." Adrian put the artichoke back on the table. "But I know of the existence of a few exceptional individuals who can, and I guess you're one of them." He turned to face Theo and tapped his cheek twice. It was uncomfortable, to say the least. "Now I'm sure you're not drawn to the dark side." Somehow, his words didn't match his face. "Of course, only those who are just…evil can never catch it."

"Like they say," Theo smiled, a weight lifting off his chest. Maybe there was hope for him yet. "You can never smell your own fart."

A pause.

"Look," Adrian whispered and put his hands on Theo's shoulders, his smile vanishing. "I don't trust you."

His eyes pulsated with dark purple while he tightened his grip, pushing Theo to his knees.

"What do you want?" Theo put his black hand on Adrian's and squeezed until Adrian jumped away.

"You and your friends can stay here tonight." Adrian stopped as he massaged his hand. "I'd like you to see something."

Theo closed his eyes, fighting Casimir's pull. "How do I know you're not gonna hurt us?" As much as he hated to have to stay there, they didn't really have anywhere else to go.

"You don't." Adrian smirked and walked away. "Room on the left. It's the only one we have." He halted and looked back at Theo. The smile still hadn't left his face. "It's big enough for all of you."

37
MIRAGE

Theo scanned the room in eerie silence. Its vast emptiness made what went unsaid feel heavier. He shivered, the discomfort creeping under his skin.

"So." Nor adjusted his sleeping bag by the wall. "Where did you go earlier?"

"What are you talking about?" Theo rested his head on the floor. "I was with Adrian in the living room. We came in together."

Morgana opened her eyes, frowning as she sat up. Scarlett followed. "There's no living room. The old man told us to come to this room—the one on the right."

"Except this room was on the left." Theo hesitated before walking to the door and gripping the knob. Was it a trap? He twisted, but it wouldn't budge. "Damn it. I shouldn't have trusted him."

"Why do we always get trapped?" Morgana tilted her head to the ceiling, likely looking for vents. "I hate this." The moment she collapsed onto the floor, the wall behind her shimmered and turned transparent—a massive window flooding the room with purple light. Not a window. A floor panel, glass-thick. A one-way mirror built into the architecture, looking straight down into the basement below.

Theo shielded his eyes, squinting against the glare.

When he opened his eyes, the lights revealed an old, decayed basement directly below them. Adrian stood on a wooden plank jutting from the wall.

"Hear me, comrades." He addressed a crowd of angry, furrowed faces that looked at him with some kind of admiration. It reminded Theo of a certain witch club he once entered with Scarlett. "I have summoned you here today to announce some potentially good news." The wild crowd turned silent. "I have found the power. Enough to get us what we deserve, what we have been waiting for." Adrian raised his fist in the air. "What was promised to our kind long ago. I will deliver it."

"Where did you find this…*power*?" A man with a disfigured face in the center of the crowd shouted out, giving Adrian a this-is-too-good-to-be-true look. "This is not the first time you have said this," he laughed. "How do we know what you say is true this time, Commander?"

Commander. Theo shuddered at the word.

The rest of the crowd roared and nodded their heads in agreement.

"Silence!" Adrian stomped his foot on the dusty board, almost breaking it. "I have it here. You could see for yourselves." He jerked his head upward with an intense side glance. Theo looked away.

"Uh-oh." Scarlett backed away from the glass as if she'd seen a ghost. "What did we get ourselves into?"

"*You* tell us." Theo walked toward her. "What is going on here?" His voice the only sound in the room. "Is this some kind of cult?"

"You could say that." Scarlett gulped down a breath as distant cheers made the ground reverberate below their feet. Theo could feel them in his bones.

"Oh my god," Nor said as he went to look at the crowd.

"Hey, you need to see this."

Theo turned around as Morgana tapped him on the shoulder, not looking at him. Her eyes were stuck on the scene before her. Theo followed her gaze. Each person in the crowd held a torch, its flames burning with the same purple hue. They were all chanting in complete and perfect sync: "*Hail the dark prince!*"—which was bad enough—and others at the front of the bunch were waving enormous banners, all had the same drawing on them. Theo struggled to see it at first, but when he did, a shock ran through his body and his hair stood on end,

"Is that—" he put his palms on the fragile glass, squinting as much as he could. The drawing was of a large white raven with pitch black eyes and dark feathers, soaring like a phoenix rising out of the ashes.

"What do you know?" Theo shook off the fascination and turned to Scarlett. "Tell me everything." She was the only one who could shed some light on their situation.

"Okay." She sighed and turned away from the window, sliding against the wall beside it. "Well, everything we've heard so far about the White Raven thing; first, it's a weapon to destroy Damian, now this whole prince and blood thing from Seth. Those were just a few of the myths that have been going around for eons." She paused, rubbing her eyes with her fingers. "I just realized. Every one of them was of the same thing. The White Raven." Eyes fixated on the ground, she shook her head and scoffed. "It had different names everywhere, but no one really knew what it was."

"That would explain what's going on down there." Morgana pointed at the glass as she eyed Nor, who was clearly trying to process everything.

"So, who are these people, really?" Theo scratched his hair frantically.

"Oh god, I hate to be *that* person," she smacked her lips together, "but, it's kinda your fault. What we see here." She extended her arms towards the window.

"*My* fault?" Theo didn't want to understand what she was implying, but it made his stomach hurt that he did. "How is it *my* fault?"

"You know, technically not you…" she hesitated. "Casimir." Her tone dropped, as if she wasn't supposed to utter the name. *His* name.

It didn't come as a surprise to Theo; apparently Casimir was to blame for every terrible thing that happened in Romania—Hell! In the world.

"These people, I think they see the White Raven as hope." suddenly, Scarlett was on her feet and facing him with her hand on his shoulder. "I've heard of them before. They associate it with Casimir." she was staring directly in his eyes as if she was searching for something. "Casmir, the savior of the witches, made a promise and disappeared." Her mocking tone was like a needle through his heart.

"How do you know all this?" With slow, careful steps, he backed away from her. No one was supposed to know that. Scarlett had been hiding some things and pretending like she was as ignorant as them. But she knew a hell of a lot more than she was letting on. Was it like this from the beginning? Was Theo wrong about trusting her?

"Whoa, what is going on here?" As if sensing the tension, Nor walked in front of Theo and stood right in the middle, blocking his view of their supposed friend. "Scarlett, what the hell are you saying?"

"Norman, stay out of this for once and stop acting like a fucking referee," she sighed, looking like she had been waiting to say that for a long time, "I don't wanna hurt you," she said on a whisper, her menacing gaze extending to Morgana who was standing far enough, leaning against a wall with her arms crossed.

"What? I have nothing to do with this." She shrugged. "What are you looking at me like that for?"

"Okay, relax, people." Closing her eyes as if the intense eye contact exhausted them, Scarlett raised her hands in surrender and rolled her eyes at Nor. A lovers' quarrel? "Let's just sit down and talk this through. I may have held out on you a little, but I'm not the bad guy here." She nodded. "Trust me."

How could Theo trust her after all this? For all he knew, she could have been pretending to be his friend, and chose him as her master, only to exact her revenge on him for some mysterious reason she didn't even bother to tell him.

His thoughts were getting out of control, and his surroundings shifted in a blur of light. It was already morning, and none of them got a wink of sleep.

"Fine, let's sit down." The words blurred with everything else. He *had to* sit down right there on the floor. "Explain yourself."

Scarlett's eyes sparkled with sadness and fear, but still a fire behind them just like when he first met her.

"I—"

The door clicked and squeaked open. "Later," Scarlett whispered, giving Theo a half nod and pushed herself off the floor.

"Oh, did I interrupt something?" Adrian shoved the door all the way open. "You all look so serious."

Theo leaped to his feet, fists clenched so tight, his nails bit into his palms.

"What do you want from us?" His voice had a dark and guttural undertone and it didn't sound entirely like him. It was as if Casimir was speaking through him. The violent urge was begging to come out. "You know what? I'm done with this bullshit." And so it did.

Theo pulled a sharp breath, and with one knee on the floor, he rested his black arm on the ground and clenched as if removing a piece of cloth. Casimir flowed through that hand. As soon as he grabbed it, the piece of the white-colored floor turned into dark, dirty rocky soil that spread through his entire arm. Theo raised it with force and plunged his fist right into Adrian's pretty face, sending him into the wall—no, through the wall. Was it another mirage? Theo's confusion lasted less than a second as the rock attached to his arm fell back to the ground. In a blink of an eye, all the walls disappeared, and he was standing in the middle of a dark cave lit only by purple lanterns held by an army of cloaked people surrounding him from all directions. Amid all the panic, Theo spotted Scarlett, who was about to fly, "Go! I'll hold them off." He gestured to her with his head. "Find the others and get out of here."

"But—" her eyes shook, trading glances between Theo and the army of people.

"I'll be fine." As much as he hated to admit it, he was happy to see a glimpse of concern and hesitation in her eyes.

Rubbing his hands together, Theo closed his eyes.

"Now or never, Cas." With a smile, he stood there in the darkness, his left foot digging into the rocky ground as he raised his fisted hands, throwing glances in all directions, waiting for a sign of attack.

But…nothing.

Time drifted, and each breath felt like an eternity. Theo pulled one last sharp breath and ran toward the crowd, which dispersed in perfect sync like machines before he could do anything, leaving him, once again, standing in the middle, unharmed.

"Calm down, Theo," Adrian walked through the crowd that was splitting up left and right at each step he took. "We don't want a fight." He snapped his fingers together, and another lantern lit up on top of Theo's head. He jumped. "There's no point in pretending, comrade. We both know what you're not saying." Theo gulped down a breath. Could he have figured out his true identity?

"What do you mean?" It wouldn't have been that bad if he had. According to Scarlett, they practically worshiped him, so it should be fine.

"Sorry, let me make myself clear…" With his hands behind his back, Adrian started pacing back and forth in front of Theo, "you use ancestral magic, you have the Ashé of a 1000-year-old, your veins are very visible, and I couldn't help but notice—" he stopped with a very visible smirk on his face, "you're missing a whole arm." He pointed at it. "What are you?"

"You're right." Of course, the arm was the giveaway. He should have known before they entered a potential enemy's house. But now he should just come out and admit it. "I'm Casimir," he said it the way he'd say anything. Too easy, like he'd been saying it all his life. Because he had.

"What?" Adrian stopped in his tracks and burst out laughing—the entire army joining him—until he fell to his knees. "Casimir? You?" That went in a whole other direction. Theo could not prevent his smile. It was better if he didn't believe him.

"Not exactly what I was expecting to hear." He stood back up, and his face turned upside down. "But this cannot stand."

"Huh?" Theo's heart was beating out of his chest as he backed away, looking at the darkened faces before him. "What are you doing?"

"Detain him," Adrian said, and the army charged at Theo at full speed, like an enormous wave in a raging sea.

Theo stood still, grounded, with his eyes closed. Reaching into his pocket, he stabbed his dagger into the ground. He spread his hands at his sides, palms up, and lifted them. His magic woke up.

A black mist rose around him, covering all the lanterns and sources of light until darkness took over. Confused screams invaded his ears as he pulled a sharp breath. Cutting through the dark like a shadow, he could predict every person's next blow, avoiding them like a feather floating in the wind. He belonged there. He was the darkness. When he stopped, he looked down at his arms. Black, razor-sharp strings were coming out of his veins. He moved them in a circular motion, creating a net that looked like a spider web, and with a move of his finger, made it fall on some people from above, capturing them and crushing them into the ground. Theo jumped away as a purple light emanating from the middle cleared some of the darkness. It was Adrian, surrounded by four huge, muscular men. Their eyes were all purple, and they held purple axes. The wave of mist rested behind Theo as he backed away with his hands in front of his face. The four men slashed into the air simultaneously, releasing sharp, shiny purple blades in Theo's direction. But the dark cloud faced them with perfectly round black holes and swallowed them up. The rest of the witches still surrounded him.

"Hey," a sharp whisper penetrated his ear. He turned to the side, beyond the witches, to see Morgana holed up behind a big rock; her face and arms slashed and her clothes ripped and torn. In that split second where Theo lost focus, one of the men charged at him and swung the axe in his face. Before he could do anything, Morgana leaped out of nowhere and blocked him with a dagger. Theo smiled and lifted his hand. His power felt lighter. He shoved his palm forward and with the speed of light, the mist turned into black swords that slashed their way to the center. To Adrian. Theo closed his palm. The swords pulled back, left floating at Adrian's neck before they could slash him right then and there. Theo fell on one knee and watched Morgana fight her way beside him; she was slicing and dicing, and jumping and rolling like a ninja. It was his first time seeing her in real action, and he couldn't help but stare.

"You okay?" She sighed, snapping him back to reality as she walked toward him, leaving a trail of bodies in her wake. Her badassery was undeniable.

"I'm out of Ashé," Theo coughed. The black arm was gone again. Just the stump, and the phantom weight he'd stopped expecting to feel. The smoke swords still hung in the air. He stood and reached out to help Morgana as she stumbled sideways.

"I'm fine." She pulled away and fell against the wall, clenching her chest.

"Hey." Theo tried to look at her, but her hair covered face. "What is it?"

"Something's wrong," she murmured. Her chest was rising and falling at an abnormal speed. She slid to the ground as her legs gave out. Theo crouched beside her, listening to her unbalanced heartbeat.

"Can I help?" The sword poked Adrian's neck, revealing blood as he interrupted. That would shut him up.

As Morgana tilted her head back, Theo spotted some white locks of hair mixed with her black ones. Although they were few, they appeared to be dominating by the second. "Your hair." Theo grabbed a few locks in his palm. "It's turning white."

She groaned as she tried to stand. "Get away from me."

Theo almost fell as she looked at him with her once-green eyes now turned gray and colorless. "Can you see?" He waved his hand in front of her face.

"Yes, I'm not blind." She slapped it away and released a sharp breath. "I'm fine now," she said after a few seconds, in which Theo's eyes failed to leave her face.

"What?"

"Um, Morgana…" Theo caught Adrian by the wrists as the mist reshaped itself into handcuffs, restraining him. "I think you should look in the mirror."

Adrian nodded.

38
WHITE RAVEN

Theo glanced around for a mirror. In an underground cave. Right.

He sighed and looked at Morgana. She stood against the wall, fingers trembling over her pale, ashen cheek, eyes fixed on the floor. Her shoulders slumped, her gaze distant.

"Hey," Theo whispered, slapping the back of Adrian's head. "Do you happen to own an actual house?"

"I do." Adrian let out a high-pitched squeal Theo hadn't expected.

"Well, where is it?" Theo cracked his fingers and yanked Adrian's hair back. He'd be lying if he said he wasn't enjoying it.

"Here in the cave." Adrian closed his eyes and groaned. "Just go that way." He jerked his head forward in a direction Theo couldn't recognize. So he grabbed Adrian's restraints and jolted him forward.

"Lead the way…*Comrade*," Theo shot him what he hoped was a smug look.

Their footsteps echoed as the cave narrowed. Theo glanced behind him at Morgana. She dragged her feet, moving slowly, as if carrying something heavy on her back.

"You okay there?" Theo said, trying to mask his concern. She waved off with a lazy and zombie-like movement that only augmented his worry.

"We're here," Adrian breathed as they stopped right in front of another wall that was reddish and a little cleaner, if that was even possible. "Just go through it."

"You like mirages, don't you?" Theo thrust him forward, and his sigh of annoyance made him smile.

Walking through a mirage was like a caress beneath soft silk. Theo loosened his grip on Adrian as goosebumps ran down his arms. He kicked Theo in the shin and ran to a place that looked like a kitchen.

Theo dropped to his knees as Morgana caught up. She looked up after a long time of looking at the floor, her hands curling into fists.

"Hey." Her expression hardened into something Theo had never seen. "Don't touch him."

She charged at Adrian, whose eyes lit up as he fell back, staring at her in what could have been shock or awe. Her fist loosened.

"Where's the fucking mirror?" She spat.

Adrian was a small man beneath her as she towered over him. She caught his face in her palm and squeezed until he looked like a blowfish.

"We don't need him." Theo placed his hand on her shoulder after an embarrassing struggle to get off the floor and a moment of chuckling at the sight. "We're already in his house. We can find it ourselves."

Morgana's upper lip twitched as she tightened her grip, then she shoved his face away and sighed.

"Sure." She shook her head and blinked multiple times. "I don't know what came over me."

Leaving Adrian restrained on the floor, it took Theo and Morgana one turn to find a whole body mirror at the end of a long, dark corridor. Morgana ran toward it like she was running to grab a pack of limited edition deluxe daggers. Theo stayed behind as he stared at the abrupt shift in her. The white in her hair had spread to her temples, mingling with the black strands like chalk on a board. Her eyes reflected a storm he couldn't understand.

Morgana stared at her reflection, a fleeting expression of something like fear crossing her features before she quickly masked it with her usual confidence and indifference.

"You done?" To appear as unconcerned as she seemed, Theo faked a yawn, his shoulder aching as he awkwardly squatted against the cold, rough-textured wall in the corridor. He was *really* out of Ashé. "Come on, you don't look *that* bad," He rolled his eyes, recoiling at his own rudeness. "You're still beautiful."

"Of course I am." She chuckled bitterly, still facing the mirror. "You know it's not about that." She squinted at her reflection and turned to him.

"I know." He shook his head and stood back up, groaning like a grandma. "But, I don't understand what could've done this." Theo moved toward her without thinking, closing the gap. "Has this ever happened before?"

He was now right in front of her.

"I don't remember." Her voice cracked as she looked up at him. Her eyes were teary and vulnerable, like he had never seen them before.

Gulping down a breath, Theo looked down to meet her gray, lifeless eyes. He raised his hand and softly rested it on her pale cheek. She closed her eyes and inhaled a sudden, sharp breath. His gaze flicked from her eyes to her lips as he leaned closer, fingers lifting her chin.

"A little help here? My leg is getting sleepy and I can't get up."

Theo jumped at the sudden voice coming from the other room, while Morgana stepped away, clearing her throat. Theo did the same, massaging the back of his neck.

"Look. A mysterious book!" He pointed at a large purple object resting on a standing desk, almost a meter away. Flustered eyes could spot anything.

"No. Don't touch that," Adrian yelled from the other side, but it was too late as Theo grabbed the book and it burned his palm.

"Fuck!" He hissed and jumped away, letting it fall on the floor. "What the hell is this?" He gently blew at his burned fingers as Morgana hurried beside him, eying the book. Noticing her fixed gaze, he rolled his eyes.

"I'm fine, thanks for asking." Theo immediately refrained as she grabbed it, unharmed.

Morgana started going through the pages with a shocked expression, as if she recognized what she was looking at, and then stopped, staring at a colored sketch of a woman taking up a whole page. Theo moved closer to get a better look, and he couldn't believe his eyes as he stared back and forth at the drawing and the woman standing beside him. In the sketch, that beautiful raven hair she once had.

It was Morgana.

Her expression darkened as she dropped the book.

"Hey." Theo grabbed her shoulders and tried to look at her face. She turned her face away. "What is this?" His whisper came out softer than he intended, almost inaudible. "You can tell me anything."

After a while, his mouth curved into a smile as she finally turned to him and nodded. She sat right there on the floor and took his hand, pulling him with her. Theo squatted beside her, squeezed her hand, and gave her a half nod.

"It's hard to believe, but I actually saw that drawing before. When I was young." She hugged her legs and scratched her head, frowning like she was having a hard time believing the words coming out of her own mouth.

"Like, it just hit me when I looked at it. I think I unlocked a memory," she looked at Theo with a half smile. "Like you usually do."

"What did you remember?" Knowing how it felt, Theo squeezed her hand tighter.

"I remember being locked in a room, but I'm usually let out at specific times by a bunch of tattooed men," she blinked twice, "one time I was running around with some kind of toy in my hand and I saw him…" she trailed off as she rested her palm on her forehead.

Theo caressed the back of her other hand with his thumb, attempting to comfort her.

"He was sitting at the table, holding a pencil and sketching that." She pointed at the abandoned book on the ground. "I asked him who the woman was, and he smiled at me, saying, 'She's a lonely bird you'll encounter in the future'. I obviously laughed it off back then because I was a kid, but now I—" She stopped, looking at Theo intensely as if willing him to complete her sentence.

Bird. Future. Theo's eyes widened.

"Do you remember the name of this man?" The dots connected in his mind.

Morgana paused before she answered.

"It's…it's…Alix." The name slid from her lips in barely a whisper. She crawled past Theo to grab the book, opening on a letter written in small text right below the sketch.

To Birdie,

I hope you find what you're looking for and chase away what's looking for you…

Your forever guardian and friend, Alix.

A silent moment passed between them as they exchanged discerning looks and sighed at the same time. Theo failed to hide his smile at the perfect sync.

"Come on." He released another sharp breath as his arm grew back and he rose to his feet, pulling her with him, never letting go of her hand. "Let's find the others."

Morgana sighed, clenching his hand tighter. Her eyes darted from his to the ground as if she was still lost in her head, a state Theo knew all too well.

"Hey." He let go of her hand and placed his arms on her slender shoulders, forcing her to meet his gaze as he prepared a reassuring smile on his face, "it's gonna be okay. I understand what you're going through. Trust me."

Comforting someone else while unraveling himself. It was weird. But at least it seemed to be working.

Morgana blinked several times, as if she had just snapped out of a daydream. Her mouth gaped open as she fixed Theo an intent stare he couldn't avert. Her eyes had regained their color.

"I admire you," she said out of nowhere with a confident nod and a genuine smile, as if confirming something to herself.

"I admire you too," Theo chuckled, cringing at his own answer before Morgana, with a smooth, quick motion, slid her hand to the back of his neck and pulled him to her, his lips meeting hers in a confused blur. His heart pounded hard enough to rattle his ribs.

Breathing heavily against her mouth with a perfect mixture of panic and ecstasy, Theo cupped her cheeks and pulled her closer, deepening the kiss. With her eyes closed, Morgana released a soft moan into his mouth as she moved her hand to his hair, grabbing it and, with an aggressive pull, breaking the kiss to catch her breath.

Theo's head jerked backward, stinging with the aggression of her pull, but the pleasure masked the pain. With labored breaths, Theo stared into her eyes.

"What are we gonna do with him?" Morgana said as she jerked her head toward the living room, where they left Adrian.

"We'll figure it out." Theo followed her lead, though his pulse still hammered in his ears. What just happened was not supposed to happen. Not like that.

He pulled away and pointed at the open book on the ground, "But first, we need to find out what this means," he turned his head back to Morgana, hesitating for a moment, "along with everything else about you."

"This is so fucked up." Morgana sighed and grabbed the book, closing it with force. A full strand of white slipped from behind her ear. "Come on, let's find the other two."

She tucked the book under her arm as she shook her head and patted Theo on the chest. It was too much of a coincidence for a book like that to fall into their lap. Adrian was surely up to something.

With a half nod, Theo headed to Adrian in the next room, and Morgana followed suit.

"What do you know about this?" Before Theo could do anything, Morgana pushed past him and shoved the book in Adrian's face.

"Nothing." He jerked his head away. "We scavenged it from the old guardians' headquarters."

Scavenged?

"What, you and your little cult?" Morgana let out an unamused chuckle and threw Theo a glance he could not decipher. "Who exactly are you?"

"I—" A pair of loud footsteps interrupted Adrian, followed by distant, indistinguishable voices, echoing throughout the cave and making them fall silent.

Theo grabbed Morgana by the arm and dragged her behind him, making a shushing sign as he waited for more cult members to appear. Morgana looked down at his hand and pulled away, looking offended. He winced.

"Hey," a familiar voice, along with a familiar figure, came running toward him. It was Scarlett, with Nor right behind her. Theo sighed as he moved to hug her.

"You found us." Theo patted Nor on the shoulder with a smile and turned to look at the book Morgana was still holding. "You won't believe what we found out."

Theo hesitated. He was feeling strangely protective of Morgana, worried about how they would react to her identity. He didn't even know *what* Morgana was. What the *White Raven* really was.

"Me and Scarlett, we went and had a drink." Nor scratched his hair, looking everywhere but at Theo. "You know, when we got away. After we looked for you, of course."

"It's fine, man." Theo chuckled at Nor's guilty attitude. He was a true good boy. "I would've done the same."

Scarlett was strangely quiet, distracted, looking down at her own feet while Morgana was glaring at her from behind Theo.

"So," as if reading the room, Nor said, breaking the uncomfortableness of it all, "What've you guys found?" He glanced at the tied up Adrian on the floor.

"Oh, we were trying to find out things about that guy's cult." Theo scratched the back of his neck as the words struggled to leave his mouth. "No luck, I'm afraid."

He glimpsed at Morgana over his shoulder. She was looking down, spaced out.

"Come on, let's leave this dump." Scarlett spoke after releasing a loud sigh that appeared to have woken Morgana from her standing coma.

39
SEVERANCE

The front gate of the mansion loomed nearly two meters above pavement remains. The skyscraping building looked less like a house than a haunted insane asylum.

Theo stood as still as the crumbling pillars flanking the entrance. He tilted his head toward the walls of the house—*his* house. The black paint on the tainted surfaces was scratched as if something equally blunt had been dragged across it.

He pulled a sharp breath. He'd forgotten to breathe for a second. Letting his gaze fall to the ground, his hands shook in rhythm with the beating of his heart. Although the others were just behind him looking at the same image, loneliness closed in on him. The sky was black as his arm and the clouds in a chaotic battle with the sun that was slowly falling away.

"You okay there?" A pleasantly familiar voice pulled him back, soft as silk, if silk were a sound. A hand that rested on the back of his neck followed it, sending shivers like prickles all over his body. He flinched.

"Don't be scared," Morgana said in the same tone, her fingers playing with the scattered hairs on the nape of his neck.

Theo blinked the thoughts away and turned to look at her. She was staring straight into his eyes with just the right amount of smile on her face that said what words did not.

He nodded, an unintentional chuckle escaping his lips at their unspoken connection.

The moment he stepped forward, electrifying shivers rippled through him, along with a familiar sense of belonging. He walked faster with a fixated gaze on the iron gate and pushed it open, driven by that familiarity.

A haunting, echoing sound emerged from the loud squeak of the door. Theo stared at the darkness waiting for him inside, took a deep breath, and walked in. He channeled what little energy he had into a hovering bulb of blue flame.

As the place illuminated, Theo stood aghast at the hominess of it. Dozens of family portraits and old paintings filled up the walls of the entrance as he ambled along the corridor. Black wooden frames protected the paintings. Theo stopped in his tracks as one of them caught his attention; a portrait of a dark-haired woman. Her sunken cheeks and pale, blue-ish face made her look like she had one foot in the grave.

"Amarys," Theo murmured to himself, afraid saying the name louder would make her ghost appear. Her eyes were scratched off, perhaps by a knife or something similarly sharp. Goosebumps prickled his neck at the sight.

"Safe to say your family's got some haters." Scarlett shrugged as she emerged beside him, tracing her fingers against the scratched up eyes of the faces in the other paintings. Seeing one of two boys—barely twelve years-old—Theo's heart sunk into his chest and he pressed his eyes closed, willing to shake the image off his mind until he could turn his back to the wall of miserable memories.

There was no furniture in the room, other than a dusty grand piano half-covered by a white, yellowish cloth. Theo made his way toward it. Pulling the cloth free was like shoveling dirt with his bare hands. Theo coughed and waved off the dust from his face as soon as he threw the yellow blanket on the ground, as far away from him as possible.

"Wow," he said between coughs. "The shitty bastards could have at least cleaned up the place before they left." He traced the dusty keys of the piano. It was way out of tune, making him shudder.

"Hey, come see this," Morgana's sharp, loud whisper broke through the silence like a saw. "I'm not sure what this is," she said as Theo stood beside her. It was the artichoke thing, like the one in Adrian's house. Except this one was as dark as onyx and as heavy as a bowling ball when Theo grabbed it.

"This thing drained the house of magic." He examined it from all angles as the others gathered behind him. "It detects black magic and kinda eats it. I saw one at Adrian's." He placed it gently back on the ground but, for a second, it stuck to his fingers and left behind transparent black goo on them. He cringed and wiped them on the nearest cloth, which happened to be Nor's shirt.

"Hey." He backed away into Morgana, almost falling backwards, taking her with him. "Not cool."

"Sorry, man." Theo raised his hand to show the goo. "It's disgusting."

"Did it do that before?" Morgana sighed after she punched Nor's shoulder. "With the one from before?"

"No, I don't think so." Theo grabbed a handkerchief from Scarlett's outstretched hand, "The last one was empty, though. It was light."

"So, who would drain the house?" Scarlett crouched and kept staring at the artichoke in amazement. She poked it lightly, but no goo stuck to her finger. "Interesting."

"What the hell does this mean?" Theo crouched beside her and touched it again. It looked like it was melting.

"Black magic is sticky?" Morgana shrugged as she crossed her arms over her chest and leaned against the piano she almost fell on top of.

"Well, we already know Theo uses black magic." Nor nodded, thumb on his chin. "Casimir's magic," he continued. "Maybe after the house became empty, someone wanted to make sure it contained no more…" he paused for a brief second, "…residual Mortifer magic."

"Makes sense, yeah." Morgana crouched beside Theo. "Suck it dry of any Mortifer leftovers." She smirked. "So to say."

Theo chuckled and turned away from her as his face turned hot.

"Anyway," he said, pointing toward a dark corner behind the piano. "There's something."

He snapped something under his shoe as he was making his way there. The others close behind.

"Another book?" Scarlett popped her head behind his shoulder. He flinched.

Theo grabbed the book with delicacy to not tear it by accident. It was old and it fit in his palm. As he blew the dust off the cover, a tiny text appeared, handwritten in black ink.

"*Project Sanguis*?" Morgana read. "Can't tell if they were trying to be clever or they're just stupid." She snickered.

"Great." Theo could not hide his disappointment when he opened it and started going through the pages as carefully as he could, "science-y stuff."

"I'm kinda curious." Morgana snatched it from his fingers with more force than she should have. "What were you expecting to find in there?" she said, as if sensing the disappointment in his voice. She sounded genuine, which was concerning coming from her.

"Are those what I think they are?" Nor popped behind Morgana and stuck his eyes close to the tiny writing on the pages. "Blood work." He turned the page. "Pentagrams." He kept flipping. "Blueprints." he stopped and turned to Morgana. "This is it. The plans for your creation." He snatched the book from her fingers and closed it. "They must've left one of their notebooks behind. Here, for some reason."

"So." Theo looked from the notebook to Morgana, hopelessly trying to keep his panic at bay. "We can find out why they made her?"

"Well—" Nor started, but Scarlett's raised hand in front of his face interrupted him. He backed away a half step.

"Wait," she said, dropping her hand back on her side, "who's 'they' we keep talking about?" She looked around and pointed her hand to the wall Theo had finally managed to get off his mind, "What the hell happened to your family?" The aggression in her voice echoed as the question filled the air, surrounding them for a long time.

"I don't—" Theo's bones rattled. Scarlett's blame was beneath word. Could he have had something to do with his family's fall?

Theo closed his eyes and inhaled a sharp, uneven breath, letting the question hang in the surrounding somberness for far too long. Hoping it would dissolve or fade away like a simple drop of water. But it was not as simple as that. As long as he would leave it hanging there, it would envelop the air and suffocate him.

"He had nothing to do with it." Morgana stepped closer to him, and their shoulders touched. "He couldn't have." In the dim light, the white in her hair looked almost gray. It blended into the rest of her head as if it had always been that way.

As she glanced up at him, there was a new softness in her eyes Theo had never seen from her, even as she frowned. A shiver coursed through his spine as her gaze lingered on him, almost as if she could read his mind by studying his features. Regardless, he leaned into the closeness and subtly brushed his finger against her bare wrist, hanging at her side with a soft caress. She did not flinch.

"How would *you* know?" Scarlett scowled and looked Morgana up and down, a mocking smirk playing at her lips. *Some things never change.*

"I don't," Morgana snarled. "It just doesn't sound like something Casimir would do." She shrugged and crossed her arms over her chest, pulling her hand away from Theo's touch, which was left cold in the absence of contact. "We don't really know anything about him, except what we've been told by people who hate him." She side-eyed Theo, raising one perfect brow.

"Hmm," Scarlett nodded, letting out an uncharacteristically desperate breath. "You say that, yet you still defend him." She looked askance at Morgana.

The bite in her voice pierced like a poisoned thorn, spreading its venom with each breath. Theo stared blankly at the ceiling, his thoughts wouldn't settle. The noise of Scarlett and Morgana's arguing distanced itself from his ears.

Was Scarlett right to not trust him? He couldn't shake the feeling of hollowness in his heart. He buried his face in his hands, searching for solace in the darkness behind closed eyes, but finding only the haunting shadow of what was a bond unbreakable.

With a shaky exhale, Theo forced his eyes open, his mind racing with a sense of betrayal that cut deeper than he dared to admit.

"Hey!" He jumped into the middle of their quarrel, raising a hand. "I'm right here, you know? You could ask *me*." He opened his mouth, the words didn't come. The answer played at the tip of his tongue. What would they do if they knew the truth? Hate him? Abandon him? Kill him? Whatever their differences, they both would not like it.

As if sensing his hesitation, Nor's eyes widened as he stood behind Scarlett with a reassuring hand on her shoulder. Theo couldn't tell if Nor was glaring or searching for some neglected glimmer of light inside the darkness of his soul. He felt bare and vulnerable under his friend's gaze as he stared back.

"This was a waste of time." Theo backed away toward the exit, his eyes never leaving Nor's as Scarlett and Morgana looked at them in confused silence. "There's nothing for me here anymore."

He turned his back on them, following the rays of sunlight to find the front door. The heavy presence of their frozen shadows—gradually being swallowed by the unnatural darkness of the mansion—followed him through the hallway, and their crushing stillness weighed on his shoulders, putting an impending hesitation in his departing footsteps.

"Theo!" Scarlett's voice echoed as she ran up behind him, making him stop in his tracks and turn. She bent, hands on her knees. "What the hell was that?" she said between breaths.

Theo's mouth was bitter. It had been so long since they talked to each other.

"I don't know." He shook his head, and with it, all the thoughts he preferred to stay buried in his mind's own impenetrable coffin.

Scarlett stood upright and looked down at her feet in silence, her face drawn in an undecipherable expression.

"Do you still hold it against me?" Theo spouted before he could think.

Scarlett looked up at him. "I don't know what you're talking about. We're good."

"Whatever Casimir did to you—what I did. Just be honest, please."

After a pause, she took a breath and met his eyes for the first time in so long. "I need to tell you something. What I was gonna say when Adrian interrupted."

Theo blinked hard and held his breath.

"A long time ago, Casimir hurt someone I loved. Someone I considered a brother. I just don't want that to happen again with you. I didn't know you were Casimir and I regret that." She looked away. "That's all."

Theo knew very well that wasn't all of it. The lies exhausted him, especially from her, his supposed confidante.

"So do you?" He shrugged. "Do you still hold it against *me*. Theo."

"I—" Scarlett's mouth formed a grimace that was not quite a smile. "I hate that I do," she whispered between gritted teeth, her hands curling into fists at her side. "I tried not to, but I don't know how to—"

"Okay." Theo said, his voice steadier than it should have been. "Well, if you can't handle it, sever your bond with me." His heart thundered as his veins tightened, an unwanted darkness surging. "I want you to."

Silence…

"What?" Scarlett's whisper came out more like a squeal as she looked up at him. She looked down, her frown tightening her lips as she blinked back tears. "You don't mean that."

"Why not?" Theo turned his face to the side, swallowing a lump forming in his throat as his eyes burned. "You've been weary and distant for months, going around me in circles for whatever goddamn reason."

As much as he hated to admit it, part of him was relieved. Mostly at Scarlett's reaction that echoed the clench in his chest, the headache pressing behind his eyes, the tears threatening to spill—

"How can I fix this?" A mask of unshakable determination replaced the mess on Scarlett's face. "Tell me what to do."

Theo flinched at the shift in her expression as she puffed out her chest and raised her head in defiance.

"You can't," he sighed, stepping closer. He put his hands on her shoulders and stared at her, daring her to object. As she stared back, her mask melted like iron in flames.

"You can't," he repeated in a whisper, shaking his head. His eyes never left hers.

She sighed, shutting her eyes. Theo let his hands fall back to his side as he did the same. He inhaled a shallow breath as an uncomfortable pull spread from his head to his chest.

He was suddenly aware of its existence—their bond. A bright orange rope tightly wrapped around his organs, one end coiled around his mind, the other hugging his heart.

Theo struggled to breathe as the rope quivered inside him. He heaved as it faded to ashen gray.

The rope's withering sent piercing flashes across his vision. It shrank in on itself, dwindling like a vine cut from its root.

Then it disappeared. No trace of it. Not in Theo's imagination, nor in his body. His eyes flew open as he backed away, tugging at his chest, though there was no pain.

Realization hit. Theo straightened his back and raised his eyes from the ground, only to find Scarlett was still standing before him. Looking at him—no, *through* him. Her eyes, red and glistening, were wide as saucers, unflinching. But he saw how deep their emptiness stretched. Her gaze was as hauntingly vacant as the hallway they stood in.

Theo's unmoving stare lingered at her eyes, his own tears on the verge of spilling. They stood in silence until she walked past him to the door.

Theo turned only at the fluttering sound of her wings against the wind.

It was done. It had to be done.

He stilled in the surrounding silence like one might when seeing an old friend and not knowing what to say. He scratched at his hair as his splitting headache worsened. The numbness in his heart and the sinking feeling in his stomach culminated in a frustrated growl.

His feet were oppressive anchors. Legs frozen, merging with the hard surface underneath them.

His eyes darted back to the open door every time he managed to look away. The sun was setting. The stairs were being swallowed by shadows.

Shadows.

Theo sighed and rubbed the bridge of his nose, a screaming void where the bond once was, elusive and unbearable.

He could sense Casimir mocking him, threatening his control, and pushing to come out.

Not a mistake.

His own distorted voice sounded in his head, followed by an eerily familiar laugh. Theo flinched, eyes darting. It was just in his head.

"Leave me alone," he said through gritted teeth. His eyes burned, he wanted to rip them out.

The laugh came again. Each echo, a piercing blow to his skull. Theo pressed his palms to his eyes and let out a pathetic grunt as his legs gave out. When he opened them, darkness surrounded him. He found himself on his knees, a grinning reflection cast by his own shadow, staring back at him.

If he concentrated hard enough, he could suppress him.

Theo failed to calm his frantic breath. His heart throbbed so hard it threatened to burst out of his chest. Then, his mouth, no longer his, stretched into a full-toothed grin.

Scorching hot tears streamed from his eyes like embers, tracing trails down his face and leaking all over his smile.

With stiff, numb fingers, he slapped himself. The heat on his cheek stung, but a strange, scalding cold spread all over his body.

A living corpse waiting to be summoned among the dead.

But, no…he would not take control.

"Theo?" Thundering footsteps echoed toward him. He lost all sense of space. Sitting or standing, asleep or awake—an excruciating and deprecating desire to give in was all that remained.

He hadn't realized he was looking down. Not until the shadows were at his feet. A hand touched his shoulder. Another grabbed his wrist and pulled him up. Every touch burned like being thrown into raging flames.

He had not realized when he growled and pulled his rigid arm away from the firm grip. Another hand on the other shoulder. Fierce blue eyes stared into his. Like in a mirror, he stared back. Air burst into his lungs, clearing a disgusting clot of beguiling solace.

Morgana's hand palmed his cheek, her thumb catching a tear at the corner of his eye. Nor hung back behind them, arms loose at his sides, worry etched across his pale face. His eyes drooped, barely visible above the bags under them. A heavy sense of guilt settled in Theo's chest. The thought of Nor—his best friend's concern gnawed at his conscience.

"You still with us?" Morgana's voice pulled him out of his self-tormenting thoughts.

"Yeah." Theo looked up and nodded at Nor over Morgana's shoulder, spreading a weak smile over his stiff cheeks. "I'm fine now."

"I hope you're right this time." Nor's mouth twitched as he returned a smile that never reached his eyes. After a visible struggle to avoid Theo's gaze, he turned away from them and walked outside to sit on the stairs.

"Where's your familiar?" Morgana returned her hands to her side and looked up like she was expecting to see Scarlett flying around.

The weight of what he had done hit him all over again. Morgana searched his face, and that was worse.

He almost regretted it. He shook his head and rubbed his eyes, stifling everything in a sharp exhale.

"She's not…anymore."

40
PHANTOM

"What do you mean?" Morgana frowned, her confusion deepening as she scratched her head and pulled him closer, his shadow looming mockingly behind him.

Her words hung in the air as her eyes searched his. Sweat prickled at his hairline. How could he explain Scarlett's absence, the decision, all of it?

He slid his gaze away from her face. The way she was looking at him only twisted the knot of dread tighter. The truth would only splinter outward into a thousand more questions he was not ready to face. Not when his own convictions still churned with doubt.

Memories flashed—broken promises, betrayals, manipulations. But what happened with Scarlett was different. He was the driver with his own hands controlling the wheel. He couldn't blame Casimir for what he had done. Not this time.

There was no going back. But she didn't have to know that.

"Just that we won't be seeing her for a while." His legs trembled as he put distance between them. His gaze fell on Nor sitting outside, face buried in his palms.

"I see." Morgana nodded almost too fast as she ran her hand through her hair, catching a few white strands between her fingers. She gasped, her nails digging into her palm as her hand balled into a fist.

"Give me a sec," she exhaled the words like a sigh. Before Theo could respond, Morgana turned on her heel and stumbled down the hallway, disappearing back into the room with the dusty piano. The door closed behind her.

Theo stared at the door, not sure what happened. He shook his head and wandered toward Nor, who sat on the stairs, hugging his knees. It had been so long since they really talked. Theo was not even sure how to approach him anymore.

"Hey." He lowered himself onto the step beside Nor.

An awkward silence stretched between them. Theo struggled for something to say.

"How are you?" He regretted it instantly.

The question was woefully inadequate, especially since Nor didn't know about Scarlett. Theo studied Nor's profile, wondering what was going through his mind, hoping he did not completely withdraw in a shell of those familiar walls.

"Where's Scarlett?" Nor cleared his throat as he played with a pebble on the stair.

"She's...she's doing a perimeter sweep, make sure Adrian's people didn't follow us." Theo found his own pebble, kicking it into oblivion. The lie stung, but not as much as the truth.

"I'm just worried, man." Frustration laced Nor's voice as he ran a hand through his hair, looking Theo directly in the eyes–a gaze Theo did not need to avoid this time. "About everything." He spread his arms wide.

Realizing that he was answering his previous question, Theo gulped down a breath as he tried to keep a calm exterior.

"Don't you see? We're all messed up, but we refuse to talk to each other."

Theo's heart jumped. A wave of emotions passed through him, his mouth hanging open without volition.

For a moment, he could only gape. Where was this coming from?

"Every one of us is going through something and none of us is talking about it." He gestured to the door. "Look at Morgana. Have you ever seen her like that?"

Theo shook his head and averted his eyes to the ground.

"We need to talk to each other." Nor's hand on his shoulder shocked Theo's gaze back to his friend's face. Against all his expectations, he was smiling. "We're family, aren't we?"

The door opened with a creak, jolting Theo to his feet and out of his thoughts. His unspoken answer died in his throat as Morgana stepped toward them. Her face wasn't much a mask—the slight tremble in her lips, the quiver in her voice.

"Sorry about that…just needed a moment to myself." Turmoil roiled beneath her calm exterior.

Nor stood, taking in the scene.

Theo prepared himself for the questions about Morgana's badly bandaged, bloody arm. He was not sure how much she wanted to reveal.

"I lost myself for a bit," she admitted, her voice growing stronger.

Realization dawned in Nor's widened eyes before he gave a solemn nod. Morgana crossed to the dusty old piano. The way she gently traced the worn keys, she'd found kinship with the weathered instrument. When she turned back to face them, her eyes glistened with unshed tears.

"Don't worry." There was a new resolve etched into her expression. "Let's get out of this shithole. No offense, Theo."

He could not help but chuckle at her wry addition. Whatever she was going through, it clearly did not affect her humor. Theo met Nor's gaze, seeing his own awe and respect mirrored there as they watched Morgana stride forward with purpose.

There was a slight bulge under her jacket pocket - the notebook, Theo realized. With a smile on his face, he could not hold back. He followed her out. It seemed like she was walking away from him, toward some sort of resolution. Theo wished he could find the same resolve, find his light, and get out of his own twisted cave. But—

"Wait." Nor's voice cut through Theo's thoughts. Morgana paused halfway down the stairs. "We can't just...leave. Not like this."

Theo's heart skipped. He turned to see Nor standing, his fists clenched at his sides. "We've got shit to sort out." Nor's voice trembled, his shoulders pulled tight. "Let's talk."

Morgana's shoulders slumped. She walked back up, her footsteps echoing in the silence. "Come on, this is stupid," she started, but Nor shot her a look that was undecipherable to Theo, but made Morgana flinch.

Slowly, she turned, and Theo's breath caught. Her eyes were glistening again, but there was a fire there, too.

"Fine, but..." She leaned against the wall, one hand absentmindedly tracing the notebook's outline through her jacket. "I just...I want to get out of this place. It's like—" She broke off, shaking her head.

"Like what?" Theo asked. His own voice sounded strange in his ears, raw with an emotion he couldn't name.

Morgana looked at him, really looked at him. "Like every shadow is a memory I can't escape."

Theo flinched. Shadows, clinging like parasites.

His hand went to his chest, where the gaping hole of his bond with Scarlett throbbed like a phantom limb.

"But mostly because the lighting doesn't agree with me." She chuckled. It was hard for her to not get one in.

"I get that," Nor said softly, ignoring her quip. He stepped closer to Morgana, his earlier frustration melting into something softer. "But running isn't the answer. Trust me, I know."

Theo's gaze snapped to Nor. How long had he been carrying this? How had Theo not seen it?

"I…" Nor stopped. When he spoke again his voice was steadier, his gaze fixed on a point beyond them. "After my mother died…you know. I ran away from home—from my dad. For years. Thought I could put it behind me, the pain, the guilt." He shrugged and laughed, a harsh sound that scraped Theo's nerves raw. "Turns out it makes it worse."

Morgana reached out, her hand finding Nor's arm. The gesture was so simple, yet so charged. Theo wanted to look away, to give them their family moment, but he couldn't. He was a part of this moment, regardless of what he wanted.

"What happened to her?" Morgana's voice was barely above a whisper.

Nor's laugh this time was softer, sadder. "She killed herself, and…" He trailed off, his free hand unconsciously touching his chest. "It was my fault. Well, mostly dad's."

Theo's breath hitched, a cold realization creeping in. How could he not know any of this about his best friend?

"I blamed the both of us for most of my life," Nor said, his voice thick. "I've been running ever since. Never even visited her grave on my own. Can you believe that?" He looked up, his gaze capturing both Theo and Morgana.

"I don't know…maybe I'm just saying that," he sighed, "for the first time in years, I don't want to run. That has to count for something, right?"

Nor's words hung in the air, heavy with meaning. They crashed into Theo's chest, right where the void of his bond ached. They should have been a comfort, but they only twisted the knife deeper. Scarlett had stuck with him through everything, too. And now…

"I'm sorry," Theo blurted. Both Nor and Morgana turned to him, surprise etched on their faces. "I'm sorry I didn't see…that you were hurting. That I've been so wrapped up in my own…" He gestured vaguely, unable to find the words.

"Hey," Nor's hand was on his shoulder again, grounding him. "That's what we're talking about, man. We've all been drowning in our own shit, not seeing each other."

"Well, let's change that," Morgana said firmly. She pushed off from the wall she was leaning on, tapping the notebook from above the pocket. "We're in this together, right?" She looked at the door, her resolve unshaken, "and we get out of here together."

Theo looked between them - Nor, with his hidden pain and unwavering loyalty; Morgana, with her scars and her fierce determination. He thought of Scarlett, of the bond that had withered away like a cut vine.

Theo turned away, fingers curling into fists at his sides. He opened his mouth, then shut it again, swallowing hard. "Maybe some pieces…aren't meant to fit back together," he muttered, voice barely above a whisper. "I'm not sure I know how to be…whole."

Nor's grip on his shoulder tightened. "You don't have to be whole, Theo. You just have to be here. With us."

"We'll figure it out." Morgana moved closer, standing before him, her eyes—sparkling hope and understanding—almost level with his. "That's what I'm here for."

A tiny, flickering light sparked in his twisted cave. It wasn't healing, not yet. But it was a start. He nodded, not trusting his voice.

Morgana stood, her hand outstretched. Nor's hand joined hers. They looked at Theo, waiting.

With a shaky breath, Theo reached out. His hand clasped theirs.

41
CONSEQUENCES

Theo's feet dragged as he followed Nor and Morgana. The old house loomed behind them, watching silently. He should've been relieved after everything they had just poured out to each other, but his gut was a mess of feelings he couldn't sort out.

Every few steps, he glanced back, half-expecting to see Scarlett hovering in a window. The ache of her loss was still there, raw and constant. Would it ever go away?

"You hanging in there?" Nor called back.

As he caught up, the determination etched on Nor's face made it harder to admit the truth. Both Nor and Morgana had exposed things Theo couldn't even begin to imagine. He had stood there nodding along, keeping the truth about Scarlett tucked away in a convenient hole in the twisted abyss of his being.

That word—family—bounced around in his head. He wanted to believe in it, to feel like it belonged to him. But the weight of his secrets, his unrelenting darkness—*Casimir*—worming into Theo's thoughts, that seductive whisper, promising wholeness and freedom. In his weaker moments, Theo found himself drawn to that promise.

He shook his head, trying to clear it. One step at a time. That's all he could handle at this moment.

As they turned a corner, leaving the mansion's paralyzing presence behind, the air tightened around them. The cobblestones beneath their feet were uneven, and the walls on either side of the alley loomed closer, rough and shadowed.

Theo caught a flicker of purple light ahead, near the far end of the narrow alley. He stopped dead, his breath catching.

Purple? Could it be…

"What's wrong?" Morgana tensed up, her hand hovering over her dagger. She was close behind him, her sharp eyes scanning the dim passageway.

"Saw something," Theo muttered, already moving toward the light. The alley was narrowing further with every step forward, the walls close enough that their footsteps echoed. Nor and Morgana shared a look before following, ready for whatever came at them.

The alley was narrow and thick with shadows. But that purple light…it was getting stronger, reflecting off the slick, damp walls and lighting up pairs of eyes floating in the dark ahead. Theo's heart pounded against his ribs as it clicked. Those eyes, that glow—they had to be Adrian's people. The light poured from an archway at the far end, sketching long, eerie shadows along the ground.

"Are those—," Nor started, his voice a low rumble. Then he growled, interrupting himself, the muscles of his arms rippling as giant claws burst from his fingers. He moved to Theo's right, taking a protective stance with his back to the wall.

"Oh great, that idiot again." Sighing, Morgana's hands grasped at her daggers, her stance low and ready. She moved to Theo's left side, mirroring Nor as best she could.

Theo's mind raced as instinct took over. He sensed rather than saw the attack coming. Another flicker of purple caught his eye on his left side, from the edge of the alley; eyes glowing with eerie light. The enormous beast of a man aimed a blast of blinding white energy at Nor, who was just a few feet away.

Theo's chaos condensed into a single, burning certainty, his heartbeat thundering in his ears as clarity swept over him. All the darkness growing within him, all the secrets he was keeping, could not prevent him from protecting what he cherished most.

With his blackened arm balled into a fist, Theo gathered whatever shadows slept around the alley, pulling them into himself. The shadows from the walls, the ground, even the darkness from under Nor's feet. Gritting his teeth, he threw up a wall of shadows just in time, catching the blast inches from Nor's face. Power surged through him, intoxicating and terrifying all at once. But as he channeled the shadows, something else seeped in through the cracks—Casimir's presence, stronger than before. Stronger than ever.

Yes, a voice whispered in the back of his mind. *Let me out.*

Theo's wall held firm against the attack, but inside, he was reeling. He had protected his friends, but at what cost? As the light faded, Theo met Nor's startled gaze, a mix of awe and concern etched across his friend's face. Beside him, Morgana's eyes widened, her stance shifting from battle-ready to wary as she glanced between Theo and the dissipating shadow wall.

As the shadows whipped around him, a dark flicker crossed some of the older followers. Their axes hesitated mid-swing, pausing for a fraction of a moment. A sudden hesitation broke their neutral expressions, vanishing so quickly it might have been Theo's imagination. What if they knew? What if they realized his identity amidst the swirling shadows in the alley? The thought prickled his mind like a bothersome thorn at his side.

"Not bad," Morgana breathed, jolting him back to the present.

The narrowness of the alley. The walls too close. The shadows too deep. Casimir's presence pressed against the edges of his mind, a relentless drumbeat, drowning out his thoughts. Each breath was like walking a tightrope over a pit of shadows.

In that split second between Theo's withering psyche and the collapsing of the wall, another purple attack launched from Theo's blind side, from some spot hidden in the shadows of the left wall. He could not sense it coming or even see it, not until Morgana's cry of his name pierced the air as she lunged towards him, daggers flashing.

But she was a blink too late. The axe sliced Theo's shoulder, sending him spinning. He hit the ground hard, pain exploding as he skidded across the rough cobblestones. The world tilted and the alley's walls blurred and narrowed around him. Through the haze, he heard Morgana fighting the attacker, her blades hitting against the metal of the axe with sharp, tooth-rumbling clangs. Nor's scream as he launched at something was distant, muffled as if coming from the far end of a tunnel.

As Theo struggled to push himself up, he felt it—a crack in his defenses, a fissure in his will. Casimir's presence surged forward, no longer a whisper but a roar in his mind.

Now, Theo. Let me save us.

The shadows in the corners writhed and pulsed, responding to Casimir's call, creeping up the alley walls and swirling around his fallen body. Theo's vision darkened at the edges, the pain in his shoulder fading to a dull throb as something else—something darker—was taking control.

"No," Theo gasped, but his resistance was weakening. Casimir's influence spread through him like ink in water and his axe wound burning like hot coal.

Everything around him raged in a blur of purple and red, the narrow alley turning into a battleground. For Theo, the greatest threat was no longer Adrian's people but the darkness within himself.

42
CRACKS

A resonant thud echoed in Theo's ears as he pushed against the wall to get to his feet. His eyes narrowed at the direction of the sound where the purple followers dropped their weapons.

A flicker of dread and disgust rose as Adrian's familiar silhouette emerged through the smoke near the archway. His laugh echoed between the narrow walls, loud and eerie, as if the very space was mocking them. Morgana and Nor appeared beside him, their eyes sharp with questioning looks.

"What do we do?" Nor asked, his gaze flickering to the remaining purple followers—barely half a dozen still standing—scattered among their fallen comrades, kneeling with heads bowed low. Adrian moved past the archway, arms behind his back, to tower over them. Theo clenched his fists at the bold streak of amusement dancing on Adrian's features, fighting the urge to wipe the smug expression away. Instead, he caught his lip between his teeth, biting down on it. His skin still reverberated, the shadows eerily silent and at bay—so different from their chaotic movements earlier—as if, for once, they were waiting for his command.

Not trusting his voice, Theo shook his head and raised his arm in front of Nor, preventing him from attacking. Morgana clicked her tongue on his other side, faint and disapproving.

"Hey." Adrian's voice overwhelmed him, ringing loud in the dead silence, with only the dripping sound of blood Theo could not quite pinpoint. "You've done well. Taking down my people so quickly."

Theo scoffed. The dismissive sound so foreign as if it didn't come from him. Adrian ignored him as he turned away. He was still clueless about who he was facing.

"I told you I'm Casimir." The words slid from Theo's mouth, foreign, effortless. He didn't remember choosing them. "The impudent fool that you are wouldn't believe me." He shrugged. Like it was nothing. Like he believed it, the urge to laugh nearly bubbling over. A smile tugged at his lips. Someone had to put him in his place.

Behind him, Morgana's sharp intake of breath tickled him. Nor's uneasy shift, claws flexing at his sides, startled him. They had known this truth about him, but hearing him declare it so blatantly must have been a shock.

Theo took a deep breath and walked forward. The stomping of his boots against the cobblestones filled the quiet. He could have sworn he saw Adrian flinch for a split second as he pulled his arms to his sides, fists shaking frantically.

"You expect me to believe that?" Adrian stammered, taking a few steps back. Was it Theo's presence or the growing shadow of Casimir's influence pressing down on him?

"*I* am Casimir reborn," Adrian continued, clutching his chest as though the lie could steady his tremor. With a quick series of nods, he swallowed hard, his gaze shifting between his followers. Hope flickered in their stares but dimmed in the face of fear. "I will be the one to free us." His voice layered with fragile conviction. Yet, his sagged shoulders and unsteady posture told a different story.

Theo said nothing. His feet wouldn't move. Adrian's eyes were frantic. Morgana and Nor looked bemused. They stood in silence, exchanging loaded glances. Morgana's fingers drummed against her dagger hilts, while Nor's muscles coiled and his arms twitched at his sides. They were clearly debating whether to intervene.

Part of him wanted to abandon this nightmare altogether—turn back to Brooklyn and leave it behind where it belonged. But that was impossible. Since returning to Romania—though barely two days had passed—all he had done was look back.

Another, darker part of him pulsed with the urge to end it, to kill Adrian right then and there. But that thought was not his. It could not have been his.

He shook the whispers away and looked up. The smoke blocking his vision had almost completely dissipated, and Adrian's façade crumbled before Theo's eyes. He was a boy drowning under the weight of an old, dead promise, grasping at a hope that had already faded.

"That's bullshit and you know it." Theo shook his head as he started walking again, although all he wanted to do was give him a hug. Nor's low growl of agreement rumbled behind him. Morgana had glided to Theo's left, her stance casual but her eyes sharp, watching Adrian's every move. They were positioning themselves, he realized, creating a triangle of protection around him while letting him take the lead. "You saw my arm, my Ashé…the way I caught the stench of that thing in your house."

Theo wasn't sure why he was trying to convince Adrian he was Casimir, something he himself struggled to believe and accept.

Adrian staggered further until his back smacked against the wall. He turned away from Theo, eyes shifting to the doubting faces of his comrades. Some of them shrank back, hesitant. Others stood frozen, waiting for Adrian to say something. A few still clung to his words, faces twisted in desperate denial. One muttered, "That's not true," while another took an uncertain step toward Theo.

Had they been following his blatant lie the whole time? It made sense, wanting to believe in a better future that none other than Casimir promised before disappearing off the face of the earth. Ironic that the same person now stood before them, and to their ignorance, holding nothing but painfully scattered memories and a broken persona.

Theo stumbled back to Nor and Morgana's sides, his eyes never leaving the scene before him. Adrian's followers were on their feet, their fury-laced eyes scrutinizing him. One of them, a young man in his twenties, stood on shaky legs.

"Comrade Adrian…" The young man's voice trembled, soft and uncertain, as though speaking might shatter him, his hollow cheeks and sunken eyes making him look far older than his years. "We believed in you…all this time—"

"Quiet, boy," an old man snapped, voice cracking as he shoved the younger man aside. His own face mapped the hardships of his life, twisted with desperation. "You don't know what you're saying," he said, his gaze softening as he turned to Adrian. "I trust you, comrade."

Theo's breath caught in his throat as Adrian pushed past them, the purple glow in his eyes intensifying the paleness of his face.

"It is my mission," His voice projected further than it should have been natural. His wild eyes darted between Theo and his people while his confident façade was cracking. "Don't believe this…*imposter.*"

The word cut deep, slicing through his pride. The shadows curled at his sides, reacting to the insult. But something in Adrian's eyes betrayed his words. He hesitated. Was he only attempting to guarantee his own survival at this point?

"I have almost amassed enough magic," he said, arms swinging wildly, his voice booming with unshakeable conviction, as if delivering the speech of his life. "The moment we've all been awaiting is near. With the *carceris tenebris* in the Mortifer mansion, I will free us." The brief glance at his black arm made Theo flinch. He twitched at the sudden, threatening glaze. "With a second Great War. A *bigger* war, and I assure you of our victory."

A wave of nausea raced over Theo as a nameless dread crawled beneath his skin. He glanced down, noticing the raw, bleeding gashes in his palms where his nails had been digging.

Of course, Adrian put the artichoke in the mansion. Was he seriously trying to maintain the lie, the sweat beading on his forehead a testament to his anxiety? Are his followers that naïve, or are they simply blinded by their unwavering faith?

"How long do you think they'll keep swallowing his lies?" Morgana muttered, tapping Theo's shoulder and snapping him out of his own mind fog. "It's kinda sad at this point."

A roar from the crowd rang in Theo's ears as the followers picked their weapons off the ground and, in one unified motion, turned to Theo, faces fueled with newfound resolve.

“Shit, not round two,” Morgana grumbled, juggling the daggers in her sweaty, blood-stained hands.

“Hey,” Theo said, meeting Nor’s gaze. His eyes glowed with fierce loyalty, but they were laced with worry. It sent a prickle of guilt to his heart. “Try not to hurt them.” He placed a hand on Morgana’s shoulder as a dark surge coursed through his veins, overshadowing the guilt.

“No promises.” Morgana took a deep breath and adjusted her stance, loosening her grip on the daggers. She glanced at Theo, her eyes reflecting trust with a faint flicker of doubt. His throat was suddenly dry.

The followers, fueled by the empty words of their deceiver, stood before them, preparing to attack. They were just a bunch of misguided individuals who can be saved if led by the true Casimir. But Theo was not the leader they wanted. He could never be.

The air shifted. A flicker of motion in his periphery. He barely dodged the axe swing. A tall, broad-shouldered man lunged at Theo with a resounding war scream, aiming for his head. The shadows erupted, answering a call he had not made, but one that lay dormant at the edge of his mind. They emerged like a cloud of darkness, blocking the blow and sending the weapon spinning from the man’s hands. Casimir lingered at the back of his head, and a smile tugged at his lips despite himself. The slithering blackness moved with a will of its own, piercing the man’s shoulder in a flash. As blood spattered across Theo’s face, prickling his eyes, he recognized the cling of a savage satisfaction at the sight.

The man crashed to the ground like a boulder, and the shadows glided over his wound with an almost delicate curiosity.

A snap of dizziness gripped Theo as his vision darkened around the edges, the world shrinking and dimming until it was only a small, dark circle. His skin pulsed like a beating heart as he raised his hands; black veins, like ink bleeding through paper, bulged against the paleness of his skin. His dark arm seemed to become darker, while his other arm grew almost skeletal under the blackness, skin stretching over bone.

With shallow breaths, Theo stepped back as the crowd gasped. When he looked up, they encircled him. Morgana and Nor had pressed forward, flanking him protectively despite their obvious exhaustion. Sweat trickled down their foreheads, but their stances were steady. Their tension was palpable, wavering between fear of him and fear for him as the darkness spread from his arms to his neck.

"You…?" One man walked forward. The sound of his axe clanking on the ground made Theo stagger as he held his breath, the shadows at his back catching his fall. The man's brows furrowed, and his gawk held a sense of awe and recognition that made Theo's heart race and bile rise to his throat. "No, it can't be…" he said almost to himself, as if unsure if he wanted to be heard.

Theo stiffened, like a puppet an unseen hand had seizing his strings. The whispers in his mind grew more resonant, the pressure of something darker smothering his will to flee.

The man shook his head as if snapping himself out of the trance.

"Wait!" He raised his fist and the movement of the crowd ceased. Was he some kind of leader among them? They sure listened to him. "You feel it, don't you?" A whisper that carried. "The power. It's…it's like him."

Him. There had to be a reason he was avoiding his name. Was he still unsure of what he realized?

Theo's pulse raced. The man's words, a rope tightening around his neck. A silent exchange passed through the crowd as all eyes turned to him, searching him, studying him. A murmur rippled through them. Most were nods of hesitant agreement.

The stiffness in his muscles ached, but an irresistible urge propelled him to call back. The shadows latched onto his arms, pulling at his skin, compelling him forward. To be Casimir.

"Y-yes, he *is* Casimir. The one we've been waiting for." Adrian's commanding voice cut through the murmurs. His nervousness was apparent through the frantic movements of his eyes. "He will lead us. Like he promised…" he turned to Theo, arching an eyebrow. "Right?"

They were staring at him, like gawking at a painting in an art museum. Their certainty, no longer a flicker, but their entire faces brightened like light bulbs, as if they had never picked up a weapon against him.

"We knew it was you," a soft voice came from below. The tall man he had knocked out and who almost sliced his head off mere minutes ago stood on fragile legs with the help of a few of his comrades, clutching the wound on his shoulder where blood had dried. "You have his power, his shadows. We have waited for decades."

Theo's pulse climbed into his temples, as if Casimir himself was trying to claw his way out of him, his weak prison of distorted flesh. His fingers twitched beyond control at his sides, darkness seeping further and further into his skin, like a snake shedding old skin.

"No," Theo gasped, stumbling backward, his palm suddenly to his forehead. A firm grip caught him mid fall.

"Don't listen to them," Morgana's voice cut through, muffled, but the concern visible. "Theo, you're not who they think you are anymore. You haven't been for a long time."

But, as she spoke, the crowd closed in on them, each glance at him visibly reinforcing the certainty of his identity. The shadows multiplied around him, feeding their belief.

"Ignore him. He's nothing." Adrian's voice faded as he stepped forward, grinding his jaw. His lips parted. No longer the center of attention, he was small, and as insignificant as his gullible, faceless followers.

He was Casimir, after all. The creator of the promise, holding their faith in the palm of his hand—

"Don't!" As Theo was about to take a step forward, Nor's firm hand grasped his arm. Theo's breath hitched as he realized he was out of the circle, several steps ahead. "Let's get out of here," Nor barked, still pulling at him. Even he could not hide the traces of fear in his voice.

The shadows snapped and clawed at Theo's heels as they ran through the archway, out of the alley. Their pull was relentless, begging him to turn around.

"I will bring Casimir back myself, to lead us into the new world and…" The wind carried Adrian's words, his last attempt at manipulation as he worked to guarantee his own survival.

Theo pushed forward. Fast. Faster. Hoping to outrun Casimir's presence, but it only grew deeper the more he resisted.

43
COLLAPSE

Theo's legs gave out as soon as they reached the crumbling steps of an old abandoned building. He looked up to find Morgana already trying to push the jammed door open. She gave it multiple aggressive shoves with her shoulder until it hissed open, screeching over the ground below.

Nor stood behind them, eyes alert, looking for any strays from the cult that might have followed.

From the outside, the building looked like a tower, but inside it was a dust-choked church, deserted in the middle of a sermon. The pews, their colors long faded from deep red into dusty brown, stood aligned in perfect rows. On the stage, a coat rack stood with a moth-eaten priest's robe hanging rigid, collecting cobwebs, its arms dangling like ghost limbs.

To Theo's relief, the place was too dark and stuffy for any shadows to appear. But his arm still pulsed, the veins darkening at the edges, red bleeding to black. He clenched his blackened hand into a fist as he looked down. He would have to ignore it.

"Looks like people bolted mid-session," Morgana said, coughing as she inhaled the dusty air. She let herself fall onto a pew in the middle as she gestured for Nor to come.

"Gotta keep watch." he shook his head. "Those people don't quit."

"I think they'll be too busy crucifying Adrian." Theo sighed and plopped down next to Morgana. The church seemed safe enough to stay for a few hours.

"Yeah, but they'll never let you go either way," Nor said. It was hard to hear him, even with the echo. "They know who you are now." He seemed to struggle to look him in the eye.

Theo winced. Did he hate Casimir that much?

"Doesn't matter," Theo muttered, the seat suddenly too uncomfortable. "We'll head back home soon. They won't be able to find me."

"Right." The shifting seemed to travel to Nor as his eyes wandered, studying the ceiling before pointing toward the door. "I'm gonna go keep watch. Just in case."

"Scarlett should be back by now," He muttered as he walked off, but the whisper carried, riding the echo.

Theo wished he didn't hear it.

Morgana let out a loud breath as soon as he was gone and stared up at Theo. His heart jumped in place as her eyes glistened with a smile he had not known he needed. He smiled back, a genuine smile for the first time since he could remember, a glimmer of tranquility contradicting the constant inner battle for control.

"He's really gotta learn to accept things." She turned her gaze toward the podium, fingers tapping the arm of the chair in a steady rhythm.

"Why did *you*?" He tried to match her calmness but failed, his foot drumming chaotically against the echoing floor.

"Why did I what?" she asked, letting out a chuckle she clearly tried to hold back.

"Accept me. That I'm Casimir."

Saying the name tasted like iron. It lived in his head too long, tangled around every thought.

"We all have our demons," Morgana said, a hint of a smile played at the corner of her mouth. "Some are just more visible than others." Her fingers now still, but the echo of the tapping resounded in Theo's ears.

"You seem happy about that." He narrowed his eyes and pointed at the curl of her lips.

"It's not that." she glanced down, shaking her head. "I just realized something about myself."

Her eyes snapped back to his, and he could not look away.

"The White Raven—me. It failed, you know?" She scoffed. "I'm a fucking failed experiment." Her jaw tensed as soon as the words left her, but her expression did not falter. If anything, she looked more annoyed than heartbroken.

Theo swallowed dryly and said nothing. His gaze roamed the pool of honesty and vulnerability in her eyes before settling on the stark white strands cascading over her shoulders, striking against the darkness of her hair.

"And that doesn't bother you?" Theo tried to hide his disbelief at her near-nonchalance, turning his body toward her searching for it—the pulse of misery he feared was his alone. "That you're forced to live with a damaged part of yourself you can't leave behind?" Insides twisting, lips quivering, he hated that the crack in his voice gave him away.

"That's not how I see it. For me, it's more like…" her voice drifted as she glanced toward the door where Nor had gone. Theo caught the shift. Maybe she wouldn't have wanted to say it if Nor were here.

"I see it as a part of life I have to come to terms with." She crossed her arms and tilted her head toward the podium, hovering above them like a silent witness.

"When I see it like that." She shrugged. "It's not much different from everything else I've had to live with during my twenty-eight years of surviving. Yeah, not sure I'd call it living." She huffed, her gaze drifting past Theo as if watching her life play out like a movie.

"You know when I went through that door in the mansion, I…" she pulled a sharp breath, the pause stretching as if she were choosing whether to speak at all. Theo braced himself, extending his arm, plopping it on the back of the chair behind Morgana.

"I stabbed myself." She winced as she tapped the sleeve of her jacket, where the sloppy bandage lay beneath, no doubt collecting clots of dried-up blood.

Theo's eyes grazed past her arm as he tried not to look and attempted to mask the gasp that escaped him, but the church's echo prevented any hiding.

"Don't worry." She held back a snort, lifting her hand in mock reassurance. "I swear I'm not a danger to myself or others. Well, that last one is debatable—"

"Why?" Theo said. The word dropped like a stone into Morgana's sudden silence, cutting through her rambling. She was deflecting, and no one knew how to spot that better than Theo.

"Think of it this way." She shifted in her seat for the first time since they sat down. Briefly standing, then sitting back down. "It's like a clot, right? I released that clot by cracking myself just enough for it to seep out," she groaned, a slight blush sneaking up her cheeks. "Sorry, I'm not very good at this stuff. The feelings thing." A nervous laugh slipped out as she shook her head. "Ugh, kill me now."

Theo kept quiet, holding back a smile. He settled on placing a hand on her shoulder. She relaxed beneath his touch.

"This is probably gonna sound weird," Theo said, breaking the comfortable, silent pause as she rested her hand on his. "But I'm proud of you." He sighed, knowing full well what his next words would imply. "I could never."

Morgana turned toward him so they were facing each other.

"Tell me." The words were soft, but cut deep all the same.

"I severed my bond with Scarlett. That's why she's gone." Theo avoided her gaze.

"Oh," she sighed after a pause.

When he raised his head, Morgana was looking to the side. His eyes burned as he followed her gaze and he landed eye to eye with Nor. He was standing with his hands in his pockets, frozen halfway to his and Morgana's private confessional.

"Why who's gone?" Nor said, his voice sounding much further than where he stood.

Theo wiped a drop of sweat trickling down his nose. He looked to Morgana for help, but she was already on her feet, leaning on the opposite pew, scratching the back of her head, and clearly wanting to be anywhere else.

"Scarlett," Theo coughed up her name, struggling to stay seated. He fidgeted until he was suddenly facing Nor. "She hasn't come back from her sweep yet." The words slipped out wobbly.

"About that," Nor's brows furrowed. Theo swallowed burning bile rising in his throat.

"She can't be still doing that, can she? It's been hours."

"I don't know." Theo shrugged, though it came out more like a nervous twitch. Nor's cluelessness made it harder for him to keep the façade. The way the truth would never cross his mind.

He was no longer capable of withholding anymore from Nor, the one who was supposed to be his closest friend.

"I severed the bond with her." The room tilted. His head spun, eyes losing focus. "She decided it was best to leave."

Nor's lips parted as he paused and stepped back. His eyes glowed like a cat's, doubling the sense of suffocation of the church.

"Why would you do that?" No sympathy, no hurt. Just disappointment.

"I—"

"How long have you been lying to me?" Nor said, crossing his arms and shifting his weight on his other leg. "When was this?"

"I can't explain it." Theo's voice came smaller than he would have wanted. He was a fly caught in the narrowing space between two walls, waiting to be crushed. "I-I was drowning, she…"

Excuses…excuses.

"She despises the fact she was connected to me. You didn't see her face when I—when Casimir—"

"There it is," Nor scoffed, nodding. "You're too far gone. The Theo I know—my best friend…I don't recognize you." He huffed out a breath in obvious exasperation. Theo's hands closed into fists.

"That's not true—"

"I don't care what you have to say." Nor shrugged, face twisting with indifference. "I don't trust you anymore." It landed like an elbow to the gut. "I can't bring myself to."

Theo opened his mouth, but nothing came. Not anger. Not denial. Just the cold understanding that Nor was right.

His fists balled. Feeling the veins pulse on his forehead, his jaw tensed until it ticked. He unclenched his right hand and tilted his head down to look at it, watching the veins blacken against the transparent paleness of his skin.

Someone laughed. Casimir's laugh. Theo's laugh. Distorted, ugly.

Nor retreated, sweat beading on his forehead.

"Trust? Is that why you followed me to Romania?" Theo's mouth moved. The words were not his. "I'm still me. The me I've always been."

Warm fingers slid over his bare elbow. Morgana. Her hand pushed, sizzling into his skin.

His hand caught her neck. Squeezing. Squeezing. His grasp loosened one second, tightened the next, as the world spun.

"I'm home." His own voice, moving further and further away.

"Let her go!" Nor screeched from somewhere around him. Theo's head swiveled toward him, his eyes locking on a giant, clawed hand attached to a cowering Nor.

"Don't!" Morgana called, her voice closer. His head whipped toward her again. His hand was wrapped around her neck. Theo recoiled, tearing his hand away, leaving a red palm etched into her porcelain skin.

His breath caught as Morgana massaged her neck. He stumbled into one of the pews with a thud loud enough to wake the dead.

Theo looked at Nor, but Nor turned away, staring down at his shoes, veins bulging on his forehead. Morgana coughed, her hand pressing against her upper arm where the bandage lay hidden beneath her sleeve.

"I'm sorry." Theo buried his face in his hands, still warm from her throat, and suppressed a silent sob.

He dreaded looking up and facing them. Their silence told him everything. The only sound was Morgana's ragged breathing.

"Who died?" A voice broke through the heaviness, making Theo jump out of his own skin, the shield of his hands slipping from his face.

Scarlett was leaning against the edge of the door, her arms crossed. "Took me a while to find you. But I got some help from a friend."

She was frowning, but something was different about her. Her eyes did not carry the heaviness they usually had ever since he met her. She looked happy.

Happy without him.

44
ASCENT

She uncrossed her arms. She touched the door. She was there.

Scarlett's frown deepened as she entered deeper into the place, her walk becoming a stalk. She had that look of well-masked exhaustion that seemed to have slipped with the crushing weight of the silence. Her eyes wandered from face to face, Theo looked at the floor every time they found him.

The next thing he knew, Theo was on his feet. The sound of his boots against the dirty floor distorted the stretching silence. His eyes wandered from Morgana to Nor, but their expressions were either unreadable or stuck in shellshock.

Morgana stared blankly, either at Scarlett or past her as the door squeaked shut behind her. Her hand was frozen, still resting across her collarbone.

Nor was the first to break the hypnosis as he blinked and walked with vast strides to Scarlett, enveloping her in a tight embrace.

Theo regarded the scene from a distance, unfolding farther away by the second. Casimir tickled the edge of his psyche. The air, thick with the poison of darkness, clogged his throat.

He opened his mouth to speak, but what came out was a strangled cough. All eyes were on him. Scarlett flinched at the sound, though she tried to hide it.

"Theo." With each step she took toward him, goose bumps climbed across his right arm, while the other pulsed, the sensation making him taste bile.

"It was a mistake." He flinched as she reached for him. "I wasn't myself, I—" Lies. He was aware when he made the decision, aware when going through with it, aware when she walked past him and did not look back.

Scarlett looked at him for a long moment like she was deciding something. Then let out a slow breath.

"I know." The smile didn't reach her eyes. "There's something I need to tell you. Something I should've told you a long time ago."

Theo's muscles locked, the dread of whatever came next climbing into his bones.

"Let me start with the easier part." She rubbed her knees with her palms, a nervous habit Theo had come to recognize too well. "I know I could've stayed with you guys," her intense gaze finally left Theo and extended to Nor and Morgana, who stood as stiff as Theo like guards awaiting orders. "But I left to talk to someone, actually. He lives here in Romania. Old friend of mine." her breath hitched as she nodded to herself, "A good friend." she paused and Theo felt pressured to say something, but it seemed like her pause was not intentional, but she just got lost in her head for a second.

"Anyway," Proving his suspicions, she blinked, waving a dismissive hand in front of her face. "He made me realize that

I was…wrong," the word came out quieter, like someone dipping their toe into cold water before diving in.

"Wrong to see you as the same person—you and…and Casimir," she said, struggling more and more with every word.

Theo's lip twitched into a half smile before he stopped it. Words lodged in his throat, tangled and useless. A laugh curled in his skull.

Oh, how wrong she was.

Looking uncomfortable with the silence and lack of reactions, Scarlett flattened her palm on top of the nearest bench.

"You know what?" She leaned her whole body on it, slanting like she was about to fall. "I need to speak to you. Alone."

"Hey," she said, jarringly soft, and immediately turned her gaze to Nor who was already taking clumsy steps toward her. "I'm sorry about this," her voice fell to a whisper that was clearly meant for Nor's ears only.

"Could you and Morgana just leave for a bit? I can't bring myself to say what I need to in front of you guys." she grasped his hand, holding as if it was fragile glass, and turned to Morgana with a nod. Morgana sighed, but nodded back. Theo, unsure of what he was supposed to do at that moment, froze in his place, trying to ground himself in the comfort of a softness that was not meant for him.

"Scarlett, you left and you—" Nor started, putting both her hands in his. The coldness in his eyes from moments ago melted into hurt, overwhelmed by unbridled affection.

A breath grated his lungs. A hiss escaped. Theo hoped no one was paying enough attention to him to notice.

What an adorably sad pair.

"We can talk about this later." Scarlett removed her hand and placed it on his cheek. "I love you."

The urge to smack the shit out of them both slowly invaded him. Squeezing his eyes shut, hoping to banish it, Theo stumbled on something, almost doubling-over.

He tsked, feeling a set of eyes on him as he looked down to wipe his boot. As soon as he raised his head, he was met with Morgana's piercing eyes, and a subtle smile he did not deserve. How could she smile—how could she even look at him after what he did to her? Even the wound was still visibly fluorescent against her pale skin, glaring at him from beneath.

At her first attempt to speak, she cleared her throat as her voice came out gravelly and huskier than usual.

"Come on, bro," she said, finding her voice. Though she was addressing Nor, her eyes never left Theo's. "They have things to settle."

Nor blinked and walked out beside Morgana, both gazing longer than they had to. For different reasons, for different people.

Once alone, the silence in the empty church pressed against his eardrums like wet cloth.

Theo's frenzied breathing became his rhythmic clock, keeping him from imploding as Scarlett searched for her words. She sat, she stood, she walked in a circle, and she stopped and heaved.

"Well?" Theo said, loud and erratic. The noise and ugliness of the word breaking his clock.

"I'm thinking!" Scarlett settled on sitting, her voice surpassing his. "You want me to tell you or not?" She looked down and said something under her breath Theo could not make out. "This is hard for me, okay?"

"Waiting this long was hard for me, too." The words slipped out, sharp and low. Let her hear him. *Let her choke on them* after what she made him go through. The silence. The distance. The resentment.

"What was that?" Scarlett raised her head, that was resting on her clasped hands.

"I said just get it over with." The blackened arm's constant stinging and pulsing increased. He had to give it a rest—or get it out of his sight. He sucked in a breath and it faded from existence. Now, he stood one-armed and feeling awkward, lodging his remaining hand in his jacket pocket.

Scoffing, Scarlett lay back against the bench she sat on and gestured to the one beside it as she crossed her legs.

"You can sit—"

"I'm good here."

"Fine." She sighed, raising her head to the ceiling. "It was about fifty years ago." She winced like recalling the memory put her in physical pain. "I bonded with my first master ever. Colt."

She shifted, rubbing her palms together. Theo let out a slow breath he did not realize he'd been holding, as the name rang a dreadful, unwelcome bell in his head. He shook his head, clinging to the small hope that it was a coincidence, and walked as quietly as he could manage to face Scarlett. She jumped, startled, as they locked eyes, perhaps at Theo's change in position, as if she was too immersed in her memories she lost all sense of her surroundings.

"Almost two hundred years I've been alive, an untethered familiar. An oddity, but…" She shrugged. "I liked it that way. Being unattached, not responsible for another life. Then Colt…" her gaze darkened as she turned her face to the window where the light of the rising sun concealed half her face.

"He was a young man, barely out of his twenties, a witch prodigy, though he would deny it," she huffed, a sorrowful smile creeping up her face.

"Anyway, four years after our bond settled, we came here to Romania one time. The high priestess was holding a summit, as I like to call it. It was those events you felt honored to be invited into. In retrospect." Her leg bounced. "The one on that day, I think, was about reviving some movement or another. Whatever her excuse was." she swallowed, waving a dismissive hand. "He had to go. Invitation and all that fancy shit. You know how that goes."

Theo nodded, breath catching in his throat. The image of Iliana's dead body flashed in his mind like a blinding light.

"When we got there, I left him when the thing started," she scoffed. "There was no way I would've sat through god-knows how many hours of politics without hurling." Her breath caught, her brows pulling together as she shook her head, refusing to look at Theo. "I just went for a fly around the property."

A cold gust prickled his bones. Scarlett paused, watching him.

"When I came back, there was—" She sniffled, swiping an aggressive hand across her eyes. Theo's fist clenched, holding back the urge to extend a comforting hand, which was not his place anymore—*If it ever was.*

"There were people running all over the place, dispersing in every direction. I got down and walked inside." Her sniffling abruptly ended on a haunting, shaky sigh. "And there he was." As she finally looked up, meeting Theo's eyes head on, he almost choked on nothing and his hand started to shake. "And there you were, hovering over him, both arms black." she paused, "Casimir. His back was turned to me. I didn't see your face." she bit her bottom lip as her voice cracked. "He was strangling Colt, and then Colt was at your feet. Not moving, coughing up blood, red and thick."

Theo held his breath, the strain needling his lungs.

"I tried to run there—I did." Scarlett's voice rose in defensiveness, but she squeezed her arm as if holding herself back. Her shoulders dropped, and she settled on a shrug as her distant gaze landed on the space where Theo's arm would have been.

"Why?" Her voice trembled.

Time slowed, Scarlett was miles away. Theo's jaw tensed as his arm sprouted back against his will, limp, but beating and twitching with new purpose.

He looked down at his alien hand. The fresh blood, the blood-curdling scream. The splotch of a body falling into a pool of red liquid at his feet. *He deserved it.*

Something soft and warm touched the pulsing hand, the sensation of the contact strange and unnatural like two same-pole magnets being forced together. The warmth searing his skin, Theo's head snapped up.

"Hey," Scarlett was speaking. He squinted through the distortion of her face, seeing nothing but a grinning shadow lingering on her shoulder. "I'm telling you this cause I know now. You're not him." Her voice cascaded in waves, swishing past him further and further away. "I forgive—" the words faded.

He was on his feet, towering over her, grasping her hand and shoving it aside along with its chilling softness.

Come here.

The exit called to him. Was that the exit?

His feet walked him to the door, his only way out of the strangling grip of the shrinking space.

Scarlett's broken voice. His name was being called. *Theo.* Was that it?

He gripped the cold handle of the door and stepped onto the grass, squishing under his boots.

Two faces emerged in front of him. Confused, waiting for him to speak. *Nor and Morgana.* Did they ask him a question?

Theo lurched past them. Behind him, their voices called—Theo, Theo—but that name was not his. He walked, walked, and walked.

He was a tornado invading the tranquility of the dawn-laced streets. His feet carried him back there. He had to return. It was home, after all.

He stopped in front of it. Absolute stillness. His head tilted back, looking up.

The mansion looked different with a half sun rising behind it, making it seem like his memory had conjured it. Its bones drooped and sagged like a starved creature, scarred by centuries of abuse and neglect.

He strode toward the stairs. His foot lay suspended on the first step. Theo gripped the handrail, almost crushing it to dust.

"Let go," he growled through his teeth, the sound foreign and familiar at the same time. He stumbled up the stairs, falling to his knees as he reached the door. He held on to the knob like a crutch as it squeaked open. Dust fell from the hinge and settling under his boots. As he crossed the edge of the door, a gust of wind welcomed him.

The hallway, touched by the breeze, carried whispers of memories, lost in time, insignificant.

He squeezed his eyes shut, tasting the life of it; Alexandru and Adrian chasing each other one moment, lying in pools of their own blood the next. Amarys on the couch. Irene and Damian conspiring near the piano.

His hand sprinted up, smacking his temple. Theo's legs buckled, his knees thudding as they touched the ground, disturbing the dust.

"Get out of my head," he hissed, the words came out desperate, and dripping with exhaustion in a call-and-response with the roaring floorboards.

His head shook, turning his already dark surrounding into a black blob of nothing.

"*You* get out. You don't want to be here." Theo's mouth moved, the words unfamiliar like a foreign language.

Straining for breath, Theo fell to his side; shadows ganged around him, soft and slow, covering him in a bubble. What did he have left to exist for, anyway?

Nothing—

Nor rejected him. Scarlett resented him. Theo… just hated Theo.

A piercing sound invaded his ears. He crawled forward, but his vision betrayed him, as reality distorted into a cacophony of highly saturated colors that shouldn't exist in a house succumbed to dreadful blackness.

Were his eyes even open?

The sound came again. Inside his head. The clanging of a chain against steel. Mina's necklace flashed at the corner, rusted, dangling, and fragile. He turned his head—nothing.

It was not real. His shaking hand fished Mina's pendant out of his pocket, where it had sat since Ovidia pressed it into his palm. He crushed it flat beneath his fingers, the once beautiful shape ugly and deformed.

Mina was not real—*Mina was your fault.*

He tossed the useless metal away. A mocking, low chuckle, jarring, made his head throb, pulsing with its own heartbeat. Up, down, up, down.

Theo reached with his hands. He found a wall, cold and harsh. The blackened arm spun unnaturally, twisting to shove away something at his side. Too close. A person?

His back hunched and limbs numb, he heaved his head.

Morgana was the one he shoved. Scarlett was there, even Nor. their faces somber, eyes bulging in shock, their mouths moving simultaneously, no sound emanating. The only voice emerging was his own, a dark tilt, too close for comfort.

His name was Colton Skeins.

"Colton Skeins," Theo repeated, a muffled sob escaping his lips, passing the dry desert of his throat.

The name slipped past him. Not pushed, stepped over.

"He put up a good fight…" he trailed off, eerie stillness hovering above him, emanating from Scarlett, no doubt. No, that was not what he meant to say.

Let her eat herself from the inside.

An echo of his own exhale filled his clogged ears, leaving visible cold breath dissipating with the airlessness of his surroundings.

Casimir's head, too tensed, too heavy, fell back. He was staring at his hands, covered in dust that highlighted the blackness of his veins.

Monstrous—*exhilarating.*

As his breathing steadied, he pushed up to his feet, wiping the dirt from his coat. He sighed, massaging his sore shoulder and wiping a lone tear leaking down his cheek.

Erratic breathing and whispered exclamations violated the quiet. Casimir craned his neck toward the sound and they were looking at him—Theo's bunch. Clueless, their expressions glowed with piteous hope.

"Guys." He crossed his arms and put his index finger on his chin, giving it light, pondering taps. This was going to be epically funny. "Is there something on my face?" He softened his voice and pulled his eyebrows together. "It's me, Theo."

They took a few steps back at the same time, like a well-oiled machine. It sent a shiver down his spine when their faces fell, leaving behind a terrified despair, a complete, uncontrollable relinquishing of their hope and expectation. Except for Morgana, she held a calm exterior, composed, and almost unfazed. He paused, watching for her eyes to slip into that same terror. But nothing came.

"Well. Busted." Casimir brushed it away and smiled, raising his hands in mock surrender.

With his head tilted toward the sky and his eyes squeezed shut, Casimir inhaled through his nose.

The release.

www.ingramcontent.com/pod-product-compliance
Lightning Source LLC
LaVergne TN
LVHW100512110826
845146LV00002B/606